Raves for RITA Award–Winning Author Barbara Metzger's Romances

"A doyen of humorous Regency-era romance writing."
—*Publishers Weekly*

"Funny and touching—what a joy!"   —Edith Layton

"Lively, funny, and true to the Regency period . . . a fresh twist on a classic plot."   —*Library Journal*

"Absolutely outstanding . . . lots of action, drama, tension . . . simply fantastic!"   —Huntress Book Reviews

"The complexities of both story and character contribute much to its richness. Like life, this book is much more exciting when the layers are peeled back and savored."   —*Affaire de Coeur*

"Remarkable . . . an original, laugh-out-loud, and charmingly romantic read."   —Historical Romance Writers

"A true tour de force. . . . Only an author with Metzger's deft skill could successfully mix a Regency tale of death, ruined reputations, and scandal with humor for a fine and ultimately satisfying broth . . . a very satisfying read."   —The Best Reviews

"[Metzger] brings the Regency era vividly to life with deft humor, sparkling dialogue, and witty descriptions."   —Romance Reviews Today

"Metzger has penned another winning Regency tale. Filled with her hallmark humor, distinctive wit, and entertaining style, this is one romance that will not fail to enchant."   —*Booklist* (starred review)

ALSO BY BARBARA METZGER

Christmas Wishes

Barbara Metzger

A SIGNET ECLIPSE BOOK

SIGNET ECLIPSE
Published by New American Library, a division of
Penguin Group (USA) Inc., 375 Hudson Street,
New York, New York 10014, USA
Penguin Group (Canada), 90 Eglinton Avenue East, Suite 700, Toronto,
Ontario M4P 2Y3, Canada (a division of Pearson Penguin Canada Inc.)
Penguin Books Ltd., 80 Strand, London WC2R 0RL, England
Penguin Ireland, 25 St. Stephen's Green, Dublin 2,
Ireland (a division of Penguin Books Ltd.)
Penguin Group (Australia), 250 Camberwell Road, Camberwell, Victoria 3124,
Australia (a division of Pearson Australia Group Pty. Ltd.)
Penguin Books India Pvt. Ltd., 11 Community Centre, Panchsheel Park,
New Delhi - 110 017, India
Penguin Group (NZ), 67 Apollo Drive, Rosedale, North Shore 0632,
New Zealand (a division of Pearson New Zealand Ltd.)
Penguin Books (South Africa) (Pty.) Ltd., 24 Sturdee Avenue,
Rosebank, Johannesburg 2196, South Africa

Penguin Books Ltd., Registered Offices:
80 Strand, London WC2R 0RL, England

Published by Signet Eclipse, an imprint of New American Library, a division
of Penguin Group (USA) Inc. Previously published in Signet and Fawcett
Crest editions.

First Signet Eclipse Printing, November 2010
10 9 8 7 6 5 4 3 2 1

Hey, Judy, this one's for you.

Chapter One

*J*uneclaire wished she did not have to spend another Christmas at Stanton Hall. "You would have liked the way Christmas used to be," she told her companion, Pansy. Pansy just grunted and continued her investigation of all the parcels being wrapped and put into baskets for the servants' and tenants' Boxing Day gifts. Bright ribbons, shiny paper, and mounds of presents and treats were spread on two tables and the floor of the rear pantry Miss Juneclaire Beaumont was using to assemble Lady Stanton's largess. Lady Stanton was being very generous this year. She had directed her niece Juneclaire to knit mittens for all the children, to hem handkerchiefs for all the footmen and grooms, and to sew rag dolls for the little girls on the estate. Juneclaire had also been sent to the nearby village of

Farley's Grange to purchase new shawls for the tenants' wives and whistles and tops for the boys. All
week she had been busy helping Cook bake plum
cakes, decorate gingerbread men, and create marzipan
angels, after tying colorful ribbons around pots of jam
from the berries she had collected all summer and fall.
She also made sachets of the lavender she had drying
in the stillroom and poured out rose water into little
bottles for the maidservants. The orchards provided
shiny apples, and Uncle Avery Stanton provided shiny
coins. Oh yes, and Aunt Marta Stanton provided a new
Bible for each of the servants, whether they could read
or not. Last year the gift was a hymnal, the year before
a book of sermons. Aunt Marta was very consistent in
her Christian charity.

Lady Stanton was so consistent, in fact, that her own
niece would receive one of the Bibles and a shiny coin
as her Christmas gift and naught else.

It wasn't that she minded being treated worse than
the servants, Juneclaire reflected, pausing to share one
of the crisp apples with Pansy. Nor did she mind all
the work, though that was considerable at this time of
year, with helping the maids air the unused rooms for
holiday guests and directing the footmen in hanging
the greenery after Juneclaire fashioned it into wreaths
and garlands. No, she was used to being useful. What
she could not and would not get inured to was being
used, to being considered a serf with no salary or self-
respect. Juneclaire acknowledged that she was a poor

relation and that she owed Lord and Lady Stanton her gratitude for the very roof over her head. How could she not accept the fact, when Aunt Marta reminded her daily?

"Still," she told Pansy, pushing a soft brown curl back under her mobcap, "they could have been kinder." Pansy was too busy redistributing a pile of apricot tarts to notice Juneclaire wipe a suddenly damp brown eye with her sleeve. "Here," Juneclaire said, looking over her shoulder, "you'd better not let Aunt Marta see you nibbling on those or we'll be in the briers for sure." She tied a bow on a pair of warm knitted socks and sniffed. "She could at least have let us stir the Christmas pudding and make a wish with everyone else."

Lady Stanton did not believe in such nonsense. She thought such superstitions were heathenish and not at all suitable for a Stanton of Stanton Hall or one of their household. She could not stop the kitchen staff, naturally, not if she wanted a smooth pudding to serve her guests, but she could see that her niece was kept too busy for any pagan rituals. If it were up to Lady Stanton, Christmas would be spent on one's knees, in church. There would be none of this mad jollity, this extravagance of entertaining and gifting. Aunt Marta was religious, proper, strict—and cheap. She wouldn't even distribute Boxing Day gifts if it were not for Lord Stanton and the fact that to discontinue the tradition would disgruntle the dependents and, worse, make her look paltry in the neighborhood. Lady Stanton was very careful of her standing among the local gentry, especially since her own roots did not bear close scrutiny, with their ties to Trade. She had worked hard to earn that "Lady" before her name and intended to enjoy its rewards. If being accepted as the first family in the vicinity meant showing off her generosity once a year, Juneclaire could handle the details. If it meant giving hearth space to her misbegotten waif of a niece, Juneclaire could at least be put to work and molded to Lady Stanton's measure.

Juneclaire kept wrapping bundles, trying to make a happy Christmas for those less fortunate than she was. At least she tried to convince herself that the servants were less fortunate, even though they got an actual wage and could move to another position; the tenants were less well established than Juneclaire, although they worked to better their own lives and had families who cared about them.

"Things were not always this way," she informed her companion. Aunt Marta would have been horrified to see Juneclaire's hands go still while she recalled earlier Christmases, when Maman lifted her up to stir the pudding and make her wish. Papa used to smile at the English ways and tousle her curls. He always knew her wish anyway, and he would laugh. His *petite fleur* only wanted a puppy or a kitten or a pony. Juneclaire received gloves and combs and books and dolls and sweets and, at last, a pony, despite a lack of funds.

Then she and Maman returned to England without

Papa, without her pony, to this cold and damp Stanton Hall with its disapproving ancestors frowning down on her from their portraits on the wall. That year she wished that the horrors in Papa's homeland would be over soon and he would send for them. Maman gave her a locket to wear, with a tiny painting of her and Papa in it. Juneclaire touched it now, under her worn brown wool gown.

The next Christmas, when they knew Papa was not coming for them, Juneclaire wished Maman would be stronger in her loss, but she was not, and then Juneclaire was nine years old and alone. For the next ten years she tried not to wish for what could never be.

Juneclaire tried to be grateful for the grudging charity, truly she did, winning the respect of the servants, at least, with her quiet acceptance of her lot. They considered Juneclaire a true lady, sweet and caring, not like some they could mention, with jumped-up airs. Of course, Juneclaire's being a lady set her apart. The staff could take pity on the orphaned chit, and they could be kind to her when Lady Stanton was not looking, but they could not be her friends, not if they wanted to keep their positions. Aunt Marta did not condone familiarity between the classes. For the same reason she did not permit her niece to play with the village children. Juneclaire wasn't good enough to merit a governess or new frocks or a maid to wait on her, but she was too genteel for the locals: her mother was a Stanton. So Juneclaire had no friends.

She did have her cousins, however, if two loud, unruly imps of Satan could be consolation to a gentle female. She was as relieved as everyone else on the estate except Lady Stanton when Rupert and Newton finally went away to school. In earlier days they had made her life an endless hell of creepy things in her bed, slimy things in her slippers, crawly things in her porridge. She was the unwilling plunder when they played pirate, the dragon's victim when they played at knights. They tied her up, locked her in closets, terrorized her in dark attics. And if *her* hair got mussed, *her* pinafore got soiled, she got a lecture from Aunt Marta and no supper. Dearest Rupert, Juneclaire's age, and baby Newton, a year younger, were just high-spirited, according to their fond mother. The Root and the Newt, as their not-so-fond and often-hungry cousin termed them, had no redeeming virtues whatsoever, except that she could listen in on their lessons and ride their ponies when the boys outgrew them.

If Christmas seasons were never joyous for Juneclaire at Stanton Hall, now they were less so when the boys came home for holiday with the only knowledge her scapegrace relatives seemed to have absorbed at Harrow: carnal knowledge.

At age eighteen, Newt was a thin, spotty-faced budding tulip, with yellow pantaloons, high shirt collars, and roving hands. Nineteen-year-old Root was short and stocky, with sausage fingers and damp lips with which Juneclaire was growing altogether too familiar. She'd taken to avoiding dark corridors and to carrying a darning needle slipped through her lace collar as a weapon. Even if Juneclaire were willing—and hell would freeze over first—she thought she'd be without more than her supper if Aunt Marta caught her in one of her darlings' embraces. Root and Newt were so stupid, though, they thought she was just playing hard to get, as they nursed their various pinpricks.

Aunt Marta would not have anything as indecorous as a kissing bough in her house, of course, but the brats had discovered a patch of mistletoe and took great joy in bedeviling Juneclaire in public places, where she could not retaliate. Unaware of her own prettiness, Juneclaire could not understand why they did not share their ardor with a willing housemaid, the way Uncle Avery did. She did not think she could mention this to the randy rattlepates, however, nor could she complain to her aunt, who would only find Juneclaire at fault for her wanton looks. No matter how hard Juneclaire stared at her mirror, she could find nothing sirenlike about brown hair, brown eyes, and thick brown eyebrows. Her mouth seemed too full and her nose too short, especially in comparison with her beautiful mother's miniature. And Juneclaire knew for a fact there could be nothing seductive about the shapeless, drab gowns she wore at Aunt Marta's insistence. They were so high-necked and loose-fitting that Root was eighteen before he even discovered she had a bosom. Unfortunately, octopus-armed Newt was not as mutton-headed.

Juneclaire could have gone to Uncle Avery with her problems, she supposed, but he would likely have patted her head and handed her a shilling, the way he used to when he found her in tears. Now she stood taller than the short, portly frame Root had inherited, and she had a fair stock of shillings. She also felt too sorry for her uncle to bring him more difficulties. The poor man hated what he called mingle-mangles, which meant he avoided his lady and her sons every chance he got, contenting himself with his pigs and sheep and cows—and housemaids. To say he was henpecked was a vast understatement. If he were a slice of bread, there'd be no place to spread jam. So Juneclaire made sure her door was locked at night and wished every year would be her last Christmas at Stanton Hall. This year just might be the one.

"What, are you still at this foolish task, you lazy girl? You should have been finished hours ago. I need you to make out the place cards for tomorrow's dinner, Claire." Aunt Marta could not bring herself to give Juneclaire her proper name, considering it too foreign, too affected for one in her niece's position. Lady Stanton unwrapped an apricot tart and held it up to her sharp nose before biting into it. She poked her bony fingers into the various boxes and trays. Lady Stanton had as much meat on her bones as she had human kindness in her heart. "I am placing you between Captain Fancroft and Squire Holmes. You may ask the captain about the war, but remember that no gentleman expects or wishes a lady to be knowledgeable. Whatever you say, do not disagree with him. Squire Holmes is interested in his children and the hunt. You shall *not* express your queer notions of sympathy for the fox. Do you understand, miss?"

"Yes, Aunt Marta. No, I shan't, Aunt Marta," Juneclaire replied from long practice.

"And see that you don't take off your gloves. No need for anyone to see your hands ain't as smooth as a lady's."

"But I *am* a lady, Aunt."

"Hoity-toity, miss. You'll stop putting on airs, too, if you hope to snabble an eligible *parti*."

Juneclaire rather thought she did, even if she wouldn't have used those terms. This year she was being permitted to join Aunt Marta's annual Christmas Eve gathering, in hopes that she would attract some gentleman's eye. There was to be no London Season for Juneclaire, not even a come-out ball in her honor, for Aunt Marta was too nipfarthing and too ashamed of this product of a runaway match between Miss Clara Stanton and her dancing master. Even if Jules Beaumont had been son to a *duc*, he was the third son of an early victim of the Terror, the family wealth confiscated by the upstarts. Juneclaire saw nothing to be embarrassed over in her heritage, even if her parents did not marry until reaching France, and in a Catholic church at that.

Now she raised her chin and said, "I do not think my birth will count against me with a true gentleman, not if he cares for me."

"Poppycock, just see that you don't give them a disgust of you. Holmes needs a mother for his brats, and Fancroft wants an heir while he can still sire one."

"But . . . but aren't there to be any younger men at the party?"

"Not for you there won't be. What did you think, some storybook hero was going to fall in love with your doe eyes? Young men don't offer marriage to dowerless chits with tainted names. They offer *carte blanche*." Aunt Marta checked the hems of the handkerchiefs.

Ah, well, perhaps the captain would be knowledgeable on closer acquaintance, or the squire kindly. She wouldn't mind children, not if it meant a house of her own, away from Stanton Hall, if the gentleman Aunt Marta picked out was nice. She made the mistake of asking.

"Nice? What has that to do with it? You'll take the first one that offers for you or you can go to the poorhouse, for all I care. It's time and enough someone else paid your bills and bought your clothes."

Juneclaire knew the threat of the poorhouse was only that. Aunt Marta would never let the neighborhood see her treat a blood relation in so miserly a fashion, nor would her aunt part with an unpaid servant so easily. No, Fancroft and Holmes must be warm enough in the pocket to offer Lady Stanton handsome settlements for her niece's hand, which meant Juneclaire dared not refuse. And what choice did she have, after all, but to marry a man of her aunt's selection? She never met any strangers, sequestered away at the Hall and traveling no farther than Farley's Grange, and she was ill equipped for anything but marriage. She was not well-enough educated to go for a governess, she was too shy to go on the stage, and she did not sew quickly enough to be a seamstress. Mostly, she did not have enough patience to continue on as her aunt's lackey.

With the optimism that came with youth and the season of surprises, Miss Beaumont hoped for better than an aging roué or a beleaguered widower. If only Juneclaire could have made her pudding wish, she would have asked for a handsome cavalier, no matter what Aunt Marta said.

At least she had her pretty new gown. White velvet it was, with a high waist and low neck and tiny puff sleeves. Aunt Marta meant her to look like a debutante of the ton: respectable, virginal, à la mode. If all went well, she could be married in the same dress, avoiding additional expense. Juneclaire had spent some of her precious shillings for green ribbon to trim the gown and had woven a crown of holly for her hair. She thought she would do very well, with her mother's pearls and the Norwich silk shawl she knew Uncle Avery meant to give her. Perhaps there would be a young beau who did not need to marry for money or consequence. Aunt Marta didn't know everything, Juneclaire thought with a smile. She didn't know about Uncle Avery's housemaids.

Lady Stanton was checking the names on the filled baskets, peevishly hurrying Juneclaire along toward her next chore. She removed the bottle of rose water from the package marked Lily; Juneclaire's smile faded. Then Aunt Marta caught sight of Pansy.

"What is that . . . that *creature* doing here?" she shouted, her thin frame going rigid in anger. "I told you yesterday Cook was looking for her in the kitchens! I abhor these unseemly friendships you insist on striking up, Claire, and I won't have it. What if Squire Holmes found out? Captain Fancroft would be revolted, I am sure. I won't have your disobedience. Do you hear me?"

Juneclaire was sure the whole kitchen staff heard her, and she blushed with embarrassment. Pansy ran to hide behind Juneclaire as Aunt Marta slammed the door behind her. Lady Stanton stomped off, insisting for the rest of the household who might have missed her earlier screaming that she hadn't raised up a penniless orphan out of the goodness of her heart just to be made a laughingstock, and where was that bobbing-block of a husband of hers when she needed him to do something about his niece and her willful ways.

"Don't worry, Pansy," Juneclaire whispered, leaving the boxes and baskets, leaving the pantry, but not leaving Pansy in the kitchen.

Now, Juneclaire might have been willing to sacrifice her hopes and dreams on Aunt Marta's altar of greed and meanness, for she was a dutiful girl. She might have put on the prettiest gown she'd ever owned and put herself on display for her aunt's guests, hoping to impress them with Lady Stanton's beneficence. She was even ready to try to charm some overweight old seaman into a declaration to please her aunt. But not Pansy. She would not let Aunt Marta sacrifice Pansy just to puff off her own consequence, just because Pansy was little and lame.

Well, wishing hadn't brought Maman or Papa back, and it would not bring her any handsome and wealthy knight riding to her rescue. Wishing was certainly not going to save Pansy. That Juneclaire had to do herself. So she did. She gathered her few belongings, including the velvet gown and her heaviest cloak, a gray wool that used to be her aunt's. The rabbit lining looked more like rat fur after all these years, but she would need the warmth if she and Pansy were to reach London, where Mrs. Simms, the old housekeeper, resided. Juneclaire hastily estimated that by nightfall she could reach the market village of Strasmere, where not many people would recognize her, especially with the hood of her cloak up. Tomorrow she could find a farmer going to Bramley, the nearest posting stop, and then in a day she would be in London. She counted out her hoard of shillings and nodded. They ought to be enough. June-claire wrapped half of them and her mother's pearls in a stocking, which she tucked inside the loose bodice of her gown. The rest she placed in her reticule, along with Mrs. Simms's last letter. She wrapped a white muffler around her neck, knotted off an unfinished pair of mittens, and put them on, not caring that one was shorter than the other. Then she went to the kitchens, where she filled every nook of her carpetbag and every pocket of her cloak with bread and cheese and apples and sliced meats. "For the poorhouse," she told the gaping scullery maid. "So they have a better Christmas, too."

Juneclaire left Stanton Hall without looking back. She did not leave a farewell note. She did not leave for her aunt's Christmas dinner.

Unfortunately, Juneclaire's almost-instant planning did not take into account Pansy's lameness. The poor dear couldn't walk far or fast. Miss Beaumont had also not considered that many others would be on the road for the holidays and that there would, indeed, be no rooms at the inn at Strasmere, or the next down the road, or the next. Sheltered as she was, Juneclaire never would have guessed that most innkeepers and their wives would not accept a single woman, traveling without servants, on foot, and in dubious company.

"I run a respectable establishment, I do," she heard over and over. "I'm not having the likes of such a one at *my* inn. I'm not."

Juneclaire raised her determined chin and lowered her thick eyebrows. She was not going back to Stanton Hall, not even if she had to sleep under hedgerows. She would get to London, even if she had to walk the whole way, carrying Pansy.

Chapter Two

*L*ord Merritt Jordan, the Earl of St. Cloud, wished he did not have to spend Christmas at home. He flicked the whip over the leader's left ear as the curricle straightened after a turn that sent the outer wheels two feet in the air. His groom, Foley, took the liberty of long years in service, and a short glimpse of eternity, to speak up. As soon as his insides righted themselves, Foley shouted from his perch behind the driver's seat that he'd rather eat his mincemeat pie than be one. "An' the way you been cursin' about havin' to be somewheres you don't want, I can't figure why you're drivin' like the Devil hisself is behind us, my lord, and catchin' up fast."

St. Cloud frowned, not at the familiarity but at the truth. Damn and blast, he was in no hurry to get to the

Priory in Berkshire. He obligingly slowed the pace a
fraction. "Now the Devil won't have to run so hard."
Why should he, when hell was waiting up ahead?

Foley shook his grizzled head but relaxed a little.
Now they were traveling at death-defying speed, not
necessarily death-wishing, and there was no one he'd
trust with the ribbons more than his master. If Lord
St. Cloud didn't have the lightest hands with the reins,
aye, and the surest eye toward horseflesh, besides the
truest aim with a pistol, the neatest right in the ring
and the sharpest skill with the pasteboards of any gentleman in St. James's Street, Foley would eat his hat. If
it hadn't blown off a mile outside London. Blister it, if
Lord St. Cloud didn't have his black moods like now,
he'd well nigh be the best employer in London Town.
He was fair and generous, not toplofty, and he didn't
truck with women.

Foley had no fondness for the female species; they
only distracted a man from the important business in
life, like war and wagering. What with their weeping
and clinging and flirting and spending every groat of a
chap's income, they were more trouble than they were
worth, by half. It was a good thing, in Foley's opinion, that Lord St. Cloud was not in the petticoat line.
Not that the silly geese wouldn't be littering my lord's
doorstep if he smiled on them. With his wealth and title, the debutantes would be pawing each other aside to
catch his attention. With his wealth and finely muscled
frame, the demireps would be clawing one another's

eyes out. And with his dark, brooding looks and well-chiseled features, green eyes and cleft chin, every other female from sixteen to sixty would be gnawing on him like a bone, with or without his incredible wealth. If he smiled at them.

Luckily for Foley's misogynistic peace of mind, Lord St. Cloud seldom smiled at anyone, and at women least of all. The groom spit over the downwind side of the careening carriage. Give him his horses anytime. Many years ago, when Foley was a jockey, a waitress at the Green Knight had run off with a linen draper's assistant; the shop boy's hands were clean, she said, and he didn't smell of the stable. That's why Foley frowned if a pretty gal looked his way. Foley never understood about his master's dour expression and dark humors.

"I don't see what's got you in such a takin'," he muttered now, hanging on for dear life as the earl dropped his hands for the grays to pass a mail coach. "After all, it's Christmas and you're goin' home."

Foley couldn't see St. Cloud's sneer from his position at the earl's back, even if the groom's eyes weren't shut as they missed the coach by inches. Home, hah! Merritt Jordan had felt more at home on the French prison ship. At least there he'd had friends among the other captives. He'd only had to worry about disease, vermin, and hunger—not his relatives. Spending any holiday at St. Cloud Priory at Ayn-Jerome outside Thackford, much less Christmas and his birthday, was more like doing penance for being born.

They would all be there, all the vultures. His mother would see to that, filling the moldering old pile with relations, guests, and hangers-on, just so she did not have to face him alone. And they'd all want something of him, as always: money, favors, compliance with *their* standards for *his* behavior. Cousin Niles would have his usual sheaf of tailors' bills and gambling debts to be paid, and Cousin Elsbeth would still be whining for a London Season. Lord Harmon Wilmott, their father and St. Cloud's uncle, would shake his jowls and issue another lecture on St. Cloud's duties and responsibilities. St. Cloud was the last of the Jordan line, Uncle Harmon would intone; he owed his ancestors a continuance. Mother's brother undoubtedly meant that the earl should marry Elsbeth, saving Lord Harmon the expense and aggravation and keeping the wealth in the family, the Wilmott family, that was.

St. Cloud clenched his fists, and the horses took exception. When he had them back under his perfect control and Foley had quit muttering, he returned to his musings of what lay ahead. Grandmother, blind as a bat for the last five years, would be nagging at him that she wanted to see her great-grandchildren, and soon. And every female in the county who could scrape up an acquaintance would be calling, with hopes of becoming the next Countess St. Cloud, by come-hither hook or by compromising-situation crook. He dare not walk in his own shrubbery without an escort or sit at ease in his own library unless the door was locked.

Hell and damnation, he thought, not for the first time. The Priory already had enough Lady St. Clouds, and those two did not even speak to each other, not without his grandmother, the dowager, shouting, or Lady Fanny, his mother and current countess until he married, weeping.

The closer his carriage got to the Priory, the more St. Cloud understood how a winded deer felt surrounded by wolves. But he was not defenseless, he reminded himself. He was no longer a child who had to abide by adult rules. He was a grown man, twenty-nine years of age, and Uncle Harmon was no longer his trustee or warder. St. Cloud had made that plain four years ago, the day he came into his majority, after waiting a young lifetime of oppression.

Merritt Jordan had, like most of his class, been raised by wet nurses, nannies, and nursemaids. He seldom saw his parents, his mother being too high-strung for the duties of motherhood and his father not being interested. Then came his father's "accident," as they called it, and subsequent death two years later, when St. Cloud was seven years old. Lady Fanny's nerves deteriorated to such an extent that she could not bear to have her son near her. He was too noisy, too active. He might break something.

Her father took over the management of the estate since there were no male Jordan relatives. Lord Wilmott and Grandmother had such rows about raising the new tenth earl that Lady Fanny took to her bed for a year.

Lord Wilmott moved his own family from Motthaven
next door into the Priory, and the elder Lady St. Cloud
moved to the dower house. Uncle Harmon took over
the guardianship when he ascended to his father's bar-
onetcy and later brought his own motherless children
to reside under the Jordan banner—and checkbook.

Niles and later Elsbeth could run wild over the estate; St. Cloud had to be groomed for his future digni-
ties. Niles could go off to school at thirteen; St. Cloud
at the same age was too delicate to jeopardize among
the other sons of the upper ten thousand. Of course his
life was precious to the Wilmotts. Without St. Cloud
they would have to live on their own neglected property, within their own modest means, for the earldom
reverted back to the Crown.

On the one hand, he was wrapped in cotton wool,
given the fattest, most placid ponies to ride, kept away
from guns and swords, swaddled like an infant prone
to croup. On the other hand, he was force-fed a rigor-
ous education by one sanctimonious, sadistic tutor after another. The last was a young curate, Mr. Forbush,
who licked his lips when he birched the young earl at
every excuse. Lady Fanny cried and did nothing. She
was as in awe of her overbearing brother as she had
been of her dictatorial father and her grim husband.
Uncle Harmon saw nothing wrong with beating the
impertinence out of a young boy who questioned his
trustee's cutting in the home woods, raising the tenants' rents, or selling off the Thoroughbred stud farm.

He approved of Mr. Forbush to such an extent that when St. Cloud finally went to university, Uncle Harmon kept the curate on as the family's spiritual adviser. The hypocrite rained hellfire and brimstone down on the household every Sunday in the old Priory's chapel of St. Jerome of the Clouds. Lady Fanny was confirmed in her belief that she would burn in purgatory, and Uncle Harmon was convinced his self-righteous sacrifices on his nephew's behalf would be rewarded in the afterlife.

The earl enjoyed the partial freedom of university life. He excelled at his studies, but he also found outlets for the years of anger and neglect in athletic pursuits, honing his whip-tight muscles and deadly skills. None of the other lads was foolish enough to think St. Cloud was merely competing for fun. Fun did not seem to exist in the young peer's vocabulary.

St. Cloud's dream, when he came down from university, was to join the army like his deceased uncle George Jordan, whose name was never mentioned. The dowager ranted, Lady Fanny wept, Mr. Forbush prayed. And Uncle Harmon refused. Merritt Jordan was still the last St. Cloud. No Corsican upstart was going to capsize Wilmott's gravy boat.

Defeated, St. Cloud threw himself into Town life like a sailor on shore after months at sea. He followed his frivolous cousin Niles into gaming dens and bawdy houses. He surpassed him in reckless wagers and hey-go-mad stunts. He ran up debts and ran with light-skirts. He skirted the law with innumerable duels and became known as Satan St. Cloud, a deadly rakehell who took his pleasures seriously. Except that he found no pleasure in such an existence, beyond aggravating Uncle Harmon.

On his twenty-fifth birthday, St. Cloud waited until Mr. Forbush had given his Christmas sermon, not about the Holy Child and Peace on Earth, but about the sins of the fathers, blasphemy, adultery, murder. Forbush stared at St. Cloud and licked his lips.

One step outside the chapel doors, the curate found himself in an iron-hard grip, being dragged to the gatehouse, where the Earl of St. Cloud celebrated Christmas his own way, beating a man of the cloth to within an inch of his life, then tossing him over the gate like a sack of refuse.

St. Cloud strode back to the house and his astounded relatives with a look on his face that could have been a grimace on anyone else's. London bucks would have recognized it as the St. Cloud smile and fled. The earl notified Uncle Harmon that his services were no longer required; a bailiff had been hired. With a green-eyed look that could stop molten lava in its course, St. Cloud informed him and Niles that the London solicitors were already advised to direct Wilmott bills to Motthaven, not the Priory. He told his mother that if she did not put off her blacks and cease the weeping after nearly twenty years, she could very well go live with Lady St. Cloud in the dower house.

Having turned the Priory nicely on its ear, the earl returned to London to purchase his own commission. Prinny himself refused the request, unless and until St. Cloud had assured the succession. He almost went to marry the first Covent Garden doxie he could find, out of spite, but not even Satan St. Cloud could go through with such an affront to his ancestors. Besides, in the nine months it would take to beget a son, Boney could be defeated. Or the child might be a girl.

Instead the earl took the offered position of liaison between the War Office and the quartermaster general. The Regent asked him to accept, to see why the troops were not properly outfitted, why ammunition did not reach Wellesley's men in time. A request from the Regent was as good as a command, so St. Cloud became a paper merchant, by damn! He saw enough graft and corruption to disgust even a politician and ended by using some of his own blunt to expedite orders. Three months later he convinced his superior that the only way to see where deliveries were running afoul was in person—St. Cloud's person.

With every intention of joining up with some regiment or other in Spain, St. Cloud boarded a convoy ship for the Peninsula. The ship was attacked and sunk. The earl was wounded and captured and imprisoned on a French barque, without ever touching Spanish soil. Whitehall was not best pleased to have to trade four French officers of high rank for his release, and St. Cloud was furious that part of his parole—

negotiated by Uncle Harmon, indubitably—was his word as a gentleman not to take up arms against his captors again.

No longer in good odor at the War Office, St. Cloud took his seat in the Lords and did what he could there for the war effort, for the returning veterans. Fusty political pettifoggery satisfied him as little as bumbling bureaucracy, so he resumed his Town life, but with some new moderation. Merritt Jordan had nothing left to prove and only himself to aggravate with outrageous behavior, like now, when the headache he had from too much drink and too little sleep was pounding in his temples with each beat of the horses' hooves. He should have known better than to start the journey so late. Hell, he thought, neatly turning the grays into the courtyard of the Rose and the Crown with inches to spare between them and an overladen departing carriage, he should have made some excuse to avoid the Priory altogether. He usually did.

While the grays were being changed for his lordship's own matched chestnuts, sent ahead three days ago, St. Cloud was ushered into the inn's best private parlor, also reserved. Over a steaming mug of the landlord's renowned spiced punch, St. Cloud mused that no matter how much he struggled, some bonds never came undone. When Uncle Harmon tried to inflict his opinions on his nephew, St. Cloud could stare him into silence, without even hinting at irregularities in the trust's bookkeeping. St. Cloud could control the wilder excesses of his basket-scrambling cousin Niles with pocketbook governance, and he could challenge any man whose loose tongue overcame his instincts for self-preservation enough to probe the St. Cloud family history. But he could not deal with his womenfolk at all.

He could not frown them into submission, for Grandmother was blind and Mother always had her eyes covered with a damp cloth or a lace-edged handkerchief, albeit not a black-bordered one any longer. He could not affect their behavior through the purse strings either, since both widows' jointures were generous, and he could certainly not still their querulous demands with threats of physical violence. All he could do was stay away.

For two groats he'd have spent the holidays in London, where his latest mistress would have found some way of enlivening his birthday. Instead he was on the road to Berkshire to face the ghosts of his past, literally.

Tapping in the wainscoting, wailing through the chimneys, disappearing foodstuffs—the Priory ghosts were walking the halls. Murdered monks, squirrels in the secret passages, or bats in Lady Fanny's belfry, his mother's letters had gone from her usual vaporish complaints to hysterical gibberish about divine retribution. And company coming.

St. Cloud tossed back another cup of punch and

called Foley out of the taproom. At least he did not have to travel in state, cooped in a stuffy coach for endless hours. His bags and valet had gone on ahead yesterday, so he could have the pleasure of tooling the curricle and his priceless cattle through the cold, barren, winter-wrapped countryside. The dreary scenery matched his mood, and Foley knew better than to complain about the speed again, until the chestnuts showed off their high spirits by nearly wrapping the curricle around a signpost.

"I thought you meant the beasts to make it through the next stages an' on to the Priory without a change," Foley shouted over the wind. "They'll be blown way 'fore that, at this rate."

"I think the horses have more heart than you do, old man," St. Cloud replied. "They'll do. I intend to slow down before long to give them a rest anyway, but you want to get to a warm bed tonight, don't you?"

"Aye, and I'm thinkin' there'll be some eggnog and spice cake waiting. So I'd as lief get there in one piece, if it's all the same to you, my lord."

Eggnog and spice cake and Christmas carolers. Marriageable women, skittish women, swooning women. Ghosts and ghouls and noises in the night. "Bloody hell."

The expletive may have been for Foley's impudence, or it may have been for St. Cloud's black thoughts, or perhaps for the tree fallen across the roadway. Foley did not know. He got down to assess the situation as soon as the chestnuts came to a halt, and St. Cloud reached into his greatcoat pocket. Too late. Two men rode out of the screening bushes, and one of them already held his pistol on the defenseless groom.

"Stand and deliver."

Chapter Three

"*B*loody hell."

"Nothing to get riled over, Yer Highness," the man with the gun called out from Foley's side. He was big and broad and had a scarf pulled up over his mouth and a slouch hat pulled down low over his eyes. "Just raise yer hands up slowlike, and everything will be aces."

The other highwayman had dismounted and was holding the chestnuts' bridles. He was also bundled past recognition, but he was smaller, slighter, and as nervous as the horses he was trying to calm. He did not have a weapon in sight, so St. Cloud weighed the odds.

"None of that, Yer Highness," the first man said, catching the earl's tentative movement. He used the butt end of his pistol on Foley's head, then turned the barrel on St. Cloud.

The other robber jumped. "What'd you go and do that for, Charlie? You never said nothing about—"

"Shut your mouth, boy. Do you want to make him an introduction? Can't you see the toff is a real out-and-outer? He was going to go for the gun sooner or later, and much help you'd 'a' been. I couldn't keep both of 'em covered, now, could I?"

"But you shouldn't've hit him so hard. What if he's dead?"

"If he is dead, Charlie," the earl said in a voice that was like cold steel, "your life is not worth a ha'penny."

"Fine words for a gent what's got his arms up in the air," Charlie blustered, but he dismounted and nudged Foley with his toe until the little man groaned. "There, now can we finish this argle-bargle and get to business? You toss the pistol out first, real slow so I don't get twitch-fingered. And remember, I ain't tenderhearted like my green friend here."

St. Cloud's wallet was next, then his gold fob, quizzing glass, silver flask, and emerald stickpin.

"And the ring, too, Yer Highness," Charlie said, searching Foley's pockets for the groom's purse but never taking his eyes, or the gun, off the earl.

"It's a signet ring with my family crest on it. No fence would give a brass farthing for the thing, for they could never resell it; if you're ever found with it, it's your death warrant for sure."

"Let it be, Charlie," the youngster begged. "We have enough."

"Chicken gizzard," Charlie grumbled, leading his horse closer to the curricle to pick up the booty from where St. Cloud had thrown it to the ground. A quick shake of the earl's leather purse had him agreeing and getting back on his horse. "Reckon it's a good day's work, and it is the season for givin', ain't it? Stand back, boy."

The youth let go of the horses, but before St. Cloud could lower his hands and find the ribbons, Charlie fired his pistol right over the chestnuts' backs. "Merry Christmas, Yer Highness," he shouted after the rocketing curricle.

The thieves were long gone by the time St. Cloud could catch up the reins and slow the frenzied animals, then turn them back to find Foley. The groom was limping toward him along the verge, holding a none-too-clean kerchief to a gash on the side of his head. St. Cloud jumped down and hurried to him, leaving the chestnuts standing with their heads lowered. There was no fear of their spooking anymore this day.

"How bad does it hurt, Foley?" he asked, pulling off his own neck cloth to make a bandage. "Can you hold on to the next inn or should I come back for you with a wagon?"

"Don't fatch so, m'lord. I'll do. 'Tain't my head what's botherin' me as much as my pride anyways.

The chestnuts could've been hurt in that panic run. And you, too," he added as an afterthought, seeing the twitch in the earl's lips. "To think I was taken in by that old trick like a regular Johnny Raw, why, I'm slumguzzled for sure."

St. Cloud helped the older man back up to the curricle, wishing he had his flask, at least. "Whatever that is, don't blame yourself. I shouldn't have been wool-gathering either, but who would have thought there'd be bridle culls on this side road in Berkshire?"

"Amateurs, they was, you could tell."

"Yes, I was able to convince them to leave my ring, when any flat knows the thing can be melted down for the gold."

The groom spit through his teeth in disgust. "An' only one gun between them."

"It was enough," the earl answered, trying to keep the chestnuts to the least bumpy portion of the road. "And now they have mine." He was trying to recall how soon they could expect to come upon the next inn. He'd lost track of their position in the headlong rush and in truth hadn't been paying proper attention before then. There had to be something closer ahead than the Rose and the Crown was behind, even a hedge tavern. He didn't like Foley's color.

The groom was barely conscious when St. Cloud turned into the yard of a place whose weathered sign-board proclaimed it the Fighting Cock. Dilapidated, in need of paint, and with one sullen stable hand to come to their assistance, this inn was a far cry from the Rose and the Crown. There was a vast difference in their style of arrival, too. Now the horses were lathered and plodding, the curricle was scraped and spattered, the earl was disheveled, and his groom was bloody and sagging on the seat. And there was no pocketful of coins to grease the wheels of hospitality.

Their reception was commensurate with their appearance. The earl had to rub down the horses himself while waiting for the doctor. He had to leave his signet ring as pledge for the surgeon's bill and the laudanum he prescribed as well as for Foley's bed and baiting the horses. The innkeeper offered to throw in some stew as part of the bargain, but St. Cloud was too furious to eat. There were no horses to be hired, not on tick, and no room for the earl, not on Christmas Eve.

"You can't mean to set out so late," Foley complained from his rude palette behind the kitchen stairs. "And without me." He tried to sit up.

The earl pushed him back down. "Stubble it, you old hen. I'm not your only chick. There are a few hours of daylight left, and we're not that far from St. Cloud. Anyway, it looks to be a clear night ahead. I'll send a carriage back for you at first light."

"But the chestnuts, m'lord, they're tired."

"They've had their rest, and I'll travel slowly. Besides, I wouldn't leave my cattle in this cesspit."

Foley grinned as the laudanum pushed his eyes closed. "Aye, but you'd leave me."

St. Cloud tucked the thin blanket around his man. "No choice," he told him. "Lady St. Cloud is frantic enough as is. If my bags arrive and I don't appear as promised, she'll send out the militia. Blast all females and families."

"And footpads and fools."

"And clutch-fisted innkeepers."

St. Cloud was still furious an hour later. Two hours later, when he got down again to lighten the load as the chestnuts strained up yet another hill, he was furious, footsore, and hungry.

Some other traveler must have had trouble with the incline, he observed, spotting a small pile of books by the side of the road. The books were neatly stacked on a rock, off the damp ground and in full view, as though waiting to be picked up. St. Cloud did not think they were left for anyone in particular, for night was coming on, this country byway was practically deserted, and the books were neither wrapped nor tied. No, the chap must simply have grown weary of carrying the heavy volumes. The earl picked them up, thinking that if he came upon his fellow traveler, he could offer a ride and restore his belongings.

Oddly enough, the books were all religious in nature. Who would bother to carry a hymnal, a Bible, and a book of sermons, only to discard them on Christmas Eve? A heretic making a quiet statement? A distraught mourner abandoning his faith? With nothing better to occupy his mind but his own sour thoughts as he paced beside the horses, St. Cloud idly thumbed through the pages. More curious yet, the Bible was written in French, with no inscriptions or dedications. What, then? A spy shedding excess baggage as he fled the authorities? No, a fugitive would have hidden his trail, not left the evidence for the next passerby to find. Furthermore, the French pedestrian could not be a spy; St. Cloud had had his fill of adventure for the day.

The earl chided himself for his flights of fancy, using some poor émigré bastard to take his mind off his own empty pockets and empty stomach.

That poor émigré bastard had food. Midway up the next hill St. Cloud discovered an earthenware jug on an upturned log, with crumbs beneath it that the forest creatures hadn't discovered yet. "Damn," he cursed. The jug was empty, naturally. All that was left was a whiff of cider, just enough to make St. Cloud's mouth water. He stowed the jug under the floorboard, next to the books.

So the Frenchman was too poor for wine, and he was not far ahead. He could read, bilingually, and he was countryman enough not to leave an empty bottle where it could injure a horse and rider. St. Cloud hoped to catch up with him soon and hoped the fellow had something more to eat, to trade for a ride.

The earl stayed afoot, looking for signs of his would-be companion. If he had been mounted or traveling faster, he would have missed the next bundle, a paper-wrapped parcel carefully placed in the crook of a tree.

The earl looked around then, feeling foolish. He shrugged his broad shoulders and untied the string holding the soft package closed. Then he felt even more foolish for the previous observations he'd considered astute. Either the Frenchman was going to have a cold and lonely holiday after abandoning his *chère amie's* Christmas gift, or the Frenchman was a female. She would come just about to his chin, St. Cloud estimated, shaking out the white velvet, with a delicately rounded figure indeed, he knowledgeably extrapolated. The gown was not up to London standards, though an obviously expensive piece of goods, in good taste and the latest fashion.

Not even St. Cloud's fertile imagination could figure a scenario for a young woman—the gown was white, after all—strewing her possessions about the countryside on Christmas Eve. If this was some local ritual, it was a dashed dangerous one, with shadows lengthening and highwaymen on the prowl.

He rewrapped the parcel and took it to the curricle, where the chestnuts were cropping grass. This time he climbed up and set the pair to a faster pace. The sooner he had some answers, the better—for his own peace of mind and for the woman's sake.

Nothing prepared him for the answers he found around the next bend. Hell, the answers only led to more questions.

The woman trudging ahead was covered head to toe in a gray hooded cape. She carried a tapestry carpetbag over one elbow and an infant slung over her shoulder! What in the world would a mother and child be doing out alone miles from nowhere?

Then she turned to face the approaching carriage as he pulled rein alongside of her, and all rational thought fled from his mind. She was exquisite, with a soft, gentle look to her. Thick eyebrows were furrowed to mix a touch of uncertainty with innocence in her big brown eyes. The babe's head was covered by a blue blanket, reminding him of nothing so much as a Raphael masterpiece. He expected a donkey to trot out of the bushes at any moment to complete the tableau.

Instead the woman noticed her dress parcel on the seat beside him and smiled. "Oh, you found my gown. I was hoping someone would, who could use it." She was well-spoken and her voice was low, with no French accent or country inflection.

"Had you tired of it, then, ma'am?" He lifted the books from beneath his feet. "Or these?"

She smiled again, a quicksilver thing, like sun peeking from behind clouds. "You must know it was no such thing, sir. I simply had not realized when I set out how few wagons I would meet along the road, nor how heavy Pansy would seem after a few miles."

"You have been out on the road by yourself for more than a few miles? I would say that is remarkably poor planning indeed," he said in an angry tone. "Almost criminally cork-brained, in fact, considering, ah, Pansy."

Juneclaire took a step back, wondering at this stranger's hostility and wondering what else he thought she could have done about Pansy. As her heavy brows lowered in displeasure, she informed him, "We are not so far from Bramley now, sir, so I shall be on my way."

Bramley was at least two hours away, by carriage, and in the opposite direction from the Priory. St. Cloud cursed under his breath at the idiocy of what he saw before him and at what he was about to do. There was no decision, really. Not even the most stone-hearted care-for-naught could leave a fragile, gently bred mother and her baby on the road alone, afoot, in the dark, on Christmas Eve. Not if he was any kind of gentleman. "I am headed to Bramley myself, ma'am. May I offer you a ride?"

Juneclaire had been hoping for that very thing, but now she was hesitant. The man's accents were those of a gentleman, but he was scowling and speaking as if he thought she enjoyed her difficult situation. Did he think she would have left herself open to insult from every passing sheepherder on a whim? She was not reassured by his travel-stained appearance either. His greatcoat was caked with dust, and his cravat was missing altogether. The carriage was none too neat, and the horses were spent. A gentleman down on his luck, Juneclaire decided, no one she should know. Which was too bad, she regretted, since the dark-haired stranger might be very attractive if only he would smile. She bobbed a shallow curtsy with Pansy still in her arms and said, "Thank you for your kind offer, but it would not be proper for me to accept."

"Not proper? How can you consider propriety at this late date? And even if you were some innocent miss who had to protect her good name at all costs, how could you put such thoughts ahead of her welfare?" He nodded toward the blanketed bundle in her arms.

Now that was unjust! Juneclaire turned her back on him and set off down the road.

St. Cloud cursed the caper-witted female, then drove the chestnuts up to her. He started to get down, but he saw the woman shrink back and glance furtively to either side, as if seeking a way to run. He sat down, hard, his green eyes narrowed. "You're afraid of me," he stated matter-of-factly.

Juneclaire bit her lip. "You are angry."

"I am always angry, ma'am. Now I am enraged. I have been set on and robbed, my groom injured. I have been treated worse than a horse trader at a miserable inn, and my feet hurt. I am tired and hungry and dirty. Soon I will be cold. If that's not enough to try the patience of a saint, which I am not, I come upon a woman in circumstances no female should be forced to endure. *That* makes me furious."

"You are mad for my sake?" Juneclaire asked quietly, disbelievingly. No one had ever taken her part in anything before.

"I have been trained since birth to recognize damsels in distress, ma'am. The books never tell you they are so reluctant to be rescued, nor that they might be more afraid of the knight errant than the dragon. Truly, I only wish to spare you the dangers and discomforts of the road."

He was not looking nearly so fierce, Juneclaire thought, and the holdup could account for his bedraggled appearance. She realized that although his voice bespoke education and refinement, he could still be a plausible villain, but the very idea of highwaymen in the vicinity sent a shiver down her spine.

He saw her tremble and held out his hand. "Come, ma'am. At the rate you were going you would have no possessions whatsoever by the time you reached Bramley. And I don't eat babies, I promise."

She looked down at Pansy and smiled, then took a step closer to the carriage. She had the feeling that her stern-faced savior would not take no for an answer anyway.

"There, why don't you hand the baby up first?"

She flashed him a quick grin that was more naughty schoolgirl than dignified matron and lifted Pansy to his waiting arms. The earl had a hard time tearing his eyes off the enchanting sight of her dimples and transferring his gaze to the unfamiliar burden.

"I've never held a—"

Christmas pig.

Chapter Four

*S*t. Cloud threw his head back and laughed. Then he looked at Pansy on the seat beside him, a bristly black-and-white Berkshire pig with stand-up ears, little pink eyes, and a pink snout wriggling up at him. He recalled his promise not to eat her and laughed till tears ran down his eyes.

Juneclaire clambered up and took Pansy in her lap, laughing, too. She was right—he was attractive when he smiled. Actually, he was the most stunningly good-looking man she had ever seen, but since she hardly saw any men except for the farm workers, the vicar, and her uncle, she thought her judgment was suspect. The smile took years off his age and made his green eyes sparkle. He no longer wore that hooded, forbidding scowl, and Juneclaire settled back on her seat, contentment easing her tired muscles.

St. Cloud patted Pansy on the head before giving the horses the office to start. "Thank you for the joke. That was the most fun I've had in years."

"You should laugh more," Juneclaire said, then followed the startling familiarity with an explanation of sorts. "She really is a fine pig, you know, and a very good friend. I've had her ever since Ophelia stepped on her by mistake."

"Ophelia?" His lip quirked. "Never tell me that's the sow? Then the boar must be Hamlet?"

"Of course. It wasn't fair that Pansy should be the runt and lamed, too, so McCade—he's Uncle Avery's head pig man—gave her to me to feed and raise."

"She seems, ah, well behaved, for a pig."

"Oh, she is. And smart and clean, too. I bathe her in buttermilk to keep her hair soft, and then she licks it up for a snack."

"How efficient," he teased, knowing full well what was coming next, with a tenderhearted girl and a tender-meated piglet.

"Yes, well, you can see then how I could not hand Pansy over to the butcher just so Aunt Marta could impress her fine London guests. She wanted a boar's head, the way she thinks things used to be done, but McCade wouldn't part with Hamlet, of course."

"Of course," he solemnly agreed, his eyes on the road so she could not tell if he was bamming her again.

"Then Aunt Marta settled on a suckling pig, with an apple in its mouth, but there were no new litters. It isn't Pansy's fault she's so small, but Aunt wouldn't listen. All she cares about is putting on a show for the toplofty London titles visiting in the neighborhood, without spending a fortune. The peers only come for the party anyway. Those snobs will never accept her in the highest circles no matter what she does, in spite of Uncle Avery's title. Aunt Marta's father was in Trade," she confided.

St. Cloud was suddenly sobered, the habitual frown again marring his fine features. His passenger wasn't a mother, a matron, or a married lady. She wasn't a seamstress or a serving girl. By the Devil's drawers, she was a cursed highborn virgin, a runaway, and a pig thief! Oh Lord, what had he got himself into now? Perhaps if he knew the family, he could just sneak her back with no one the wiser.

"I'm sure your family must be worried about you, Miss . . . ?"

She must have read his intent, for she sat up straighter. "No, they are not. They never did before. And it's June-claire. One word."

"Very well, Miss Oneword, I am Merritt Jordan, at your service." He was not about to put notions in her head by mentioning his title. He couldn't bear to see that typical calculating gleam come over her guileless brown eyes. Besides, she seemed to have a low-enough opinion of the shallow Quality already. Heaven knew what she would think of Satan St. Cloud. For some reason her thoughts mattered.

Juneclaire was studying him, fitting his name to the strong planes of his face, the cleft in his chin. "I suppose your friends call you Merry?" she asked doubtfully.

Friends, relatives, acquaintances, everyone called him St. Cloud and had since he was seven. "Only my uncle George used to call me by a pet name. 'Merry Easter, Merry,' he used to say. 'Merry Christmas, Merry.' That's my birthday," he told her, not examining how easily he revealed personal details to this chance-met waif. He doubted if anyone outside his immediate family knew his birthday or cared. And he never mentioned George to anyone, ever.

"How wonderful for you! I suppose Christmas is your favorite day of the year, then."

"Hardly. That's the day Uncle George died."

"Oh, I'm sorry. I didn't know." Juneclaire was upset, thinking sorrow turned his lips down.

"Of course not, how could you? And no, the rest of my doting family does not call me anything half charming," he went on. He heard the bitterness in his own voice and saw regret in her serious little face. Dash it, the chit felt sorry for him!

The earl quickly turned back to the horses to hide his scowl, but Juneclaire huddled deeper in her cloak, squeezing Pansy to her so hard the piglet squealed in protest. She did not understand this man at all, and his uncertain temper unnerved her.

"I told you I don't bite," he said gruffly, then added, "I would be honored if you called me Merry, if you like. If your chaperon"—a nod toward Pansy—"permits this breach of etiquette. I think the circumstances are such that formal rules need not apply." There, she was smiling again. St. Cloud released the breath he didn't know he'd been holding.

"Thank you. My family calls me Claire, or Clarry. I hate both of those," she confided in return.

"Then I shall never use either," he vowed, again enraged at the way the girl's family seemed to hold this rare treasure in so little esteem, so careless of her feelings and well-being. If she was his . . . sister, he'd be out scouring the countryside. For sure he would have found her before some stranger with who-knew-what on his mind could offer a ride. Or worse. The earl masked his outrage at her poor treatment as best he could, with so little practice at hiding his ill humor. He'd quickly realized his little innocent could be startled by the slightest hint of anger, like some wary forest creature. He made a conscious effort to ease the set muscles of his face into an unfamiliar smile. "I shall call you Junco, then, for a gray-and-white snow bird in the Colonies." He reached over to touch the gray cloak and the white muffler she had wound around her neck. His gloved hand briefly grazed her cheek. "It's not quite the *rara avis* I think you are, but a brave and cheery little fellow. Do you mind?"

Juneclaire shook her head. Then, to hide the color

she knew was rushing to her face at his words, at his touch, she bent to the carpetbag at her feet. "Would you like something to eat, Merry? I have some bread and cheese and—"

"I thought you'd never ask!"

Later, after a silence broken only by the steady beat of the horses' hooves and Pansy's vocal table manners, the now-content earl asked, "You do have friends waiting for you in Bramley, don't you?"

He had a hard time holding on to his temper and his new resolve not to look like thunderclouds when she gaily answered, "Why, no, I am just going to meet the coach to London there. I was hoping to make the afternoon mail, but now I shall have to wait for tomorrow morning."

St. Cloud ground his teeth in an effort not to curse. "Tomorrow is Christmas; no coaches will run."

"Oh, dear, I hadn't thought of that."

"I warrant there are a lot of things you hadn't thought of, miss. Do you have enough brass for a respectable hotel? For sure I cannot help you there. The thieves barely left me the lint in my pockets."

Juneclaire suddenly found a need to inspect behind Pansy's ears. The piglet complained loudly, which hid Juneclaire's whispered "No."

"Did you say no? You ran away without enough blunt to hire a carriage or put up at an inn? Of all the cork-brained, mutton-headed ideas, why, I—"

Juneclaire was pressed against the railing at the edge of her seat. St. Cloud took a deep breath and unclenched his jaw. "Forgive me, Junco. I am just concerned for you."

Concerned? He looked ready to strangle her! "The money doesn't matter. I do have enough for my London coach fare and a night on the road, Mr. Jordan, and perhaps an inn in Bramley, although not the finest. But the inns are all filled with holiday travelers, and they don't seem to want unescorted females at any price. Or pigs."

There went St. Cloud's plan to drop her off with some respectable party in Bramley and proceed on his way before anybody recognized him. "Just what had you intended to do, then, if I might ask?"

She didn't like the sarcasm and raised her straight little nose in the air like a duchess. "I intend to sleep under a hedgerow as I did last night, for your information. It's not what I would like, but don't worry—Pansy and I shall manage."

Don't worry? Tell the Thames to stop flowing! Didn't the chit know what kind of villains roamed the roads? Thieves, beggars, gypsies—if she was lucky. Didn't she understand that she was ruined anyway? One night away from home was enough to shred her reputation. One hour in his company had the same effect, and that's how well she managed.

He could make up some Banbury tale about being brother and sister and pray no one recognized him, the chestnuts, or the crest on the side of his curricle. That close to St. Cloud? Hell, he may as well pray the pretty bird-wit turned into a bird, in fact, and flew off. And her damned pig with her. St. Cloud could hire her a coach and four and send her on her way, except that the banks would be closed, and tomorrow, too! What a coil. For twopence he would take her home, beat some sense into her relations, and be back on his way before midnight. He would, if the chestnuts weren't spent and she did not look so appealing, with her brown curls tumbling around her hood and a crumb on her chin.

"How old are you anyway, little one?" He wondered if he could throw her back, like a too-small fish.

"Not so little. I am nineteen, old enough to be out on my own."

"So ancient." She looked younger, he thought, with that untouched look. She did not have the brittle smile or the coy simper of a London belle years younger. "If you are such a mature age, how is it that you are still unwed? Are the men around here blind?"

"I do not go out in Society, so I do not know many men. But thank you for the compliment, if such it was."

Gads, she couldn't even flirt, and she was going to make it to London? "It was, Junco. But are you in mourning that you had no come-out?" he persisted.

Juneclaire picked at the unfinished hem of her mitten. She'd have the thing unraveled if he did not stop asking his probing questions, but she felt she owed him her answers, for his caring. "My parents died many years ago. Aunt is . . . embarrassed. They ran away, you see, and their marriage was irregular by her standards. But I am not quite on the shelf. Aunt Marta is looking for a husband for me, among the widowers and older bachelors."

No, he would not take her back, even if he knew her direction. He noticed that she was careful not to mention an address or a family name. At least the peagoose had some sense. St. Cloud wondered if she would trust him enough to hand over her coach fare so he could hire job horses and drive her to London himself. It meant a long, uncomfortable night, but he'd had worse and she would be safe, he thought. "Who is it you go to visit in London, Junco? You and Pansy?"

"Mrs. Simms, our old housekeeper. I thought she might find me a position in the mansion where she is employed."

Juneclaire had to grab Pansy to keep the pig from falling off the seat, the curricle stopped so suddenly, and she was sure the words coming from Mr. Jordan's lips were not meant for a lady's ears. She knew he would have that ugly look on his face, but by now she was confident enough that he was not going to turn violent on her. He simply had a volatile temper, no patience, and a colorful vocabulary. Juneclaire had nearly reached the end of her tether, too, however. "I know my plan is caper-witted," she shouted back at him. "But I have nowhere else to go. And not just for Pansy's sake. I'd rather go into service—be a scullery maid or such—than be married off willy-nilly to some over-weight sea captain or a snuff-drenched squire whose only conversation is about what animal he killed last. I have no choice! I am not a man who can join the army or take religious orders or read the law. No one will even teach me a trade! All I have is Pansy. What am I supposed to do?"

Two days on the road had taken their toll on Miss Beaumont's courage. A short tirade against this scowling stranger was the best she could manage before tears started to well in her eyes. Silently St. Cloud handed her a fine lawn handkerchief and then clucked the horses into motion.

That tore it, he conceded. There was no choice but to take the chit to St. Cloud Priory, but heaven knew the little pigeon deserved better than the flock of vultures there. He'd get fresh horses at Bramley one way or another and then turn around. The earl did not know how Miss Juneclaire Oneword was going to accept his high-handed decision. Not well, he guessed from her last burst of indignation. He'd face that hurdle once they reached Bramley.

As a matter of fact, where the hell was Bramley? They had turned off the Thackford road miles back at a cross sign and should have reached the town, he thought, although he did not know the way so well from this direction. "Ah, Junco, is this the road to Bramley?"

"How should I know?" she snuffled into his hand-kerchief. "I've never been here before."

Chapter Five

*T*hey were lost. Juneclaire was glad she could not see her companion's face in the gathering darkness. He was on foot, leading the horses up an uneven dirt track they were hoping led to a farmhouse. So many muffled imprecations came back to her through the cold night, Juneclaire began to wonder if Mr. Jordan had ever been a sailor. He certainly was not a countryman, stubbing his toe on every stone.

"Oh, look," she called out to distract him, "the evening star. Let's make a wish."

"Ouch! Bloody bastard bedrock." She'd distracted him too much. "I wish you to Jericho, Miss Juneclaire—ooph."

The one word he uttered was not even in her mental dictionary, thank goodness. With her breath making clouds in front of her face, Juneclaire stated, "Then I shall have to wish for you. I shall wish for your heart's desire."

"Right now my heart's desire is a hot tub and a warm brandy. If you can produce those, Junco, I shall believe in leprechauns, genies, and brown-eyed goddesses. Otherwise, wishes are for schoolgirls."

She made her wish anyway, not for his bodily comforts but for his troubled soul. The man might be an aristocrat, but he was not happy. Juneclaire had finally taken a better look at the cut of his coat and the quality of his horses, after she got over being terrorized at his arrogant ill humor. She refused to be embarrassed by her earlier remarks about the nobility, not if he was unabashed at his profanity. He *was* toplofty, refusing to let her go on alone, looking down his distinguished nose at her plans. He was obviously not used to being disagreed with, she thought with chagrin, recalling the row that had ensued when he tried to blame her for getting them lost, as if she should have known to bring a map with her when she left home. He had not demurred when she called him "my lord" either.

No matter, Lord Merritt might have everything in the world he wanted—not at this moment, of course—with no need to make wishes, but Juneclaire thought otherwise. She thought he was so cynical, he'd lost the capacity to believe in miracles. Perhaps he had been disappointed too many times. Juneclaire mightn't have a home or a loving family, a fortune or a settled future, but she still looked for magic. So she made her wish for his inner contentment.

Ice-cold well water for washing and tepid lemonade for drinking were not what Lord Merritt requested, his lowered brows reminded Juneclaire, but she smiled complacently. He was much happier now that they had found this old barn. He even whistled while rubbing down the horses. There were no lights at the farmhouse, but the barn was half filled with workhorses. St. Cloud thought the family must be off visiting for the holiday. He put his chestnuts in a loose box near the end of the row and swept out two other stalls with no signs of recent occupation. There was fresh hay for the horses, straw for their own beds, and a lantern by which to eat the rest of her hoarded food. Pansy was having a wonderful time, rooting around in the corn-crib, and Juneclaire was pleased.

"Why are you wearing that Mona Lisa smile, Junco? We are miles from nowhere, with an irate farmer liable to burst in on us at any minute, and our next meal has just eaten more than her fair share of this one."

Juneclaire wasn't worried, since he was scratching behind the little pig's ears while he spoke. "This is a great improvement over sleeping under a bush," she told him, then lowered her eyes. "And I feel safer with you here."

He snorted, or Pansy did. "I daresay I am more protection than the porker, but not much. Some hero

I have been. In one day I have gotten myself robbed and lost. I have no money, no pistol, no map, and I am eating your food."

"And you shouted at me."

"That, too. You should be demanding my head on a platter instead of feeding my pride. Any proper hero would have found you a proper bed."

Juneclaire settled into the straw and began to take her hair down. "But you found me just what I wanted. I have always dreamed of staying up all night in a barn on Christmas Eve to see if the animals really do speak at midnight, as the old tales say."

"Do you believe they will?"

She did not notice the way his eyes watched her, green glitters in the lantern's light. "Goodness," she said after removing the mouthful of hairpins to her pocket, "I have no idea and won't until I see for myself. Aunt Marta would never let me, of course. She was petrified that I might find myself alone with the grooms and stableboys. Aunt Marta is a terrible snob, you see."

"I daresay she would be relieved that you are alone with a wellborn rake," he noted drily.

Juneclaire paused in her efforts to brush her hair out of the thick braids that had been wound into a bun at her neck. "Are you really a rake?"

St. Cloud leaned back in the straw, a reed in his mouth. He watched the way the lantern cast golden highlights through her soft brown hair, way past her shoulders, covering her . . . cloak. He sat up. "I suppose I was, once. Now? Maybe it depends on one's definition. Are you afraid for your virtue?"

She looked like a startled fawn, those brown eyes wide open, thick brows arched high. The thought had never occurred to her. "Should I be?"

The earl had given over thinking of Juneclaire as Madonna-like hours ago. Now he was rearranging his impression of this hobbledehoy waif. The translucent beauty and the purity were still there, but Miss Juneclaire was no child. She was a damned desirable woman. He could think of few things he'd rather do than run his hands through those silky masses or feel her soft lips smile with pleasure under his kisses or—

"No," he answered curtly, getting up to snuff out the lantern. "I don't seduce innocents."

"Oh." Juneclaire could not keep the wistfulness out of her voice. She'd never even met a rake before and was hardly likely to again. She sighed and thought she heard a chuckle from his makeshift bed in the neighboring stall. She must be wrong. Her stone-faced savior was not much given to light humor. "Merry?"

"Yes?"

"Don't you find me attractive?"

That was a definite chuckle, followed by his own sigh. "Very, minx, but I find I am still somewhat of a gentleman. You are under my care, and that means you are safe, even from me. Especially from me. So stop fishing for compliments and go to sleep, Junco. It's been a long day and you must be tired. I am."

He rolled over in the straw. Juneclaire pulled Pansy closer for warmth but did not shut her eyes. She could see starlight through the chinks in the barn's roof. Every now and again one of the horses would stamp its foot.

"Merry?"

He turned around again, bumping his elbow on the wooden partition. "Blast. Woman, do not try my patience."

"But, Merry, I do not wish to sleep. Then I will never know about the animals. Won't you talk to me a bit so I stay awake?"

He grumbled, but she could tell he sat up. "What do you wish to talk about?"

"I don't know. . . . What do you do all day? Usually, I mean, when you are not traveling about the countryside saving silly girls?"

So he told her about his clubs and his wagers, Gentleman Jackson's and Manton's, the House and the War Office, agricultural lectures and investment counselors. He told her about the opera and the theater and balls, thinking that's what a rural young miss might care about. None of it whatsoever seemed interesting to him: neither the telling nor the living. Juneclaire, however, seemed to be swallowing his tales as eagerly as Pansy relished the windfall apples stored in another unused stall.

Juneclaire was thinking that she was right: he was indeed a man of means. His lordship's life was full and glamorous, dedicated to his own pleasure. He was as far above her as the stars overhead. She never felt her lowly status so much as when he asked what she did all day and she had to tell him about going to church and visiting the sick, helping Cook and directing the housemaids, mending and polishing and tending the flower gardens.

St. Cloud thought again of seeing her relations drawn and quartered for turning their own flesh and blood into a drudge. They hadn't managed to ruin her spirit, though, for he could detect the pleasure she derived from her roses and her sugarplums, the pride she took in seeing her aunt's house run well. Juneclaire was a real lady, and a rakehell such as he was not fit to touch her hem.

That did not keep the earl from moving his pile of straw to her side of the partition, though, so they could talk more easily. Juneclaire scrunched over to give him more room. St. Cloud did not want to talk about tomorrow, when he would have to force unpleasant decisions on her, and Juneclaire did not want to discuss the future, when this enchanted interlude would be only a memory to savor. So they talked about the past, the happier times before his father was injured and her father was killed, before his mother turned him over to tutors and hers slipped away. They talked of Christmases past.

"When we were in France, the whole family gathered in the kitchen to stir the Christmas pudding. Did yours?" she wanted to know.

"The children, sometimes. I doubt my mother even knows the way to the kitchen. What about you? Aunt Marta doesn't sound like one to take her turn after the potboy."

"She thinks it's all pagan superstition," she said regretfully, then added, "but I used to sneak down and have my turn anyway. Cook would call for me last, just before it was done."

"And would she put in the ring and the key and the penny? I cannot remember the other charms that were supposed to bring luck or wealth or whatever."

"No, Cook never dared to put the lucky pieces in the pudding she made for the family. I think she made another just for the staff."

"It was rigged in my household anyway. Aunt Florrie always got the little silver horse. She would cry otherwise. Aunt Florrie is not quite right," he explained, wondering if he should also mention his vaporish mother, wayward cousin, devious uncle, blind grandmother. No, he decided. Why chance giving the chit nightmares? And that was without reference to the ghost. He pictured Juneclaire crying out in the night, her hair tumbled over her shoulders, throwing herself into his arms in the straw. He shook his head. Unworthy, St. Cloud. "Oh yes, and once she was permitted at the table, Cousin Elsbeth always managed to receive the piece of pudding with the ring in it. It never helped, for she is twenty and still unwed."

"Then she must not have wished hard enough."

"I suspect it has more to do with her ambitious expectations and her shrewish nature. But I am certain you must have made a wish, fairy child that you are. What did you wish for?" He thought she'd confess to seeking a visit to London, fancy clothes and balls, like Elsbeth.

Suddenly shy, Juneclaire answered, "Just the usual schoolgirl fancies, I suppose." She was not about to tell him that her wish was going to be for a handsome cavalier to rescue her from the corpulent captain or the smelly squire. That had already come true, without her even making the wish! "I know," she declared, changing the subject, "let's make our Christmas wishes anyway. No, not for a hot meal or anything silly like that, but something special, something important. It's supposed to come true by Twelfth Night if you are deserving, so your wish must be for something worth being good."

"Do you mean only the righteous can have their wishes answered? I thought those were prayers," he teased.

Juneclaire considered. "Being good never hurts."

Oh, doesn't it? he wondered, pondering the ache in his loins to think of the dark-haired beauty not two feet away from him and two lifetimes apart. "You go first."

"I suppose I should wish for an end to the war and peace for everyone."

"No, no. That's being too good. Take it as a given and wish for something personal. After all, it's your one and only Christmas wish, practically in a manger. It's bound to come true, little bird." He reached over and found her hand.

"Do you know what I wish, then? I wish for a place of my very own, where I am wanted and welcome and no one can send me away or make me ashamed to be there."

He squeezed her hand, there in the dark. "I think . . . Yes, I think I wish for fewer people dependent on me, fewer responsibilities, and not having to listen to them tell me what's right for me. Then I mightn't feel so inclined to do the opposite."

They were quiet for a moment, lost in their own thoughts. Then Juneclaire started to hum a Christmas carol, and Merry joined in. They went through all the old songs they knew, English and French. His fine baritone held the tune better than her uncertain soprano, but she knew more of the words. They might have done better the other way around, but the horses and the pig did not complain.

Despite Juneclaire's determination to stay awake, her eyelids were too heavy to hold open when they ran out of songs. She had put in two long, hard days, even for a country girl used to physical exertion and fresh air. They drifted into sleep nestled in the straw, their hands entwined, the pig between them.

Chapter Six

*V*oices! It was true! Animals really could—a hand was clapped over Juneclaire's mouth before she could sit up and exclaim over the wonder of it all. The lantern was lighted, so she could see Merry's face inches from her own, scowling at her. He shook his head no. She nodded and he took his hand away but stayed so close, Juneclaire could feel his breath on her cheek. There were miracles and then there were—

"I tell you, Charlie, old man Blaine will have our hides for using his horses."

"Shut up, boy. Who's to tell him? He'll come back tomorrow an' be none the wiser if you bed 'em down proper. Left you in charge, didn't he? 'Sides, it wouldn't do to take my own cob out, now would it? I swan, you got less brains'n a duck, Ned Corbett. Riddles is back in the livery over to Bramley for all the world and his brother to see. For aught anyone knows I'm tucked up tight, and you been here watching the Blaine place all day and night just like you ought to be."

"That last carriage was too close to here, Charlie. Magistrate'll be here in the morning asking questions."

"Not on Christmas Day, he won't. Lord Cantwell likes his stuffed goose too well. And if he does, you didn't hear nothing anyway. 'Sides, that last coach was a bonus, you might say, for a good day's work. Who'd expect some widder lady to wear all her diamonds to midnight service? Finish up with them horses, boy. I want to divide up the take and be gone."

"I still don't like it. I wish you hadn't gone and hit that groom this morning. He dies and we could hang, Charlie."

"Stop worritin' at it, Ned. We could already hang for highway robbery, boy. What do you think, they hang you twice?"

"And you never said nothing about pulling a gun on no swell."

"What did you expect, boy? His nibs was going to hand over the blunt if we asked him pretty please? You're acting like a bloody schoolmarm."

"I never wanted to go anyways, Charlie. My ma finds out, she'll die."

"You're forgetting why you agreed to help me in the first place. You needed money for medicine, 'member, else she'll die. Sounds like she's going to cock up her toes anyway. May as well go in style."

"You leave my ma out of this, you makebate! She always said you'd end on the gallows, and she was right."

Juneclaire could hear the sound of a scuffle. She moved to poke her head over the wood to see, but St. Cloud quickly held her down with his body across her chest. All she could hear was heavy breathing. No, that was hers.

"Let that be a lesson, boy. No one messes with Charlie Parrett. You just cost yourself an extra yellow boy I was going to throw in for your ma. You'll think twice about giving me lip next time."

"There ain't going to be no next time, Charlie. I ain't going out with you again."

There came the sound of a heavy slap. "You ain't with me, boy, then you're against me. I'd never know when you'd give my name over to Cantwell for the reward money. O' course, the second they take me up, I'll shout your name so loud, your ma will hear even in heaven."

"I wouldn't cry rope on you, Charlie. I just don't want to do it again."

"You already been on the high toby, Ned, so there's no backing down. You don't come with me, I'll have to leave town and this easy-picking territory. Afore I go, naturally, I'd be sure to send a message to Cantwell, asking him where you got the ready for your ma's doctorin'. Now stop your sniveling and take your money, you poor, tender little dewdrop. Why, you're nothing but a whining pansy."

So Pansy went out to investigate. She slipped past St. Cloud while he was still lying across Juneclaire. Juneclaire held him and her breath.

"What's that?"

"What do you think it is, you looby, the lord-high sheriff hisself come to arrest you? It's a bloody pig."

"Farmer Blaine doesn't keep pigs."

The next sound Juneclaire heard was the cocking of a pistol.

After that, a blur. St. Cloud hurtled out of the stall with a shout, and Charlie swung the pistol around. The earl was on the bigger man before the thief could take aim. Ned jumped up, but Juneclaire hit him on the back of the neck with a bucket. The two older men fought for possession of the weapon, one hand each on the gun, St. Cloud's other hand going for Charlie's throat, Charlie's trying to gouge at St. Cloud's eyes. Juneclaire was ready to brain Charlie Parrett with her bucket when she had a clear shot. Ned started for the pitchfork near the door but tripped over Pansy and went down. Juneclaire hit him over the head again. When she looked up, his lordship and Parrett were rolling on the ground, the pistol between them.

They rolled into the upright where the lantern hung, sending the light flying. Now they struggled in the dark, with harsh panting noises and grunts the only sounds, till Juneclaire heard the crinkly rustle of loose straw catching on fire. Then Ned was rushing by her, stamping at the burgeoning flames. The horses started to kick at the walls of their stalls, and Pansy was squealing. Juneclaire found the other bucket, the one she'd washed with, and tossed the water on the fire. Then she took her cloak off and threw it over the sparks and started stomping up and down on it while Ned scraped the unlit straw away with his hands, leaving just bare dirt that could not burn. Then the pistol went off.

Juneclaire froze in place. Not Merry, she prayed, not even thinking of her own devilish situation if the enigmatic gentleman was hurt. There came the scrape of flint and a tiny glow. Whatever was keeping her knees locked upright, whether bravery, fear, or stupidity, gave out when she saw who lit another lantern. She sank to the ground on top of her wet, charred cloak and hugged Pansy so hard, the pig squealed loudly enough to wake the dead, but not Charlie Parrett.

Ned dashed for the door, to be stopped by an iron-hard clasp on his wrist. The boy made retching sounds, and St. Cloud shoved him toward one of the buckets.

"I guess I should have let him go," he said in disgust, watching Juneclaire hand the boy a handkerchief—St. Cloud's own. "Are you all right, Junco?"

"Yes, I think so. The fire is out. And you, my lord?"

"All in one piece, at least." He gingerly explored a bruise on his chin, which, from its feel, would add a less-than-festive touch to his appearance by the morning. Juneclaire thought he looked more human with his hair all mussed and his face dirty. He certainly was more endearing, though she could not go toward him to wipe away the smudges or push the dark curls back off his forehead. Not with Charlie at his feet.

"Is he . . . ?"

"Quite. We've saved the county the price of a trial." St. Cloud dragged the limp figure into one of the empty stalls, out of sight. He came back to poke through the pile of loot. His silver flask went into his greatcoat pocket, along with his fob, gold quizzing glass, and stickpin. He kept his pistol in easy reach and his eye on Ned while he counted out coins and bills. "Of course, this leaves us with a tad of a predicament, my dear, especially since I am sure you wish to be involved with investigations and your name to be brought out at inquests as little as I do. It could be much simpler, really. You know, a falling-out among thieves . . ."

"Merry, you wouldn't, just to save yourself some trouble!"

"Please, my lord, my ma—"

St. Cloud gave the youngster a look that sent Ned back to the bucket. "We heard all about your mother, sirrah. How proud she'd be to see her baby now," St. Cloud said with a sneer. "How much her health would improve to see you hang."

"But, Merry, he's just a boy!" Juneclaire pleaded.

"Just a boy who terrorizes the countryside, robbing

and injuring innocent travelers. What about justice, Juneclaire?"

"But it was Charlie who hit your groom. And Ned said he wasn't going to do it again, and he did help put out the fire. And we can give the money back now. What's the justice in hanging a boy who looks after his mother the best way he can? Someone should have been helping them before, the parish or landlord. Then this wouldn't have happened."

St. Cloud had a dark inkling who was the title holder for these miles around St. Cloud Priory, in the vicinity of Bramley. It was only an inkling, mind, so he thought he'd keep it to himself while Miss Juneclaire waxed eloquent. Ned must have appreciated her defensive oratory as well, for he looked up and said, "Thank you, ma'am. It's Miss Beaumont, from Stanton Hall, ain't it? My aunt keeps house for the vicar at Strasmere, and we visited once before Ma took sick. She mentioned a Miss Juneclaire Beaumont, who decorated the church and taught Sunday school to the children."

So much for squeaking through this coil without trumpeting their identities to the countryside, the earl thought, angrily stuffing what he determined his share of the thieves' haul into his wallet. He checked to make sure his pistol was loaded.

"No!" Juneclaire screeched, rushing to put her hand on his sleeve, having correctly interpreted the earl's aggravation if not his intent. "He won't tell anyone I was here. Will you, Ned?"

"No, ma'am. Never. I'll do anything you say, my lord."

St. Cloud patted her hand, taking a moment to think. "Very well, Junco, you've won your case. Ned, you'll take Farmer Blaine's horses out again, with a lantern and your friend Charlie. You'll ride to Lord Cantwell's house to head him off from coming here. Tell him you were asleep . . . where? The loft over the cow barn? Fine. You heard a shot, went to investigate, and found this suspicious character dead in the stable, the horses in a lather, a sack of jewels and gold next to him. You don't know anything else, did not see anyone run off, but suspect it was as we mentioned, an argument over the split. The other chap must have shabbed off when the shot woke the house. You had no pistol, so you couldn't give chase.

"That should keep Cantwell happy, with the money returned." The earl fixed Ned with a penetrating stare. "And be assured, bantling, I know exactly how much is left in that sack to be returned to the victims."

"You don't have to worry, my lord. I wouldn't touch a groat. Not now."

"Very well, I believe you. How long should that take?"

"No time at all. Bramley's right over the next rise, around the bend."

St. Cloud called curses down on the vagaries of fate while he searched in his pockets for a pad and pencil. "When you are finished with the magistrate, you will have to ride back to the Fighting Cock. I am sure you can get there and back before morning riding cross-country, even in the dark."

Ned nodded, while St. Cloud tore a page from his book. "The note is for my groom. You needn't see him, just give it to the innkeeper and redeem my signet with the purse I will give you. If you are back here with my ring, say, an hour past dawn, we can forget the whole bumblebroth. If not, young Ned, I will go straight to Lord Cantwell. And you can bet your bootstraps that Uncle Hebert will take my word over yours."

Ned was nodding, swearing on his mother's head that he'd do everything his lordship ordered, as fast as the horses could fly. He'd try to hold back dawn for an hour, too, if his lordship wanted.

"But what *about* his mother?" Juneclaire wanted to know. "They'll be in the same mess."

"I'll see that the mother is taken care of," St. Cloud promised, "if I see the son in the morning."

Juneclaire was satisfied. Her knight's armor wasn't tarnished.

"Oh, by the by, Ned, there is no need to mention me or the lady in any context whatsoever. If, however, someone is looking for her by name, you may inform him or her that Miss Beaumont's fiancé was escorting her to his family home for the holidays when there was a carriage accident."

Juneclaire's contentment shattered into rubble. Her knight's armor must have been made of cheesecloth instead of chain mail, that he received such a grievous blow to the head to addle his wits.

Ned knew there had been no female in the curricle that morning, but he also knew he was lucky to get out of the barn with his skin on. This devil could best Charlie, who was bigger and a dirtier fighter, and he had a look that could freeze a fellow's blood right in his veins. If the swell wanted him to swear, Ned would say his lordship was marrying the pig!

The earl helped the boy take the body out and tie it to one of the horses. Juneclaire tried not to look. She draped her cloak across one of the partitions in hopes it would be dry by morning. Then she started shivering.

When St. Cloud came back, Juneclaire found it the most natural thing in the world that he should hold his arms open and she should walk into them. He wrapped his greatcoat around her, rubbed her back, and feathered kisses on the top of her head until the trembling stopped.

"I'll never be a disbeliever again, Junco," he murmured into her hair, sending shivers through her again, but not from the cold this time. "And you must have been very, very good to compensate for my wickedness, to get our wishes answered so quickly."

"I don't understand." She didn't understand any of the feelings she was feeling either.

"Your wish, Miss Beaumont, for a place of your own. It's cold and dreary, but I'm sure you can change that in jig time with one of your smiles. They work for me, you know."

Juneclaire looked up at him in such muddled confusion, he had to kiss the tip of her nose, which was cold, so he held her closer still. "My house, goose. Your house when we marry."

She pulled back as far as his arms would let her, perhaps a quarter of an inch. "Oh, pooh, you don't have to marry me. I know you were being honorable and all that for Ned's benefit, but he'll never talk. You put the fear of God into him."

"God would be more forgiving if he doesn't get back. And I was not being honorable just for Ned. I am a gentleman, as I keep reminding you. The boy won't talk soon, but someone might see us in the morning, and sooner or later he'd mention your name. You have to be a respectable married lady by then."

"But you cannot want to marry me."

"To be honest, I haven't wanted to marry anyone, but why not you? You are kind and brave and loyal, and handy with a bucket. You're beautiful and you make me smile. What more could I ask? You'll be getting the worst of the bargain, but I need you to make my wish come true."

"All those responsibilities and people dragging at you?"

"Exactly. One of my responsibilities is to produce an heir, and now you'll keep me safe from all the matchmaking mamas and predatory females."

"Silly."

No one had ever called the Earl of St. Cloud silly before. No female had ever fit so perfectly next to his heart before. No matter what he told Juneclaire, he'd known their fates were sealed from the moment she stepped into his carriage and proved to be a lady. The matrimonial noose had been tightening around his neck with every mile until he could barely draw in his last gasps of freedom. Now the idea did not seem so bad, as he whispered reassurances in her ear until she fell asleep in his arms, his greatcoat spread over both of them. The pig whiffled in the corncrib.

Chapter Seven

*T*he earl awoke to the sound of church bells. The sun was well up, but St. Cloud did not want to disturb Juneclaire by searching out his fob watch. She still slept next to him under the greatcoat, not even the top of her head showing. St. Cloud shut his eyes again to savor the feeling. He almost never woke with a woman in his arms, never caring to stay the night with any of his paramours. Now he thought he might enjoy starting the days this way. Not with unfulfilled desires, naturally, but a special license would take care of that problem. He expected the other, the feeling of comfort and joy, just like the old carol they sang last night, to last for the next fifty or sixty years. God rest ye merry gentlemen.

Time didn't matter anyway. St. Cloud was already

long overdue at the Priory, and Juneclaire had no coach to catch in Bramley, even if they were running. And the boy had returned. He could hear Ned whistling about his tasks and jingling harness. Tactful lad.

St. Cloud wondered what Juneclaire would be like in the mornings. Some women, he knew, were querulous if roused early. Not even the earl dared approach the dowager Lady St. Cloud until Grandmother had her fortifying chocolate. Others, like his cousin Elsbeth, were vain of their looks until safely in their dressers' hands, and his mother had to lie abed all afternoon if forced to bestir herself before noon. Junco was not temperamental, conceited, or missish. St. Cloud could not wait to find her reaction to being kissed awake like Sleeping Beauty. He himself woke up amorous.

He raised the coat to stroke her smooth cheek— and his hands touched hair more bristly than his own side-whiskers. His eyes jerked open to stare into little red-rimmed beady ones, with absurdly long white eyelashes.

St. Cloud jumped up. Pansy jumped up. St. Cloud shouted: "What the hell!" And the pig raced off with a piercing whee that sounded like the gates of hell swinging shut.

"Stop that, you confounded animal," the earl ordered. "You weren't hurt, so quit overplaying your part, you ham. Your mistress must be out talking with Ned, so you're wasting your time trying to get sympathy." St. Cloud felt he was the one who deserved pitying, denied the pleasure of waking his bride-to-be. On his way out of the barn he tossed Pansy an apple saved from Juneclaire's hoard the night before. "There, and don't tell anyone I tried to kiss a pig good morning!"

Juneclaire wasn't polishing tack with Ned. She must be using the convenience, or be out by the pump, washing. This would be the last time in her life she'd use icy water or sleep on the ground, St. Cloud vowed.

Ned jumped off the upturned barrel and touched his cap. Then he fumbled in his pocket and withdrew St. Cloud's ring. "Here, my lord. I was back by first light, I swear, but you didn't say nothing 'bout waking you up."

The earl could see that the curricle was clean and shining in the wintry sun. The boy must have been back for hours, working outside in the cold. "Thank you," he acknowledged, nodding toward the equipage, and Ned blushed with pride. He was no more than twelve or thirteen, St. Cloud saw now by light of day, though tall for his age. He shouldn't have been out riding the roads all night, damn it, but he shouldn't have been mixed up with highwaymen either.

"Did you have any trouble?" the earl asked.

"Nary a bit. That widder lady went back toward Bramley, and the innkeeper sent her to Lord Cantwell at High Oaks to report the robbery. She was still kicking up a dust over to the manor. Magistrate was having to give her hospitality for the night, it seems, 'cause she was too afrighted to go back on the roads and had no money for the inn. He was right pleased to see me with the widder's purse and sparklers, I can tell you that."

"And what did he say about Charlie?"

"He said good riddance to bad rubbish, is what. Charlie'd been poaching up at High Oaks for as long as I can remember, only Cantwell's man could never catch him. His lordship being magistrate and all, he had to have proof. Charlie Parrett was too smart for that."

"If he was so smart, he should have stuck to poaching instead of going on the high toby."

Ned scuffed his worn boots in the dirt. "I reckon. Anyways, Charlie was right about his lordship and his Christmas dinner. Magistrate said he'd come out tomorrow to look over the place. No hurry today, with Charlie dead and the killer long gone, he said. And the widder had her money back, so he could stop her caterwauling and send her on her way before she curdled the cream for his pudding. Takes his supper serious, Lord Cantwell does."

"Very well, and if you just volunteer as little information as possible when he does arrive, the whole thing should blow over shortly. You can play dumb, can't you?"

The boy grinned at him. "Seems I've had a heap of practice, my lord."

"Quite. And did you do as well at the Fighting Cock?" He hadn't put his ring on yet, just turned it in his hand. "Did that innkeeper give you any trouble?"

"Nary a bit, once he saw the brass. And I saw your groom, too." Ned looked away. "I wanted to make sure he was, you know, not mangled or nothing. He was sitting in the taproom, happy as a grig, Wilton's daughters making a fuss over him on account of the bandage on his head. Said he slept the day through, then woke up for supper right as rain. He was glad to get your letter, I could tell, and wanted particular to know the horses was safe."

"Trust Foley to care more for the chestnuts than for me."

"Prime 'uns they are for true. I brushed them down quietlike this morning while you were sleeping. But he asked about you, too. Said he didn't recognize me a bit, so I was thinking I was home free, till he wanted to know why I wasn't wearing livery, and if I wasn't from the Priory, where'd I meet up with you and where'd you get the blunt to pay his shot and hire him a carriage. I didn't know what you wanted me to say, him being your man and all, so I did what you said just now and played dumb. He thinks I'm stupider'n a rock," Ned complained, "what doesn't even know its way home." He paused to look up at the man who towered over him. "Is it true you're St. Cloud? The earl hisself, who owns half the county?"

St. Cloud cursed. He wished Foley's head had been hit just a mite harder. "I am the earl, yes, but nowhere near as wealthy as all that."

The boy whistled through his teeth. "St. Cloud hisself," he marveled. "And I brushed your horses. Wait till I tell Ma."

"You'll tell her nothing of the sort," the earl ordered, but knew the boy would burst if he didn't tell his mother, so tacked on, "until I am long gone. You'll have to figure a way to tell her without mentioning the robbery. A carriage accident, I think, and you helped. That way you can explain about the money for her doctor." He flipped the boy two gold coins. "But don't mention the lady with me."

Ned looked confused. "The lady?"

"Excellent, boy. You'll have that rock perfect yet. Now tell me, did you send Miss Beaumont to the farmhouse to freshen up? We should be on the road soon, lest Cantwell decide to do his civic duty between meals after all."

Ned was shaking his head no, and St. Cloud suddenly felt an emptiness in the pit of his stomach that had nothing to do with hunger. "She's not at the house?" He raced around the barn to the well, Ned and Pansy on his heels. St. Cloud spun back and grabbed the boy's thin shoulders. "Tell me you gave her directions to a stream or something where she's gone."

White-faced, Ned shook his head again. "She . . . she wasn't here when I came back, sir. I thought you knew."

The earl ran back to the barn to search the stalls in case she woke up and realized the impropriety of sleeping next to him. Maybe he snored. Maybe . . .

Her things were gone, except for Pansy and the blue blanket. And a page from his notepad, stuck on a nail in the stall where they'd slept. St. Cloud sank down on a bale of hay while he read.

Dear Merry, Happy birthday and Merry Christmas. You are an honorable man, and under other circumstances I would be proud and happy to be your wife. Circumstances were such that I feel I can call you Merry, instead of Lord Jordan or whatever your title, but I cannot marry you. I cannot take advantage of your nobility and generosity and am therefore leaving. I have nothing to leave you for a Christmas gift or to thank you for your kindness, except that I might help grant your Christmas wish after all. Now you shall have one less responsibility, one fewer persons hanging on your sleeve.

For your birthday I am giving you Pansy. I cannot travel well with her, and she would not be happy in London, but that is not why I am leaving her with you. She is a very smart pig, and I know you will care for her, but mostly she will make you smile. I defy any man to be a sobersides with a pig as a companion. She likes sticky buns and having her ears scratched, but I expect you already know those things.

I have borrowed five shillings, so you do not need to worry about my reaching London. I shall return them to you in care of the postmaster at Bramley as soon as I am able. I regret taking them without your permission, but you would have argued about my decision to leave, and I could not bear to see you angry again. I shall remember you sleeping instead. Thank you for your kindness and best wishes to you. Sincerely, Juneclaire Beaumont.

St. Cloud cursed and threw his ring across the barn, the ring he was going to give her as proof that *her* Christmas wish was coming true. Pansy chased it, chuffing at the new game, nosing in the straw until she found it.

"Botheration," he raged. "The blasted animal will likely eat the damn thing and choke. Then Junco will have my head for sure." As he traded the last apple for his ring, St. Cloud realized he was thinking of Miss Beaumont in the future, not the past. Never the past, gone and forgotten. He was going after her.

He wiped his slimy, gritty ring on his sleeve—the once elegant greatcoat was ready for the dustbin after these two days anyway—then put it on his own finger, until he found Juneclaire and could place it on hers. After he strangled the chit.

"Fiend seize it, she must have been gone for hours! She could be halfway to London by now if Bramley is as close as you said." The boy nodded from the doorway, miserably aware that he should have awakened the gentleman ages ago. He wiped his nose on his shirtsleeve, to his lordship's further disgust. The earl stomped back to the stall where his pistol and his flask lay.

"After all my efforts to keep her out of this scandal-broth," he growled, "she has to go make mice feet of her reputation. The Devil only knows what she'll say about Charlie Parrett or you."

Ned was inching along the railing in the barn, not sure whether to flee his lordship's wrath or stay to take the pig home after the furious gent butchered it. Ma'd be right pleased to have fresh ham for Christmas dinner and bacon for Easter. Mention of Charlie Parrett stopped him in his tracks. "Me? You think she'll go to the magistrate and turn me in?" His voice was so high, it cracked. "But she didn't want to last night."

"No, brat, she won't peach on you on purpose. She's got bottom. But if she comes from this way, the good citizens in Bramley are bound to ask if she saw anything. And how is she going to explain being on her own? And if I go after her, there are certain to be more questions."

"Naw, no one'd dare quiz a fine swell like you." Ned didn't mention that most of the villagers would run inside and slam their doors rather than ask such a fierce-looking, arrogant nobleman what he was doing in their midst.

St. Cloud was pacing the length of the barn, the piglet trundling after. He was talking more to himself than to Ned, who was filling buckets for the horses. "But if they don't talk to me, I'll never find out where she went. And if I don't give some answers, they'll make them up. I know village life. It's the same as London gossip. No, I'll have to hope no one recognizes me."

"What about your uncle Hebert, the magistrate? He has to know you."

"Prosy old puff-guts always hated me, too. He's not even a real relation, just by marriage, his sister to my uncle. The dastard's bound to ask a lot of questions."

"Like what happened to your face."

"I haven't even seen how bad it looks." The boy's grimace told him. "A carriage accident."

"And where did you sleep?"

"Under a hedge."

"And what were you doing Bramley way, when everyone knows the Priory is clear west and north?"

St. Cloud started leading out the chestnuts, and Ned ran to help. "I was meeting Miss Beaumont to escort her to my home. And if anyone asks where is my groom or her maid and how did I mislay a female in my care, I'll tell them it's none of their deuced business. Especially not Hebert Cantwell's."

Ned whistled, impressed in spite of himself. "Guess it's no wonder they call you Satan St. Cloud, telling all those bouncers, and on the Lord's birthday, too! But they're going to wonder all the same, a top-of-the-trees gentleman like yourself all mussed up and Charlie Parrett laid out dead. What'll you say if anyone asks if you killed him?"

"The truth, brat, that he was such a bungler, he shot himself with his own pistol."

Chapter Eight

Juneclaire was on her way out of Bramley before St. Cloud was aware she was gone.

How silly he was, she had thought on the short walk toward the village earlier that morning, as soon as the cock crowed in predawn light. How silly and how sweet, to think about saving her from gossip. But ruination was only for ladies of the ton, not poor females. Indigent misses could not afford to worry overmuch about their good names, not when they had to consider their next meal. As for Juneclaire, she had no name to speak of, so how could she lose it? Her aunt already considered her no better than she should be because of her parents' marriage. She made it plain no respectable man would have Juneclaire to wive without good reason.

Merry, Lord Jordan, though, with all his talk of heirs
and London, was Quality. He was of the ton, and he
respected Juneclaire enough to offer marriage when
he need not at all. He thought she was good enough
to bear his own name, bear his children. No one else's
opinion mattered.

He said she was beautiful and brave. The thought
kept her warm on the way to Bramley. She was not feeling very courageous, once wagons and carriages started
passing her, local people on their way to church dressed
in all their finery, staring at the outsider. She was truly
alone now, without even Pansy to talk to, to watch out
for. Her own solitary state seemed much magnified
without the little animal, now that she was coming
among strangers. Merry would look after Pansy, she
assured herself, before she fell into a fit of the dismals
with missing her companion. The pig, not the man, she
tried to convince herself. He was a real gentleman—the
man, not the pig—so Pansy would be safe. Juneclaire
did not think he'd bring that formidable temper of his
to bear versus an innocent creature. Not that his ill humors were a sham, she admitted, but they seemed more
an ingrained habit than from genuine meanness. He
was kind. He had been mostly gentle with her and more
than fair with Ned. He was concerned about his groom
and worried that his people were fretting at his late arrival. He was a good man. He wasn't appreciated by his
relatives either, which was just about the only thing he
and Juneclaire had in common, besides a night in the

barn. Her mind had come full circle. That was enough to dream about, not enough to marry on.

"Do you need a lift into town, miss? Bells are starting to toll." An old couple in an antique tilbury had pulled up alongside her while she was woolgathering. "I be Sam Grey," the man said, "and this be my Alice."

Alice took in the odd condition of Juneclaire's cloak, as well as the quality of its cut and fabric. Juneclaire felt those old eyes missed nothing, not her tapestry bag, the muddied half boots, or the mismatched mittens. Juneclaire bobbed a curtsy, lest these good people think her manners as ramshackle as her appearance, and smiled. "A happy day to you, sir, ma'am. I am Juneclaire Beaumont, and I would be delighted to accept your kind offer."

Alice smiled back at Juneclaire's pretty behavior and moved over on the seat. Her black dress crinkled as she moved, so starched it was. She had a new green bow on her black ruched bonnet, and Sam wore a sprig of holly in his lapel. "Can't think what folks is about," he groused now, clucking the equally ancient horse into motion, such as it was, "passing a little gel like you up on the way to church, and this being a holy day and all."

"You know what it is, Sam. What with highway robberies and shootings, folks think they can't trust anyone. Little Bramley has never seen the like. Our Johnny brought the news this morning, Miss Beaumont. Such goings-on."

Juneclaire only had to nod and exclaim "How terrible" a few times while Sam and Alice speculated on the unmourned demise of Charlie Parrett. Sam spit over the side of the carriage. "Should end any of this bobbery about a gang of footpads in the neighborhood. Charlie Parrett was ringleader, mark me, and you'll see no more lawbreaking roundabouts, and a sight more rabbits and grouse on Lord Cantwell's estate, to boot." He laughed and coughed and spit again.

Alice patted his hand, then turned to Juneclaire. "A nice young lady like yourself hadn't ought to be alone on the roads during such uncertain times."

There was no censure in Alice's remark, just a great deal of curiosity. Juneclaire knew her face would turn red if she tried to lie to this shrewd little woman, and her tongue would twist itself in knots. It always did, so she told the truth. "I have no choice, for I had to help a friend in need, and my own situation was intolerable, so I am going to London to seek a position. I have coach fare and a bit extra."

Sam spit again but Alice *tsk*ed. She didn't know about any friend, but she could imagine what kind of trouble bedeviled such a pretty gal. "Well, you won't find the men are any different in London, Miss Beaumont. I can tell you, for Sam and I were in service at one of the great houses for years, we were, till the master pensioned us off and we came here. I suppose you have references and appointments and friends to stay with till you are settled?"

Juneclaire stared at her mittens, wishing the right

one could grow an inch up the cuff. "No, ma'am, just the address of our old housekeeper. I was hoping she might—"

"Without references? You must have come down with the last rain, Miss Beaumont. And if Bramley sounds bad, with talk of highwaymen and poachers and murderers, you should see London. There's cutpurses on every corner, and that's not the worst of it. Why, a pretty girl like you would get swallowed up the second your foot touched pavement. There are folks there who meet the coaches looking for just such ones as yourself. They offer the little country girls jobs and rooms and rides—and do you know where the girls end up?"

Juneclaire didn't, but she could guess. Aunt Marta had preached about the fleshpots of the city often enough. Feeling slightly ill, Juneclaire thanked Mrs. Grey for her warning. "Now I shall know better how to go on."

"You've never been in service, have you, dearie?" Alice guessed, shaking her head.

"Not that I ever got paid for, no. But I cannot go back. Pansy—"

While Juneclaire was realizing that she no longer had to worry about Pansy's future, Mrs. Grey was bemoaning a world where gently bred females—and she did not hesitate to declare Miss Beaumont a lady—had to leave home and hearth to see their virtue intact. Alice didn't doubt this Pansy had been seduced and abandoned by some rakish lordling or other, and Miss Beaumont was next.

"Don't fret, missy. I'll talk to Mrs. Vicar Broome right after service. She knows everything that's going on in the parish, so she'll find you a ride toward Springdale. That's the next closer coaching stop to London, and folks in Bramley have lots of relatives there. Someone's bound to be going off for Christmas dinner. And we'll fix you up with some kind of letter of introduction. I still have lots of friends in London, though I wish there was another way."

During Reverend Broome's reading of the Nativity, Juneclaire thought about another way. Would she rather be a servant in someone else's household or a drudge in her aunt's? Servants got paid pittances, barely enough to repay Merry's loan, and that was assuming she found a position at all. Back with the Stantons, though, she did have a room of her own, the use of Uncle's library, all the food she wanted to eat—and no strangers whispering about her in church.

She knew she was an object of speculation, but she would have been horrified to hear her tale so embroidered. By the time Mrs. Broome had pressed a hot roll and a shilling into her hand, Juneclaire was escaping a ravening monster and ravishment. Pity the man who pursued Miss Beaumont to the hitherto peaceful little village.

Juneclaire was bustled toward Mr. Josiah Coglin, who was waiting with his wife and daughters for their coach to be brought round from the inn. The owner of the mercantile and his family were bound for Spring-dale, where Mr. Coglin's brother ran a similar enter-prise. Mr. Coglin was all sympathy to Juneclaire's plight, quickly whispered into his ear by the efficient Mrs. Broome. Of course, the vicar's wife would never be indelicately explicit, but Mr. Coglin got the idea. So did Mrs. Mavis Coglin, who thought the drab little chit with heavy eyebrows must have invited any insults, since her looks had nothing to recommend her. Mrs. Coglin saw no reason to chance such a questionable miss with her own blond-haired, blue-eyed angels, or her husband. Miss Beaumont could ride on the seat with the driver and footman, she declared, lest the la-dies' skirts get crushed. Further, if the chit wished to go into service, she'd better learn her place.

Juneclaire clutched her carpetbag in one hand—no one offered to take it for her—and waved goodbye to the Greys and Mrs. Broome with the other. Once the Coglin ladies were settled inside, the grinning footman took his seat, nearer to Juneclaire than she could like. She was already pressed against the coachman on her other side, and that man's watery eyes were more on her than the horses.

Could Stanton Hall be worse than this?

They stopped at an inn about an hour later when the younger Miss Coglin complained of queasiness. The footman, whose name Juneclaire had learned was

Scully, hopped down smartly to lower the steps. All the while he was handing out the ladies and Mr. Coglin, he kept his leer on Juneclaire, hoping to catch a glimpse of ankle when she clambered down from the box without assistance. Mrs. Coglin turned her back on Juneclaire with a flick of her ermine tippet and demanded a private parlor, instantly. Mr. Josiah Coglin looked back at Juneclaire with a shrug of regret, either for his wife's manners or for missing a pretty sight.

Juneclaire brought her satchel, thinking she might take the opportunity to freshen up, but the innkeeper's harried wife was quick to direct her toward the kitchens, where the help ate.

"I am not a servant," Juneclaire stated. "Not yet, at any rate." And she vowed never to accept employment with such jumped-up mushrooms. She took a seat at a window table in the common room so she could see when the carriage was ready to leave. Mrs. Coglin might just forget her guest the same way she forgot to invite her to share the early nuncheon her strident voice was demanding.

When Juneclaire managed to get the attention of the serving girl, she asked for tea and a quick snack. The maid, who looked none too clean and none too happy to be waiting on a solitary female who looked as if she hadn't a feather to fly with, took her not-so-sweet time before plunking down a tepid pot of tea, a watery egg, dry toast, and a rasher of bacon. Bacon! To keep the tears from her eyes, Juneclaire looked about the room at the other travelers. To her right was a large, noisy family whose children never stayed in their seats long enough to count. One small girl toddled over to Juneclaire, so she gave her the bacon, receiving back a runny-nosed, gummy grin. To her left snored two sheepherders, judging from their smell, with their heads on the table. Across the way was a party of loud young men still on the go from last night's wassail or this morning's ale.

One of the men was looking at her the same way Scully had looked at her, and she felt dirty again. She left a coin on the table and went to find a place to wash.

The innkeeper's wife met her in the hall and thrust a tray into her hands. "Here, you may as well be useful. Bring this in to your mistress." She jerked her head toward an oak-paneled door and bustled back toward the kitchen before Juneclaire could repeat, "But I am not a servant."

The tray had a steaming pot of tea, lovely biscuits, and golden currant buns. Juneclaire sighed. She tapped lightly on the door, balancing the heavy tray in one unaccustomed hand, and went in.

"Put it there," Mrs. Coglin directed, again not offering to share the room or the food with Miss Beaumont. She didn't say "Thank you" either. Even Aunt Marta, the worst snob Juneclaire had ever known prior to this, always said "Thank you." She might pay her staff nipfarthing wages and treat them as interchangeable mannequins, but she always said "Please" and "Thank you."

Juneclaire demonstrated her own manners and breeding in inquiring as to the health of the younger Miss Coglin. That beribboned miss did not answer, too busy cramming biscuits into her rosebud mouth as fast as her dimpled fingers could snatch them away from her sister. Juneclaire turned to go, declining to curtsy.

"You can take this with you," Mrs. Coglin instructed, indicating yet another tray. This one held a single glass and a bottle of some reddish restorative cordial. Juneclaire thought of refusing, of giving her oft-repeated line like a bad drama, but then she thought of the miles to Springdale. She took up the tray.

Scully was coming out of the kitchens, wiping his mouth, when he spotted Juneclaire in the dark hallway with her hands full. Before she could begin to guess his intent, he grabbed hold of her and was slobbering damp kisses on her neck and cheek as she struggled to avoid his mouth on hers.

"Come on, pet, it's Christmas. Give a fellow a kiss now."

It was all of a piece that such a self-inflated shopkeeper as Mrs. Coglin would have a loose screw for a footman. Juneclaire didn't have a darning needle about her person, so she pushed at him, but he was too strong. Or the ale he'd been drinking was.

"What's the matter, lovey? Who're you saving it for? That last gent couldn't've been any good if he sent you on the road. Scully'll show you a better time."

What Scully showed her was that he was bigger, so

she'd better be quicker. Scully was Mrs. Coglin's servant; let *him* carry the blessed restorative, drip by sticky, sugary, reddish drip. Down his face, down his shirt, down his ardor.

Now she couldn't go on with the Coglins.

Juneclaire fetched her bag and left the inn just as that noisy family was departing. A gaunt woman with an infant in her arms was trying to herd her brood onto the back of an open wagon half filled with boxes and bundles and two chickens in a crate. The father chewed on the stem of his pipe and patted the workhorses hitched in front while he waited. The patient beasts' noses were pointed west, toward Strasmere, toward Stanton Hall.

"Pardon, sir, but could I ride along with you for a bit? I can pay my way, and I won't mind sitting in the back with the children."

Juneclaire was going home. Uncle Avery would never let her be thrown on the dole, and Aunt Marta would just have to take her back. It might be too optimistic to hope Lady Stanton would appreciate her niece more, now that she had a day or two of running the Hall by herself, but no matter. Juneclaire was good at it. What she wasn't good at, it seemed, was facing the world on her own. She wasn't quite that brave, no matter what Merry thought.

Despite what she saw as a grievous flaw in her character, and a disappointment to Merry if he should find out, Juneclaire was determined not to be cowed by her relations. She would *not* marry a fusty old man of her aunt's selection, not after turning down the most handsome, most intriguing rake in England. She would *not* be harassed by her cousins, not after routing Scully, and not after spending a night safe and unafraid in the arms of a true gentleman.

Juneclaire pulled the little runny-nosed moppet toward her and curled up on the hard wooden wagon bed, her satchel under her head as a pillow. She'd just rest after her adventures, and she would *not* cry.

Chapter Nine

*S*t. Cloud thought he'd leave the pig. Then he thought of trying to convince Miss Beaumont that he was a worthy candidate for her hand without that blasted pig in his. There was no way he could look into those soulful brown eyes and tell her that he'd found Pansy a good home. Not when he was bound to recall Ned's thin frame and hungry, hopeful expression every time the boy glanced at the porker.

Then the earl had to consider that he couldn't spring the horses without seeing if pigs really could fly. Those little trotters weren't meant for clinging to a swaying bench going sixteen miles an hour, nor was St. Cloud willing to dawdle. Neither could he manage the chestnuts, fresh as they were, with one hand.

Rope, that's what he needed. Ned almost lost his

front teeth, grinning at the impatient nobleman, but he did fetch a coil of hemp. St. Cloud made a harness of sorts, looping the rope under Pansy's legs, across her belly, and over her chest, around her neck, meeting in a sailor's knot on her back. The other end was snubbed to the arm rail, over Pansy's vociferous protests. The shoat was even more unhappy when, not three yards from the barn door, she slid off the seat to dangle inches from the wheels, all four feet kicking in the air. The volume of noise coming from the baby swine was far out of proportion to her size and was only equalled by St. Cloud's curses.

"Is there a crate around, boy?" he demanded of Ned, who was thrilled to be enlarging his vocabulary. Ned shook his head, then learned a few more new words.

St. Cloud gave up. He unbuttoned his greatcoat and stuffed the piglet into his waistcoat. Pansy stopped complaining immediately. The earl rebuttoned all but two middle buttons of the outer garment so Pansy could stick her snout out and breathe. No one in London would believe this.

No one in Bramley would either.

It had surely been an eventful Christmas morn in the little village: that widow screeching about highwaymen; then Charlie Parrett riding in facedown, and a slip of a thing running off to London to save herself from a fate worse than death, now this bedlamite. The fellows brimming with Christmas cheer in the inn's taproom couldn't decide if the raggedy chap with the thunderous look was Charlie's killer and confederate, a rapist, or just a raving maniac. Then the hostler who led the horses away reported a well-known crest on the curricle. Worse yet, he was Satan St. Cloud.

Now, coincidences were one thing, but not one of the men gathered at the bar doubted for an instant that all the day's unlikely events circled around this nasty-looking nobleman like steel bits near a magnet. From his reputation and the ugly bruise on his face, they assumed he'd helped Charlie Parrett to the big poaching preserve in purgatory. From his reputation and his query about a missing young lady, they knew he was bent on having his way with the chit. Not in Bramley, he wouldn't, not when jobs were scarce and prices were high, with him closing down the old quarry and shutting down the wood mill, and half the farmers paying him rent without ever getting to speak their piece about repairs or crops. They dealt with his uncle or his agents, and that wasn't half right. St. Cloud sure wasn't going to be helped in his hellraking, not when many of the local families sent their girls to the Priory to be maids and such. Not even rounds for the bar loosened tongues.

They drank his ale and watched out of the corners of their eyes when he poured his mug into a saucer and fed it to the pig. His reputation or not, none of them could figure out about the pig. None of the locals had any truck with the gentry anyway—queerer than Dick's hatband, all of 'em.

St. Cloud ordered breakfast for two and carried his mug and the pig's dish over to a table to wait, to think about his next move. On the way, he saw himself in the cracked mirror over the bar—and shuddered. Black hair sticking at all angles, purple bruises on his cheek and chin, no cravat whatsoever, and two days' growth of dark beard—it was no wonder the sots at the bar wouldn't give him the time of day. They most likely thought he'd steal it from them! In London the earl shaved morning and evening, bathed at least as often if he was riding or boxing or fencing, and changed his clothes from buckskins to pantaloons to formal knee breeches without a second thought. His valet, Todd, was liable to go off in an apoplexy if he saw the earl in such a state. Then he'd quit.

The citizens of Bramley might be more forthcoming if he didn't look like Dick Turpin, and he'd feel better, too, the earl decided after a satisfying breakfast of beefsteak and kidney pie, potatoes, hot muffins, and coffee. Pansy did not care for the coffee, so he drank hers also. Then he addressed the landlord about a room to wash and shave in. Money still opened some doors, he was relieved to note, although he was forced to rent the room for a day and night, payment in advance. No amount of money was going to see Pansy up the innkeeper's stairs, so St. Cloud tied her to his chair and tossed a coin to the barkeep to keep her ale flowing.

There wasn't much he could do about the bruise. Todd would have some concoction to cover it up, but he was at the Priory, likely steaming imaginary wrinkles out of St. Cloud's evening attire. And there was no hope for the caped greatcoat. It would have to be burned. St. Cloud could wash, at least, and didn't cut himself too badly with the borrowed razor. The serving wench who brought the hot water managed to find a cravat somewhere, likely some other guest's room, he didn't doubt from the way she quickly tucked his coin down her bodice. There, now he felt presentable again.

The maid must have thought so, too, for she stayed to admire the earl's broad shoulders and cleft chin.

"I don't suppose you know anything about a young woman wearing a gray cloak, do you?" he asked her, thinking she might be interested in talking.

That's not what Betty was interested in at all. She shook her head. Foolish chit, refusing the likes of this top drawer. So what if he looked like storm clouds; he was generous, wasn't he? A girl could do worse. "Why don't you stay the night and I'll ask around? Maybe I'll find something out, or maybe you'll forget about looking. The room's paid for anyways."

The earl smiled at her, if you could call a cold half sneer by that name, and walked by her without commenting. Something in his bleak look made Betty call after him, "I heard she came through town early, but she never came by the inn that I saw. You might try the church."

St. Cloud didn't know if the suggestion was for the sake of his immortal soul, his manhood, or his quest for Juneclaire, but he had nowhere else to try.

He gathered up a sleeping pig, a sack of potato peelings and yesterday's muffins, and proceeded to the church.

The second Christmas service was in progress; maybe Juneclaire was inside praying. He eagerly stepped over the threshold, then halted. Not even the Earl of St. Cloud would bring a pig to church. Pansy barely roused when he tied her to the hitching rail outside, between a dappled mare drowsing over a feed bag and a fat, shaggy pony harnessed to a cart decorated with greenery and red ribbons. St. Cloud scattered a few muffins near the piglet just in case she woke up hungry—she always woke up hungry; in case she woke up, period—and fed one to the pony. Then he went into the little church and took a seat near the rear.

Now Merritt Jordan was not one for practicing religion on a regular basis, but never since his school days had he sat on bare wooden pews with the reprobates and recalcitrants avoiding the preacher's eye. He scowled, and his neighbors on the bench scooted over. That was one benefit of two days in the same clothes, he told himself, and sharing them half that time with a pig. Now he was free to stare at the backs of the worshipers ahead of him, those too well bred to turn around to look at the latecomer.

There was Cantwell in the first pew, the one with

the carved aisle piece. St. Cloud wagered old Hebert's fat behind wasn't on any hard bench. He'd have soft cushions for himself and his family while the rest of the congregation, his people, wriggled and writhed in discomfort. Cantwell's wife was the broad-beamed lady beside him with the stuffed white bird mounted on her bonnet. What kind of hypocrite killed a dove for Christmas? he thought maliciously, flicking his gaze over the rest of Cantwell's party: two washed-out blond misses, a sandy-haired youth.

The earl studied each rear view in the church. There were five ladies with gray mantles, but two had gray hair, one had black, another was suckling an infant under the cloak, and the last one's head barely reached over the pew in front. Of the brunets, in case Junco had removed her cloak, only one was of the right height and slimness, with erect posture and neatly coiled braids. He stared at the woman's back, willing her to turn around. She did and gave him a wink from one of her crossed eyes.

The minister was stumbling over "the Lord coming among us this day," and the choir was singing the final hymn. St. Cloud turned his back to study the stained-glass windows as the parishioners filed out after the recessional. When the foot shuffling and whispers had passed, the earl turned and approached the doorway, where the vicar was shaking the last hands.

"A word with you, Reverend, if you don't mind? I'll only take a minute of your time."

Mr. Broome nodded, pushing the spectacles back up his nose. He led the way back down the church aisle and out a side door to a covered walk leading to the manse.

When they were seated in the vicar's office, the earl declined a politely offered sherry, knowing the reverend must be wishing him to the Devil, with his Christmas dinner growing cold.

"To be brief, sir, I was told you might have information about a young woman passing through here this morning."

Mr. Broome polished his glasses. The earl ground his teeth. When the spectacles were wiped to the gray-haired man's satisfaction, he looked up at his caller and asked, "And who might you be?"

The earl was trying his damnedest to hold his temper in check. "Merritt Jordan," he replied, thinking to keep his unsavory St. Cloud reputation as far away from Juneclaire as possible.

The vicar blinked, then blinked again. Yes, he had that look of his father and uncle before him. Broome had grown up with the Jordans. But the young earl was said to be an intelligent man, among other things. How could he suppose that a vicar who got his living from the family would not instantly recognize his patron's name? Didn't Reverend Broome pray for St. Cloud's reform and redemption every night?

"Ah, what might you want with the young lady, if I might ask?"

St. Cloud bit back a curse. He was not in the habit of explaining his actions to anyone, yet he knew he wasn't going to hear a word until he reassured the old dodderer. "Nothing havey-cavey, I swear. I intend to marry the girl."

Thank you, Lord. The vicar raised his head with a smile. "Do you, now?"

"As soon as I find her, damn it. Excuse me, vicar. You can perform the ceremony yourself to see it's all on the square, if you just tell me where Miss Beaumont is."

Positively beaming now, Mr. Broome rose and poured out a glass of the unwanted sherry. "I'll just go speak with Mrs. Broome for a moment. She's the one who saw the young lady off, you know. She wasn't happy about such a sweet young thing out on her own, going to London, so she'll be pleased as punch to make your acquaintance. I'll just be a second, my lord."

He was more than a second, and his wife was not pleased to be called out of her kitchen with her hair coming undone and her cheeks flushed from the oven fires. Red-faced, the vicar returned, while angry whispers sounded in the hall.

"I'm afraid my good wife is, ah, concerned. Not that I doubt your sincerity, mind, but, ah . . ."

"Get on with it, man. I don't have a special license in my pocket to prove my intentions are honorable, blast it. Do you want me to swear on your Bible?"

"I think you have sworn enough, actually, my lord,"

the vicar gently reproved, making the earl feel about six years old.

He apologized, then sipped the sherry to restore his patience. "What, then?"

"It has to do with a friend of Miss Beaumont's. Pansy, I believe."

Sherry spewed down St. Cloud's new cravat. "Pansy? Your wife is worried about Pansy? Is everyone demented? Pansy is under my care, sleeping off a drunk right now."

The vicar shook his head sadly. His wife was correct, poor Pansy's ruin was complete, and his lordship showed no remorse. "I am sorry, my lord, in that case I cannot—"

"Wait. Let me get her. You'll see for yourself, and Mrs. Broome, too."

Mrs. Broome was wringing her hands when the earl returned and dumped a tipsy piglet on her polished wood floors. Pansy tried to gain her feet, scrabbling against the shiny surface. Then she gave up, collapsed in a heap, and passed wind.

"Meet Pansy," St. Cloud announced. "You should have let sleeping hogs lie."

Chapter Ten

"What do you mean, I'll have no trouble recognizing the Coglins' coach because Miss Beaumont is riding on top with the driver?" No matter that he intended to take her up in his own open carriage, without footman or tiger. How dare anyone else treat Juneclaire so roughly! He jumped up and stalked to the fireplace.

"But, my lord," the vicar's wife tried to explain, fearing for her prized collection of china shepherdesses on the mantel, "Miss Beaumont had no maid or escort, and her clothes . . . Well, Mrs. Coglin did not see her for a lady."

"Anyone with two eyes in their head can see she's a lady! Hell and damnation, what kind of bobbing-block puts a female up on the box in the middle of winter?"

He grabbed up a paperweight from Vicar Broome's desk.

Mrs. Broome was wringing her hands again. She didn't know whether to worry most about her bric-a-brac, the goose roasting in the kitchen, likely burning without her, or the lace curtains, which the pig was now tasting. She didn't want to offend his lordship, of course, but he was not a comfortable guest. "Mr. Coglin is the wealthiest shopkeeper in town, so his wife tends to get a bit above herself."

"Very charitably put, my love," her husband noted, his eyes twinkling. His lordship's anger warmed Reverend Broome's heart, it did, showing just the right amount of pride and protectiveness. This wasn't some hole-in-corner affair; the earl really cared for the girl. The vicar sighed when Lord St. Cloud gave his graphic opinion of coxcomb caper-merchants and their encroaching, overblown wives. Not all of his prayers for the earl's salvation had been answered, then. No matter, Mr. Broome was a patient man; he did not expect miracles.

Mrs. Broome was scarlet-faced, having snatched her beloved snow globe from the earl's hands before he could punctuate his comments about toplofty tradesmen by smashing it onto the desk. "No matter where she's riding, my lord, if you miss the coach along the road, you'll find the family at Coglin's dry-goods store in Springdale. You'll want to catch up with them before Miss Beaumont parts company with them, so perhaps you should hurry. Please?"

St. Cloud considered asking if he could leave Pansy with them for a while but reconsidered when the pig started nibbling on the carpet fringe. He did beg Mrs. Broome for a large hatbox, which she was only too happy to fetch if it would see him on his way with the blessed pig.

While he waited, the earl wrote a check against his London bank, made out to Mr. Broome. He did not fill in an amount. "Here, vicar, buy some cushions for the back pews. I promise you'll have better attendance on Sundays."

Who said prayers weren't answered?

Mavis Coglin loved to visit her sister-in-law, Joan, in Springdale. Joan and her family had rooms over the store on the main street, a cook-housekeeper, and a shabby landaulet. Mavis possessed a fine clapboard house overlooking the village green in Bramley, employed four domestics, and had a traveling carriage plus a chaise for local calls and such.

"No, Joan, dear, don't apologize," Mavis oozed. "We don't mind being cramped in this little parlor, do we, Mr. Coglin? And I am sure whatever your Mrs. Burke prepares is adequate, though how she had the time with all her other duties . . . So I had my own cook fix some of her specialities. Scully is bringing them up from the coach now. That's the traveling coach, of course. You won't mind if Scully helps serve, will you? I know your dear little girls are used to passing dishes and such, but truly, Joan, it's not quite the thing." Mavis was having a grand time, especially when someone knocked on the shop door right in the middle of dinner.

"You see, Joan, dear, how inconvenient it is to live near the store? Every Tom, Dick, and Harry is forever ringing your bell when a button falls off or a ribbon goes missing. Isn't that so, Mr. Coglin? Why don't you let Scully get the door, Joan? He'll send the inconsiderate fellow to the roundabout fast enough. So much more the thing, don't you know, than sending one of the children. I never answer the door myself, of course, except when Lady Cantwell calls. Dear Lady C needed to confer with me about flowers for the church altar."

"Here now, mister, the shop is closed. Just because you went and spilled some wine on your neck cloth ain't no reason to ruin gentlefolk's Christmas dinner. I got splashed some myself and I'm still serving. And it ain't going to stop me from celebrating tonight neither, when the folks is home in bed."

St. Cloud wasn't listening, not to Scully anyway. He was hearing the sounds of the family upstairs and trying to pick out Juneclaire's soft voice.

Scully put his hand on the earl's shoulder to set him on his way. "G'wan, now, pal. Come back tomorrow."

Scully's hand was removed by an iron vise around his wrist. "You forget yourself, *pal*. I am here to see Mr. Josiah Coglin, and you shall stand out of my way."

"It's worth my job, an' I let you go up," Scully whined, his fingers growing numb from the continued pressure.

"And it's worth your life if you do not." Eyes as cold as green ice bore into Scully, convincing him. He gulped and nodded. "Here," the earl ordered, thrusting a large hatbox into the footman's arms, "guard this. And if you value your neck, don't let it out."

Don't let what out? Scully sank down on the floor between the glove counter and the lace table, staring at the hatbox. He pushed the box across the aisle with his foot and rubbed his wrist. The fellow had the Devil's own strength.

Scully did not give a thought to his employers' safety upstairs, too concerned with his own skin and what was making noises in the dread box. Weren't no bonnet, that was for sure, with moans and grunts coming from it. The greasy hairs on the back of Scully's neck slowly rose, leaving a chill right down his spine. B'gad, the thing could be a goblin or some such creature from hell, ready to drink his blood if it got out. Scully had to know.

Fellow said don't let it out, not don't look. Scully edged closer on hands and knees to where he could peer in one of the holes poked through the lid. He took a deep breath and put his eye to the opening. A red-rimmed eye with no white showing looked back. Scully was out the door before his heart remembered to start beating again. He ran around the corner, jumped into the traveling carriage, and slammed the door. He wasn't going back upstairs till that warlock left and, no matter what the limb of Satan ordered, he wasn't staying downstairs with no soul-snatching hell fiend, not in a pig's eye.

"Sirs, ladies, forgive me for intruding, but could you tell me where I might find Miss Juneclaire Beaumont? You brought her here from Bramley."

Nearly all the Coglins had their mouths hanging open. Mavis closed hers with a snap and demanded that the impertinent fellow remove himself at once, before she called for her footman.

"Your man already greeted me at the door. Please, ma'am, Miss Beaumont? Then I shall be more than happy to leave you to enjoy your meal in peace."

Mavis sniffed. "I am sure I do not know what became of the baggage. She left the inn where we stopped for refreshment without so much as a by-your-leave."

"She just left? Surely you asked her where she was going, with whom?"

"I never had the chance, sirrah. The wanton went off without a word to anyone. No one saw her leave. And you can be sure I asked, for I meant to make the jade pay for my footman's new uniform, if the stains did not come out."

A muscle twitched in St. Cloud's jaw. "How did Miss Beaumont come to be responsible for your footman's uniform?"

"She threw a bottle of wine at poor Scully. Fine return for our Christian charity, I say. Now you can leave us decent people to our meal."

"A moment more, ma'am, so I understand perfectly. You let an innocent young lady set off by herself from an inn in the middle of nowhere?"

Mavis wiped her mouth delicately with her napkin. "I told you, I made inquiries. And there was no proof that she is, indeed, a lady. In fact, the innkeeper mentioned some young bucks passing through. Perhaps she took up with them."

"Ma'am," St. Cloud ground out through narrowed lips, "were you a gentleman, I would call you out. Were you a lady, I'd see every door in London closed to you. Miss Beaumont has more ladylike grace in her little finger than you possess in your whole overdressed, overweight, overreaching self."

"Josiah, throw him out," Mavis screeched, her face swollen and splotched. "Do you hear the way this ruffian is speaking to me? Do something, I say!"

Josiah Coglin figured the intruder to be five inches taller than himself, fifteen years younger, and in fitter condition by half. Jupiter, the most exercise Josiah got was carrying the cash envelope to the bank. Besides, the fellow was right. So Josiah did something; he passed around the mashed turnips. His brother snickered, and Joan hid her satisfaction in her napkin. The children still watched, wide-eyed.

Mavis saw no one was coming to her rescue and the

rudesby was still glaring at her. "Pish-tosh," she blustered, "fine words coming from a fine jackanapes with rag manners and rags on his back. What do you know about gentlemen and ladies? Bounders like you come into the shop all the time, looking for a piece of gimcrack frippery to turn the girls' heads. For all we know, you're the doxie's fancy man. I know your kind."

St. Cloud's gaze could have withered the silk blossoms at Mavis Coglin's heaving breast if they were not already dead. "No, ma'am," he said on his way to the stairs, "you don't know my kind at all. Not many earls buy their own shoe buttons or silver polish."

Scully was still cowering in the coach when St. Cloud found him. The earl banged open the door and plucked the footman out like a pickle from a barrel. He held Scully by the collar, feet off the ground. "Why did Miss Beaumont throw the wine at you?" he demanded.

Scully was saying every prayer he'd ever heard, including the last rites. The earl shook him. "Why?"

"N-nothing, gov, I swear. She just come over violentlike."

Juneclaire, who pleaded mercy for a young robber? St. Cloud tightened his grip and shook the weasel again. "You must have done something to insult her. What?"

"A k-kiss, that's all."

That's all? St. Cloud broke the dastard's nose and darkened both his daylights, that's all. Scully was relieved the devil hadn't sent the demon in the box after him.

Damn! St. Cloud took a swallow from his flask while he tried to think through the fog of anger clouding his mind. He absently poured some of the brandy onto a roll for the pig nuzzling at his sleeve.

She could be anywhere! She could be halfway to London or asleep under a hedge. She could have taken a ride with anyone passing by that inn or been taken by the young blades for sport. Not even the brandy warmed the chill in his gut at the thought.

He needed more people to help search. He needed more money to pay them. The earl decided to drive home and organize the armies of servants at the Priory. He'd have them combing the countryside, searching every coach and cart. He'd get rid of the pig, thankfully, and saddle his stallion so he could cover more territory. He'd get to London, hire Bow Street runners, and knock on every door in London asking if a Mrs. Simms was housekeeper.

Just let her be safe until he found her.

St. Cloud stuffed the pig back in her box and whipped up the horses, wondering at his determination to locate a chit he'd only known a day or so. It wasn't just pride, he told himself, because she had refused him, and not just how he hated to be thwarted. He wanted her, but this was more than lust, more than the thrill of the chase. He had to find her to fill that empty space where his dreams had been. He had planned on showing her the Priory, her future home; he'd pictured her in the portrait gallery, the orangery, the morning room. He could practically see her there. Now he'd be looking around the corners, staring in the mirrors, waiting for her to appear like Mother's ghost. He had to find her.

But he didn't find her, not even when his curricle overtook the lumbering old wagon full of noisy children. He didn't notice the sleeping woman among the bundles and boxes and babies and crated chickens. He kept on driving.

Chapter Eleven

*M*atthew Mulvilhill shoved his brother Mark into their sister Anne, who started bawling, which woke Baby Sarah, wailing in their mother's arms. Their father, John Mulvilhill, reached behind him to clout the nearest young Mulvilhill without taking his eyes off the horses. Lucas, minding his own business, was carving his name in the planked wagon with his new pocket-knife. The knife slipped, ruining his perfect *L*, and Lucas said a word not found in the Bible. He hopped up to get out of his father's reach and tripped over little Mary, who was cuddled next to Juneclaire, who awoke to shrieks and kicks and a suspicious damp spot on her much-abused cloak.

Christmas carols held the children's attention for perhaps a mile, at the horses' phlegmatic gait. Some-

where in the middle of a wassail song Juneclaire noticed that in addition to the general bumpiness of the
wagon now that they'd turned off the larger road, and
the seeming inability of the children to sit in one place
for the count of ten, one of the bundles was moving.

"'Heigh-ho, nobody—' What in the world is in that
sack?"

"Kittens. We're taking them to Granny's."

"In a sack?"

"Sure, you puts a rock in with 'em and they go down
fast."

"A rock? You're going to drown the kittens?"

"Pa says we have too many cats. They'll eat the chickens, else."

"But . . . but it's Christmas!"

"That's why we gots to take 'em to Granny's. Our
pond is froze, but she's near a good running stream. Pa
says I can toss 'em in."

"No, it's my turn!"

"I can throw the farrest!"

"Pa!"

Juneclaire had no idea where she was. She was alone
on a wood-bordered dirt track with no habitation in
sight. She had only Mrs. Broome's roll by way of food
in her satchel, two precious shillings less in her purse,
and a sackful of kittens in her hands. And it was starting to snow.

She would *not* cry. The kittens would, and did, a

pitiful mewing that hurried her to a log under a tree whose branches offered some protection. When she opened the sack, four pairs of bluish eyes blinked up at her. Another pair of eyes would never open again, no matter how hard she tried to blow life into the tiny mouth.

She didn't have time to cry. The other scrawny babies wouldn't eat the roll; it was too hard. They were too cold, too thin, too weak from hunger—and she couldn't just leave the dead one there for the badgers and crows. She made room in her carpetbag and folded the sack on top of her belongings, then carefully lifted the kittens in. There were two gray-striped ones, a patchwork brindle, and an all-black kitten who tried to suck on her finger. She unwrapped her warm scarf and draped it over the top of the satchel, one corner turned back for air.

Crying was for children. Juneclaire cleared leaves away from a spot between two jutting roots of the tree. She laid the dead kitten on the ground, then covered it with the leaves, sticks, and whatever stones she could find. Then she placed her French Bible, the hymnal, and the volume of sermons on top of the makeshift grave and set out down the country lane, wiping her eyes. For the second time in two days she'd left her books on the side of the road; she couldn't begin to count how many new heartaches she carried with her. But those weren't tears. They were snowflakes.

*   *   *

If Juneclaire were alone, she would keep walking. She'd eat her solitary roll and walk until she found a likely cottage or tidy farmstead to seek directions or hire a cart ride back to Bramley. Sam and Alice Grey would put her up for the night, she thought, or Vicar and Mrs. Broome. She'd walk all through the night if she had to, if she were alone, rather than approach the derelict thatch-roof hovel and its broken-doored barn. This place seemed too poor for a horse or a scrap of food for the kittens or a warm fire. Goodness, the hut looked so poor, the people couldn't afford to give directions!

Maybe it was deserted, Juneclaire thought cheerfully as her brisk steps took her nearer. Maybe it was the haunt of one such as Charlie Parrett. Her feet dragged.

Then a dog started to bark. It was a big, mud-colored mongrel with a hairier strip down its back, charging out of the old barn.

"Good doggy," Juneclaire called. The dog came nearer, stiff-legged, snarling, sniffing the air. "Nice doggy," she said. The cur's ridge hairs were standing up, its teeth showing. Not a nice doggy at all.

The beast was barking and snarling in earnest now, darting up to snap at the air perilously close to her ankles. Juneclaire was going to throw her satchel at it, until she remembered the kittens. The kittens! She raised the bag over her head, shouting, "Go away, you miserable mutt! You're not going to eat my kittens, not on Christmas Day!"

The outcome was still pending when a sharp whistle pierced the air. The dog dropped to its belly as if pole-axed, though it still kept a yellow-eyed gaze on June-claire, daring her to take one more step. An old man hobbled out of the barn. Sam Grey was old; this man was old enough to be Sam's father. He was old enough to be Noah's father. He was bent, bald, and toothless, with skin like autumn leaves. But he controlled the big dog with a simple "Down, Jack. Good boy."

"Thank you," Juneclaire said. "I'll just be—"

"Don't know what's come over old Jack." He paused to think about it. "Usually it's just cats what get him so riled."

"It's my fault, then, for that's what I've got in my bag. I'd better get on my way. Good afternoon to you." She started to back away, keeping her eye on the big dog.

The old man was peering at her from under unruly white brows. His blue eyes were clear enough, though. He took a wheezing breath and said, "Hold, missy. What's a mite like you doing out here?"

With a simple hand gesture from his master, Jack was on his feet, rumbling low in his throat. Juneclaire stopped her retreat. "I . . . I was going to London to seek a position, but I decided not," she told him, thinning the story to its bare bones. She saw no reason to mention a pig, a nobleman, a highway robber, or Scully. "Only, the family that was carrying me back had all these children, and they were going to drown the little kittens. I couldn't let them, so I got off with the cats. Only, I don't quite know where I am, and the kittens need something to eat, and yours was the first place I came to."

He nodded slowly, like a rusted hinge. No words came from his sunken mouth, so Juneclaire nervously went on, "I am heading west of Strasmere, but I have friends in Bramley. I just met them today, actually, but they are nice people. They'll help me. And . . . and I can pay my way."

Still there was no response. He couldn't have frozen in that position, could he, with the dog on guard? Juneclaire imagined them all turning into snow sculptures, the whole tableau waiting for the spring thaw. "F-forgive my manners." She bobbed an awkward curtsy. "I am Miss Juneclaire Beaumont, from Stanton Hall, near Farley's Grange."

The old man bent at the waist, and Juneclaire almost rushed forward to catch him, except the dog stood between them. "I'm Little Yerby," the ancient announced once he'd straightened and paused to catch his breath. "My father was Big Yerby. He's gone, but the name stuck. Even my Aggie calls me Little." There was another halt for breathing. "She's gone off to our daughter's lying-in with the donkey, else I'd ride you to town." He scratched his bald head. "Guess you better come in, then. Coming on to snow. My old bones've been warning me for days." He turned toward the house.

"But what about Jack and the kittens?"

"Jack does what I tell him."

Juneclaire hoped so, as she followed him toward the mean cottage, only she hadn't heard him tell Jack anything.

There were two rooms inside the dwelling, both neat as a pin. Fresh rushes covered the packed-dirt floor, and calico curtains fluttered at the windows. Vegetables and herbs hung from the rafters, and a warm fire burned in the open hearth. Juneclaire observed that Little Yerby's clothes were clean and neatly mended, as he took a copper kettle off the hob. He poured some of the hot water into an earthenware pot for tea and added a little to a saucer of milk for the kittens. Juneclaire crumpled the roll into the warm mixture and put it and the kittens, on their sack, near the fireplace.

With a mug of hot tea in her hand, Juneclaire was more than content to sit and watch the kittens attack their meal. "How could anyone think of destroying such sweet and innocent babies?"

"Be worse to let them loose to starve." Little Yerby was in a cane-backed chair, warming his gnarled fingers on the mug more than drinking from it.

"But they wouldn't eat so much."

"Big family like that, they was prob'ly scraping by just to feed their own young'uns."

"But they don't take them out and drown them if there are too many!"

"World's a hard place, missy."

Juneclaire sighed. "I know."

"Next choice is worse." Little Yerby stood up in stages, then turned and gave Juneclaire a toothless grin. "Don't know what my Aggie'll say—'tain't proper with her away and all, me inviting a pretty little thing to spend the night—but there it is. You can bunk near the fire, where my girl used to sleep. There be an old quilt somewheres." He shuffled off to the bedroom and rummaged in a chest. "Here 'tis. If you'll help with the chores, I'll add some vegetables to the stew Aggie left me. Can't chew much more'n that, you know. Still, I saved some dandelion wine for Christmas supper."

He halted at the pantry. "Sorry Aggie ain't here. It's the first Christmas since we married. Sorry my girl married away, too. What was I looking for? Oh yes, the wine. Mind wanders some, you know." Then he slapped his thigh and doubled over, laughing. "Won't they talk down to the local, Little Yerby and a rare charmer. Aggie'll be tickled pink!"

Juneclaire smiled back. "And I'd be honored to be your guest, Mr. Yerby, and help with the chores."

"Yeah, the chores, near forgot. Not as spry as I used to be. You know anything about cows?"

"No, but I know a lot about pigs." Juneclaire was transferring the kittens to a basket he held out to her so they wouldn't wander too close to the fire.

Little Yerby slapped his leg again. "You ever milked a sow? There, you go on start. I'll put up the stew."

*   *   *

How hard could it be? The cows were all lined up, their heads in the food troughs. A bucket and a stool stood ready by the door. Jack sniffed at her but didn't growl or anything, so Juneclaire carried the equipment to the first animal in the line. She put the stool down, then shoved the bucket under. She removed her mittens and blew on her hands, then straightened her shoulders, sat down, and reached under the—uh-oh.

"Guess old Fred is tickled pink, too." But not as pink as Juneclaire's cheeks as she cautiously backed away.

The cows were easier. Juneclaire only got half as much on her as she got in the bucket, till she got the knack of the thing. Little Yerby skimmed off a ladle of cream and stored the rest of the milk while Juneclaire rinsed the buckets at the well.

After supper Little Yerby nodded over his pipe, and Juneclaire sat on her cloak by the fire with the kittens playing in her lap, their bellies round and full. Then Jack scratched at the door.

"Oh, dear, does he usually come in at night?"

"Just for an hour or two afore he settles down with the cows. He can stay out, though. You know, Aggie always wanted a cat. Said Jack was my dog, not her'n. Cat'd keep mice out of the pantry and the root cellar, too."

"And you have the milk for it, till the kitten can hunt on its own. But what about Jack?"

He knocked the pipe into the fireplace. "Never tried an infant before."

Juneclaire gathered the kittens on their sack. "He wouldn't . . . ?"

"Jack does what I tell him," Little Yerby answered, opening the door. "Down, Jack. Stay."

The dog lay rigid, tense, and ready to spring, the hackles at his back erect, his muzzle creased to show huge white teeth. Little Yerby nodded, and Juneclaire put the kittens down, about a foot from his nose, and held her breath.

There was a puddle of saliva under Jack's mouth by the time the kittens noticed him. He didn't move, but he growled. One kit dug its sharp claws into Juneclaire's skirts and tried to climb, one disappeared into the rafters, and another found the other room and hid under the bed. The last kitten, though, one of the gray-striped ones, arched its back and hissed. Jack raised pleading eyes to Little Yerby, who shook his head no. The kitten reached out a tiny paw and batted at Jack's nose.

"Look at that," the old man said. "Just like David and Goliath."

Juneclaire was ready to snatch the idiot cat out of harm's way, but Little Yerby told her to let them be. Jack nudged the kitten's foot, toppling the wee thing, which meowed loudly. Jack opened his mouth—and licked the kitten. Juneclaire gasped. David, as the hero was instantly christened, be it he or be it she, circled around and curled up to sleep next to the big dog's chest, between Jack's feet.

Juneclaire rounded up the other kittens and soothed them in their basket, with the familiar sack. She did not want to offend the old man's hospitality but had to renew her offer: "You have been so kind, Mr. Yerby, and I was no help with the chores at all to speak of, and David won't be feeding on Mrs. Yerby's mice for a while still, so will you not accept my shilling for his feed?"

"Nay, lass, you'll be needing it more. Howbeit you can do something worth more than gold, missy. I couldn't get to church today without the donkey, not on these old legs, and I never did learn me my letters." He handed her a worn book. "Would you read me the story?"

So Juneclaire sat on the stool by the fire that Christmas night while the old man leaned back in his chair, one knobby hand resting on his dog's head, the other stroking a sleeping kitten.

"'And it came to pass in those days,'" she began, "'that there went out a decree from Caesar Augustus, that all the world should be taxed.'"

Chapter Twelve

*H*ome for the holidays. Oh, joy.

St. Cloud meant to head directly to the stables to begin to organize the grooms' search. Instead, he saw the gardener's boy race from the gate lodge across the lawns to announce his arrival at the Priory. Oh, blast!

By the time the earl tooled his weary chestnuts through the tree-lined drive, over the bridge at the ornamental lake, past the formal gardens and the maze, a welcoming delegation was waiting in the carriage drive.

His relatives would never be so outré as to demonstrate what might be taken for affection; they'd be waiting in the gold salon having predinner sherry and dissecting his character. St. Cloud Priory kept Town hours, even though Countess Fanny hadn't been to London in years. Instead, they sent servants to wait outside in the snow. There were two grooms and Foley to help with one curricle, three footmen to carry his bags that had been delivered the day before. His valet, Todd, took one look at the earl and about-faced up the steps to order a hot bath. Talbot, the butler, remained at attention in the open doorway and a maid was there to—Hell, St. Cloud couldn't figure why a maid was there at all, shivering. He handed her the hatbox and told her to wait inside.

He waved off the footmen and let the grooms take the chestnuts, with orders to double their rations. He held Foley back. The wiry ex-jockey was pale, with a small bandage still on his head.

"Old man, am I glad to see you. How are you feeling?" the earl asked.

"Fairly, my lord, iffen I can say the same? It's a rare takin' they been in, up to the house, with me no wiser from talkin' to that boy you sent with the blunt. I was that worried about the chestnuts, I was," the older man scolded.

"They've taken no harm, I swear. Listen, Foley, I need a groom to ride to London as soon as possible, through the night if the snow doesn't get worse."

"I'll go saddle Lightning, my lord. You have a message for me to take?"

"You're not going. Find one of the other men, someone you trust."

"You mean a younger man. I'll be handin' in my livery, then."

"Don't get all prickly and puss-faced on me, old man. Not now. You've been hurt, and I need you here."

Talbot coughed from up the stairs, subtly. "Old stone britches should shut the door if he's gettin' cold," Foley pointed out, not so quietly, not so subtly.

"Ignore him. Here is the message your man is to give to my secretary at Jordan House: I want every available footman and groom out in Mayfair, going house to house, looking for a housekeeper named Mrs. Simms. Some of the knockers will be off, but they should be able to ask around for the housekeepers' names."

Foley pulled at the bandage on his head. "I thought I was the one concussed. Of all the crack-brained starts—"

"Enough, Foley. I am sure there will be more than one lecture waiting for me inside. I do not require yours."

Foley knew the short limits to the earl's patience. "Yes, my lord. And when the men find this here Mrs. Simms, what are they supposed to do with her?"

"Send for me, but give Mrs. Simms ten pounds to hold on to the lady—she'll know who I mean—and keep her safe until I can get there. I also want a man at every posting house that takes coaches coming into Town from Bramley, Springdale, or anywhere closer. They are to look for a lady in a gray, rabbit-lined cloak. She has brown hair and a smile like a Madonna. The man should follow her, find out where she goes, and make bloody hell sure she gets there safe. And send for me. I'll be in London as soon as possible. Is that clear?"

"Clear as pitch. Every man jack in London is to look for a housekeeper or a pretty chit."

"Right. Now go, get someone started while there's still light."

Foley left, shaking his head and muttering. "I take my eyes off the lad for less'n a day and there's a female involved. Should've known."

"Welcome home, my lord," Talbot intoned as he bowed the earl through the door. "Merry Christmas, my lord, and may I offer you the felicitations of the day on behalf of the staff and myself. The coincidence of your natal day with the Nativity brings double cause for joy and celebration." Talbot must have been practicing since yesterday. "The family and guests are in the gold parlor. Shall I announce you?"

"Good Lord, no. I'm not fit for company, much less milady's dinner table. Tell them to go in without me. I'll join them later for tea." He took the hatbox from the blushing maid, who curtsied and fled down the hall. "I have a great many arrangements to make, Talbot. I am sure Todd is seeing to my bath, but could you send up some dinner on a tray? Make that a large dinner. And a basket."

"A basket, my lord?"

"Large. And a decanter of that cognac my father put down. Large, if I have to face the family later."

Before St. Cloud could cross the black-and-white tiles of the huge entry hall to reach the arched stairways, his grandmother's less-than-dulcet tones floated down the hall: "So where is the scapegrace? Been home twenty minutes by my count, two days late, and nary a word for his worried kin. If I hadn't sent my maid out, we'd be sitting here like ninnies not knowing if he was dead or alive. Why, the jackanapes could have expired on the doorstep, and without an heir, mind you."

The dowager's words were punctuated by raps of her cane and, since she couldn't see what she was thumping, muffled oaths and tumbled footstools. "Sad lack of manners you taught the boy, Fanny. No sense of responsibility either, the rakehell. I've been sitting all day in this mausoleum among confounded strangers waiting for the whopstraw to show, instead of being home in my own comfort with my own people. Deuced if I'll stay here all night waiting on his convenience. Be like waiting for your haunt to come, Fanny. I'm going home. Talbot! Munch! Get the carriage! Where's my wrap?"

Before St. Cloud could flee upstairs past Talbot's stiff-spined, measured tread, the dowager's cane rapping started down the hall, followed by the crash of china. Lady Fanny's fluttery "Mother St. Cloud, please" came after. "What about dinner? Oh, I feel ill."

"Not in front of the guests, you ninny." That from

Uncle Harmon. "Who's got the vinaigrette? Where's that blasted Talbot? No, Florrie, we won't burn feathers under Fanny's nose. Give Lady Pomeroy back her headpiece, you clunch. Elsbeth, stop batting your eyelashes at the admiral. Get over here and help your aunt."

Welcome home, my lord.

St. Cloud's silent appearance in the gold salon put an end to all the commotion except the dowager's flailing cane and demands for her carriage. "I am here, Grandmother, so you can stop enacting us a Cheltenham tragedy and upsetting Lady Fanny. I simply did not wish to present myself in all my dirt."

The dowager sniffed when he kissed her powdered and rouged cheek. "I can tell why. So what fustian are you going to give us for being two days late and near missing your own birthday party?"

"Why, Grandmother, you should know me better than that. I haven't seen fit to explain my actions since my youth. Surely you don't expect a rakeshame to make excuses?"

The dowager cackled and banged her cane down on Talbot's foot. The butler did not disgrace his calling by more than a wince, St. Cloud observed, as the earl turned to kiss his mother's brow, removing a lavender-soaked handkerchief to do so. "I am sorry if I interfered in your plans, my lady. You should know better than to fret over me."

"Dear boy, how could I not? My condition . . ."

St. Cloud was already shaking hands with his cousin, ignoring the younger Wilmott's smug looks. Niles was wearing white satin knee breeches, a white satin coat, and a white waistcoat picked out with red-and-green embroidered holly. None of it paid for, most likely. St. Cloud took great care to pat Niles on the shoulder in greeting, leaving a smudge. His cousin Elsbeth presented the tips of her fingers for his salute, her nose wrinkled. "That's more than travel dust, St. Cloud."

Uncle Harmon Wilmott did not put his hand out or step closer. He nodded curtly, frowning. "I think you could show more remorse for turning the house upside down and upsetting your mother's delicate nerves."

"Do you, Uncle?" The earl spoke slowly, deliberately, watching the color rise in the baronet's pouchy face.

Lady Fanny was quick to step into the silence, although she found interchanges between her son and her brother particularly wearing. "Yes, dearest, I was quite overset to think something must have happened to you, and there was the bother of redoing the seating plan, you know. I don't see what I would have done without Harmon's support. It's been that way for years, of course, and we mustn't let Harmon think we're ungrateful, dear."

St. Cloud bowed in his uncle's direction but did not add to his mother's words. She held a gray filmy scarf to her cheek. "You really should have been here," she reproved. "Harmon had to light the Yule log in your place. You know the head of the household holds that honor."

"I am certain Uncle Harmon found no difficulty in usurping my . . . honors." He turned to greet others of the company while his mother searched for her hartshorn.

Lord, even Sydelle Pomeroy was dressed—or undressed—to the nines. Red silk with nothing under it, unless he missed his guess.

"I knew you wouldn't forsake us, my lord," she breathed, making his appearance a compliment to her undeniable beauty.

" 'Us,' my lady? How could I forsake you when I did not know you would be here?" The sultry widow had been after St. Cloud's title as long as Cousin Niles had been after her fortune. Lady Pomeroy had been Uncle Harmon's wife's godchild and milked the tenuous relationship for all the invitations she could. She and Niles made a fine pair: cold, calculating, and conceited.

Damn, he wished they were all gone! Then St. Cloud remembered Junco—he hadn't thought of her for at least five minutes—and her wishes. An evil kind of grin came over his face, lips half quirked, eyes slightly narrowed. Only Niles recognized the St. Cloud smile for what it was and left off denigrating the earl's shabby manners. St. Cloud stepped back to the hall and returned with the hat-box.

Aunt Florrie clapped her hands together. "Oh, goody! You brought us a present!"

"My gifts to you must still be with my baggage upstairs, Aunt Florrie. This was a present given to me, which I was going to take upstairs, if I had been permitted. Since you've all made me feel so welcome, I'll share it with you."

He tipped Pansy out to the floor, and the piglet headed straight for the scent of biscuits, in ladies' hands, on low tables, and under gentlemen's pumps, where crumbs were ground into the Aubusson carpet. So Juneclaire was right, St. Cloud acknowledged. Christmas wishes come true. The room was almost clear in no time, the indomitable Talbot having the presence of mind to announce dinner. Juneclaire was right about another thing: a man with a pig really did have more opportunity to smile. St. Cloud was positively beaming.

None of those remaining in the parlor seemed to share his good humor, except for Florrie, who had tied a napkin around Pansy's neck and was helping her sip from the hastily discarded sherry glasses. The dowager was shouting to know what was going on, and how could everyone have gone into dinner without her taking precedence. Niles was snickering at more evidence of his cousin's gaucherie, and Lady Fanny had collapsed back on the sofa.

"Come, Mother, they cannot start without you." The earl half lifted his mother into Niles's arms. "Uncle Harmon, I am sure I can leave you to escort Lady St. Cloud into dinner."

Lord Wilmott was seething, his jowls quivering. "How dare you, sir, shame your mother by setting an animal loose in her drawing room? How could you bring such disgrace to this house?"

St. Cloud took out his quizzing glass, blessing Charlie Parrett for treating it kindly, and surveyed the overturned furniture, the broken glassware, and, finally, the livid baronet. "Odd," he drawled. "I thought this was my house." He bowed. "My ladies, I shall see you after dinner."

Chapter Thirteen

"*H*ogwash," St. Cloud told his cousin Niles. "The man works for me. If Todd can't look after one little pig for an evening, he's not worth his wages."

The efficient, even-tempered, and elegant gentleman's gentleman was worth a fortune, which was about what it took to convince Todd to play swineherd for a few hours. St. Cloud had no intention of discussing his domestic arrangements with Niles, however, not even to rid the coxcomb of that supercilious grin.

Todd had wrought miracles. The pig was fed, walked, and bedded down in St. Cloud's dressing room, with promises that Pansy would be installed in the stables tomorrow. And St. Cloud was combed, brushed, and polished to a fare-thee-well, from glossy black curls to glossy black footwear. His cheeks were as smooth as a baby's bottom, and the bruise on his face was almost unnoticeable. With his muscle-molding white Persian knee smalls, wide-shouldered black coat of Bath superfine and stark white linen enlivened only by an emerald stickpin the color of his eyes, he made Niles look like a man-milliner and the squire's sturdy sons look like bumpkins.

Most of the guests reassembled in the gold salon chose to treat the pig incident as a fine joke, reinforcing St. Cloud's belief that an earl with upwards of forty thousand a year had a great deal of social latitude, and that Society was a jackass. It also appeared to St. Cloud that the joke became funnier the more females a man had to marry off. The admiral, with his three platter-faced chits, thought it was hilarious. He joined the squire, with one daughter and two nieces, in proposing toasts to the earl's birthday. Everyone joined in, in high good humor, especially once the lambs' wool punch was served round twice, except Mr. Hilloughby, his mother's current tame cleric, who stuck to tea, and Uncle Harmon, who was in high dudgeon.

Lady Pomeroy sat at the pianoforte, having arranged the candelabrum to best highlight her mature décolletage while shadowing the tiny signs of passing youth. She skillfully picked out carols, seemingly by heart, but purred a request for the earl to turn her pages for her.

Uncle Harmon frowned when St. Cloud acquiesced,

taking a seat on the bench so near Sydelle that a draft couldn't have come between them. Lord Wilmott wanted the earl for Elsbeth, Lady Sydelle and her inheritance for the spendthrift Niles. The older man grew perfectly bilious at the thought of his goddaughter and his nephew making a match of it, melding their fortunes while his own expensive progeny got short shrift. Being well aware of his uncle's ambitions, and dyspepsia, the earl moved closer to the alluring widow.

The reverend decided it was time for one last Christmas invocation, for faith, hope, and chastity, and a benediction for the Christ child.

"Speaking of children, St. Cloud, when are you going to provide some for this old pile?" The dowager did not wait for Hilloughby's amen. She couldn't see the blushes of the younger girls, invited for his consideration, St. Cloud made no doubt, and wouldn't have cared anyway. "It's time and past you married and got yourself an heir. I want grandchildren!" She thumped her cane down, hard, on one of the squire's chits' gowns. The girl ran crying from the room, trailing a flounce. "What's that ninnyhammer Fanny crying about now?" the dowager demanded.

St. Cloud removed the cane from her fingers. "You don't need this while you are having tea, and that was not Lady Fanny, Grandmother, but an innocent miss you have embarrassed with your wayward cane and wicked tongue."

"Humph. If all the young gels are such niminy-piminy, milk-and-water chits, it's no wonder you haven't taken leg shackles. But I can't wait forever, you know. This place has been in the Jordan family for centuries, boy, and it's your job to see it stays there."

He sipped slowly from his cup. "I am no longer a boy, Grandmother."

"And I wouldn't ask a boy to do a man's job!"

Lady Fanny tried to play peacemaker again, handing round a plate of sugarplums. "I am sure St. Cloud knows his responsibilities to the name, Mother St. Cloud."

"And to his family," Uncle Harmon put in, as blatant as a battleship. He dragged Elsbeth away from one of the squire's sons and thrust her onto the sofa next to her cousin.

Elsbeth was her usual sulky self, in a pet this evening because she was not the center of male adulation. She and Aunt Fanny had invited the plainest girls in the country for St. Cloud's perusal, knowing Elsbeth would shine in contrast. Now he and every other man in the room, including the squire's gapeseed sons and her own brother, were panting after that fast Sydelle Pomeroy. Even Mr. Hilloughby's collar got too tight when the widow walked past him, as slow and slinky as sin. Elsbeth bet the widow's skirts were dampened. Red silk, while Elsbeth sat as demure as a debutante in pink chiffon! It wasn't to be borne. Worst of all were the calf's eyes St. Cloud was making at the older woman, when everyone in the room knew he was as good as promised to Elsbeth. Papa said he was only sowing more wild oats, that he'd only offer a lightskirt like Sydelle a slip on the shoulder. Well, Elsbeth was tired of cooling her heels in Berkshire while St. Cloud was kicking his up in London.

"Yes, cousin," she lisped. "Just when are you going to drop the handkerchief?"

He dropped a bombshell, not a handkerchief. "I already have."

The admiral called for another toast. He'd wasted an evening, but the punch was good.

"No, sir, it's not official yet. I haven't had a chance to seek her family's permission, but I expect her here within a few days."

"Oh, dearest, how wonderful! Who are her people? Shall we like her?" The countess's various shawls and draperies dipped in the tea, in her excitement.

"Her name is Juneclaire, and I'm sure you'll love her, Mother. And, no, you do not know the family. They are from Farley's Grange." He pushed the tray back farther.

"Nobody who's anybody lives in Farley's Grange, boy. When do we get to meet her?"

"As soon as I can arrange, Grandmother, and her grandfather was from the *ancien régime*, not that it matters a halfpenny."

"Foreigners," the dowager muttered, secretly delighted he'd chosen anyone but that Pomeroy high flier or Harmon's brat.

"You must give me her address, dearest, so I can extend a formal invitation."

St. Cloud took a deep breath. Thinking it was better to get over rough ground quickly, he flatly announced, "I have no idea where she is."

His mother dropped her vinaigrette bottle. "You aren't bringing one of those independent London bluestockings here, are you? I couldn't bear to live with another pushy fe—" She held her gauze scarf to her mouth and looked away from the dowager.

St. Cloud patted her hand. "No such thing, Juneclaire's sweet and gentle. You'll see."

"When you find her, cuz?" Niles taunted. He was also delighted, recalculating his odds of winning the Pomeroy's hand. "How did you happen to mislay the bride-to-be?"

"There was a bit of a mix-up with the coaches. That's why I was detained," he said with a bow in his still-speechless uncle's direction. "I am not sure precisely which carriage took her up when the one she was traveling in had a spill." The spill may have been all over Scully, the footman, but St. Cloud was sticking to the truth as closely as possible. He had no idea what he would say if anyone thought to ask how he met the young lady, much less when. "There's nothing improper about it," he lied now, for the squire's wife and the rest of the neighborhood who would have the story by noon tomorrow. "She may have returned home or be staying with the vicar and his wife at Bramley. She might even have gone with her housekeeper on to London. I'll send the footmen out tomorrow to make inquiries, and I'll ride to London myself."

"But you can't send the staff away tomorrow, dearest; it's Boxing Day. All of the servants have the day off for their own feast and celebration. And you have to be here when the tenants come calling for the wassail."

"For their gifts, you mean. Damn."

"Oh, but Mr. Talbot takes care of the staff gifts, and your secretary in London remembered the check for the church alms box. And the bailiff delivers the boxes for most of the Priory tenants. They come just to see you and wish you joy of the season."

"Like feudal times, cuz, you know, lord of the manor and all that. *Noblesse oblige*."

Lady Fanny thought a moment. "I suppose Harmon could stand in for you."

St. Cloud put his teacup down with a thud. "That's all right, Mother. As you say, they are my people, and I shall be here."

The countess looked toward her brother to make sure Harmon saw what a good boy St. Cloud was. "Besides, dearest, you cannot go up to London, not with our New Year's ball next week. You couldn't have forgotten?"

St. Cloud bit the inside of his mouth. How could he, when she'd written to remind him seven times in the past month? The Priory hadn't made much of Christmas since his father's accident and Uncle George's death, but the dowager insisted that Lady Fanny had to entertain the county somehow over the holiday season, to repay all the invitations she received and to uphold the St. Cloud name. They had settled on a New Year's masquerade ball when they were out of blacks years ago, and the tradition took. Lady Fanny still wore half mourning, and she still piled all of the details for the ball on Talbot, the housekeeper, the bailiff, and her son. He hated the whole affair. "Now there I should appreciate Uncle Harmon's management. It's time Cousin Elsbeth learns how to manage a party, too. I make no promises after tomorrow, Mother."

"But you did promise to see about the ghost, son. I haven't slept easy in my bed in weeks, and that cannot be good for my health, on top of all the work for the ball. And then there was the upset about your tardy arrival and now the excitement of your betrothal. I really must have my rest. Of course I cannot be comfortable in my room. . . ."

"Blast it, Fanny, I told you I had the steward go over the whole east wing, and the fellow found nothing. The ghost is all in your head." Lord Wilmott finally found his voice with the realization that there could be no wedding without a bride. Let the boy go haring off to London while Harmon made his own investigation. There was some hugger-mugger here, and he was determined to get to the bottom of it and get rid of this upstart nobody. Elsbeth still had a chance.

For once in her life Fanny held firm, even against her

brother's wrath. "No, Harmon, it's a St. Cloud ghost and perhaps only St. Clouds can see it, although the servants have heard it crying through the chimneys. And there was *no* wind that night, so you can take a damper, Harmon."

"Brava, Fanny," the dowager said approvingly. "You can't keep the boy tied to you with your megrims or your mutton-headed mismanagement. Now you'll try things that go bump in the night!"

Fanny held the cloth to her eyes, and St. Cloud was tempted to take the cane to the dowager and his uncle. Yes, Lady Fanny was vaporish; did anyone think she was going to change now? "I thought you'd heard noises in the Dower House, too, Grandmother."

"I'm getting old, boy, not senile. You worry about finding the gel, St. Cloud. Hilloughby can say an extra prayer to get rid of the ghost. That's about all he's good for anyway." The dowager had almost given up hope that the cleric—or anybody—would offer for Fanny and get the peagoose and her Wilmott relatives out of the Priory once and for all. The New Year's ball had been her idea at first, to get Fanny socializing again in hopes of marrying the wigeon off. No one wanted her, more's the pity.

With the St. Cloud fireworks seemingly over for the night, the dinner guests took their leave. There was no reason to stay later, with the earl as good as a tenant for life and snow falling. If the snow hadn't been falling, Lady Sydelle might have ordered her carriage and headed for London. As it was, she was in such a snit, she forgot to slink on her way down the hall, after excusing herself to the family still in the gold salon. She stomped down the hall and up the stairs with such determination that she split the back seam of her too-tight dress. There was a crash below in the hallway. Talbot was not made of stone, after all, and neither was the Limoges teapot.

With only family left, Aunt Florrie wanted her Christmas gift, since she wasn't getting to keep the pig and Harmon took the sugarplums away. They all moved to the smaller parlor, where a wooden candle pyramid had been set up on one of the tables and lighted, St. Cloud's gifts on a red cloth beneath. Harmon did not hold with bringing a tree into the house, even if Queen Charlotte was trying to foist her Teutonic notions of *tannenbaum* on the London gentry. Fanny thought a tree with candles, apples, garlands, and cookies sounded lovely. Maybe next year, she thought, when there was a new countess.

She gave her son a pair of slippers with the family crest embroidered on them by her maid. He gave her a pearl-and-diamond brooch selected by his secretary. The dowager gave him her late husband's gold watch, which, besides being mentioned in the entail, was the same watch she gave St. Cloud every year. Every year he had it returned to her bed stand, knowing she hated to be without it. The earl gave her an ebony cane with a carved handle.

"What is it, boy? A snake?"

"No, you old fire breather, it's a dragon."

He gave Aunt Florrie a music box with a bear in a tutu twirling around on top, and she gave him a rock.

Elsbeth presented the earl with some monogrammed handkerchiefs. Her maid did not sew as well as Lady Fanny's. She went into raptures over the gold filigree fan that caught his eye one day as just the kind of gaudy trumpery she might enjoy.

St. Cloud next delighted his other cousin by saying he'd write out the Christmas gift as soon as Niles presented the reckoning, so Niles gave him the snuffbox in his pocket.

He and Uncle Harmon exchanged nods.

"You know, Papa," Elsbeth said, practicing her attitudes over the fan, "now that I am not to marry my cousin, can I finally have a Season in Town? I know Aunt Fanny doesn't go to London, but perhaps St. Cloud's wife can present me. Is she good ton, cousin?"

"Don't be a gudgeon," her brother told her, still in an expansive mood. "If she were a gap-toothed hunchback from the Outer Hebrides, St. Cloud's countess would still be good ton."

"Why? Aunt Fanny isn't."

Chapter Fourteen

The horses were straining in the traces, hurtling into the night. Foley rode silently beside him. No, it was Todd—no, someone else, watching him try to manage the runaway team. He couldn't do it. They were out of control. Then the carriage shaft started creaking, crunching, cracking under the stress of the wild ride. They'd be thrown, or dashed under the horses' hooves, and the passenger just watched. Then St. Cloud felt the wind and waited. His legs must be broken; he couldn't move them. The horses! Someone, help! The passenger laughed and laughed and—

St. Cloud jerked awake, gasping. He could feel the sweat on his bare chest and hear the echoes of distant laughter. The velvet bed curtains were open—and Pansy was sprawled across his legs. "Damn." There was no way the pig could get up on the huge canopied bed herself. St. Cloud even used the low stool. If this was Todd's revenge for having to nursemaid a pig, St. Cloud would have his head come morning. Boxing Day indeed. He'd give the fellow a box on the ears for this night's work. Then again, this was more like Cousin Niles's style of bobbery, foolish since the check was not yet signed. St. Cloud wouldn't even put such a prank past Sydelle, a woman scorned and all that. He sighed. Either way, he was awake.

"Are you hungry, pig? Silly question—you're always hungry. Let's go." St. Cloud lighted his candle and found his robe and new slippers. He also found where Pansy'd eaten her way out of the wicker basket. "At least that explains the crunching noises I heard."

He piled two plates with leftovers from the kitchen and led the pig into his library, where he restarted the fire and settled back on the worn leather chair. Then he heard the noise, a tapping almost like Grandmother's cane, although more regular. That must be Lady Fanny's specter, he thought, getting up to stand closer to the fireplace, where the sound was loudest. There must be a squirrel in one of the disused chimneys, tapping to open a nut or something. Maybe an owl. The noise would carry through all the grates in the place, echoing eerily enough, he supposed, to spook his susceptible parent. He didn't know why Uncle Harmon or the steward hadn't just sent for the sweeps. He'd do it tomorrow.

No, damn it, tomorrow the servants did not work, and he would be busy shaking hands and listening to speeches. Blast. All he wanted to do was get on his fastest horse and ride to find Juneclaire. He wandered toward the window, a glass of brandy in his hand. The snow was still falling, though lightly. Lord, let her be safe and warm.

He was up at dawn, before most of the household except for Cook, who took one look at her kitchen and started screeching about Priory phantoms and the walking dead. Breakfast was going to be late that morning. St. Cloud and the pig strolled through melting snow toward the stables, where Pansy, at least, could find apples and oats. The earl found his man Foley up and ready to be sent on the hunt. Word had come down from the house last night that the missing female was no less than the future Lady St. Cloud. Foley would ride to hell and back to see his lordship settled, even if he couldn't abide females personally.

"O'course I'm sure I can ride. I had my rest, didn't I? And no, us stable men don't put up with tomfoolery like them at the house, not doing their jobs 'cause it's a holiday. Horses still has to be fed, don't they? And we may as well exercise 'em on the way to somewheres as around a ring. Your message'll be in London by now, my lord, so where else do you want us to look?"

The earl wanted someone to watch the departing

coaches at Springdale and at Bramley, but he wanted Foley himself to head toward Farley's Grange by way of Strasmere, making inquiries along the way. "Ask if anyone has seen her, but if not, keep going toward Stanton Hall. Snoop around there if you can, and find out what they're saying about the Stantons' niece. The servants must have some idea of what's going on. I want you there because I know you won't add any more to the gossip than there already is. Try not to use her name when you ask along the way, too. We've got to keep this as quiet as possible."

Sure, then only *half* the county would know the Earl of St. Cloud had misplaced his fiancée.

Little Yerby made Juneclaire wait an hour for the snow to finish melting so her shoes wouldn't get wet and ruined. Then he sent her off with three well-fed kittens, a jar of milk, a loaf of bread he could spare because Aggie was coming home soon, and hope.

There was a family of gentlefolk not a mile down the road, Little Yerby told her, with a sickly little girl. "Mayhap they need someone to teach the young'un her letters, if she lives that long." He took a pull on his pipe, then coughed. "Else Mrs. Langbridge might want another lady round about. There's no family that anyone sees. Mister's a solicitor in Bramley. Tell them Little Yerby sent you."

While St. Cloud prepared to greet his household

staff and hand out their vails under Talbot's supervision, Juneclaire prepared for her first interview. She shook Little Yerby's flooring off her cloak, rebraided her hair, and kissed the old man good-bye.

Mrs. Langbridge met her at the door and tried to press a shilling into Juneclaire's hand. "Oh, you're not here for Boxing Day? Of course not. You're not a—Oh, I am sorry. There's just so much to do. Why did you say you had come?"

"Mr. Little Yerby sent me, ma'am, to ask after your little girl and to see if you might need a governess for her."

"My poor Cynthia." Mrs. Langbridge wiped her eyes with an already tear-dampened cloth.

"She hasn't . . . ?"

"Oh, no, she is just distraught over the move." Mrs. Langbridge waved a hand at trunks and bags waiting in the hallway. "She does not want to leave her friends, and her papa, of course, but the doctor thinks a healthier climate might . . . So we are going to Italy tomorrow, Cynthia, Nanny, a maid, and I. Mr. Langbridge cannot travel with us just yet, you see, so things are all at sixes and sevens, with packing and trying to leave the house in order, and Cynthia will fret so, which cannot be at all good for her. Do forgive me, Miss . . . ?"

"Beaumont, ma'am, and you must be wishing me to Jericho. I can see you do not need a governess and you do not need a stranger to keep you from your preparations. Please forgive me for the intrusion and accept my wishes for a safe journey and a swift recovery for your little girl."

"No, Miss Beaumont, please forgive my manners, after you were kind enough to call, and I haven't even offered you tea." She tried to brush away another tear. "I am sorry, my mind is in pieces, what with leaving my Tom and Cynthia so inconsolable."

"Mrs. Langbridge, you seem exhausted. Would you like me to sit with Cynthia for a bit while you catch your breath? It will be no bother, I assure you, for I am in no hurry to go home and only need get as far as Bramley this afternoon."

"Would you, Miss Beaumont? How kind. I should like to spend some time with Tom before he has to go visit a client. Some old hag called him out today, of all days! He is getting ready now and could drive you to Bramley when he leaves."

Juneclaire was removing her cloak. "That would be perfect. And could I make another forward suggestion? Don't you think that Cynthia would be happier about the trip if she could take a friend of her own along?"

"A friend? But we cannot . . ."

Juneclaire reached into her satchel and pulled out a kitten. "Why not?"

"I'll name her Holly," the little girl announced, "so we both remember an English Christmas. Do you think they have holly in Italy, Miss Beaumont?"

"I have no idea, Cynthia. You shall just have to go and see, won't you? Perhaps you shall write and tell me, so I'll know for the future." Juneclaire was pleased to see the hectic flush leave Cynthia's cheeks, although the spots of color remained, betraying her illness. The child was calm now and had taken her medicine without complaint, too rapt in watching the three kittens tumbling on her bed covers. She chose the black kitten "because Papa says everyone in Italy wears black. But, Miss Beaumont, what if Holly isn't a girl? Can a boy cat be called Holly?"

"I don't see why not. Do you know Mr. Little Yerby?"

"Of course, everyone knows Little. He brings the milk twice a week, and sometimes he lets me ride his donkey."

"Well, Mr. Little has one of Holly's brothers or sisters, and he is going to call the kitten David, no matter what."

"Oh, but if Little says his cat's a boy, then that's what it is. The animals always do what he says."

While Juneclaire was spending the morning entertaining a sick child, St. Cloud was standing on the steps of the Priory's porch, drinking wassail toasts with his tenants. By noon he was drunk as a lord, and so was the pig at his side, dressed in a ribbon-and-lace collar Aunt Florrie had stayed up all night sewing. None of his other relatives had made a showing yet, and none of his minions had reported back from the search. Two more hours of this, St. Cloud promised himself, and then he could ride to Bramley, if he could sit a horse.

Juneclaire stayed to watch Cynthia fall asleep for her nap with a smile on her thin face, and then she took luncheon with the Langbridges, at their insistence, although she did not want to intrude on one of their last moments together. They were all praise for her handling of their peevish child. "Oh, no, I cannot take any of the credit." Juneclaire laughed. "Once I showed her the kittens she was a perfect darling."

Mr. Thomas Langbridge was a pleasant-looking, sandy-haired gentleman with a worried frown. "I wish a kitten could work such magic on the client I have an appointment with this afternoon. I feel sorry for the old grande dame truly, because she is blind and has lost most of her family, but I wish she would not choose to change her dashed will every time her rackety grandson sneezes."

"And today of all days," his wife complained.

"Not even you, my dear, can accuse Lady St. Cloud of purposely selecting the day before your journey. She had no way of knowing. We must be thankful she waited past Christmas to send for me. And she keeps country hours at the Dower House, at any rate, so dinner will be early if I stay, and you know I must if she invites me, if I wish to retain her as my wealthiest client. I never understood why she did not take her business to any of the solicitors in Ayn-Jerome or even Thackford."

"Most likely she turned them off in her previous tantrums." Mrs. Langbridge was rearranging the food on her plate. Juneclaire had no such loss of appetite and busied herself with the turbot in oyster sauce.

"More likely she trusted my uncle. Try to show a little compassion for the old countess, my dear, even if she is a crusty beldam."

While he enjoyed his mutton, Mr. Langbridge's solicitor's mind was busy chewing a different bone. Somewhere over the vanilla flan he presented his idea: "You know, Miss Beaumont, you might well apply for a position with Lady St. Cloud if you are seeking employment. We would take you on in a minute for Cynthia if the situation were different. You are patient and kind, refined and intelligent. That's just what the old bat—ah, lady needs. I admit to having concerns about her, alone in the Dower House with just her old retainers looking after her. You and your kittens wrought such a miracle with Cynthia, I'd be happy to recommend you for the dowager's companion."

Juneclaire smiled and thanked him. "But I'm afraid you haven't painted a very pretty picture of your employer. I think I should rather face my own family's ill humors than someone else's."

"You can think about it on the way to Bramley. I am stopping by my office there to fetch copies of papers she wants to emend. You could drive out with me, and if you find you don't suit or she is not interested, I shall simply bring you back to town on my return trip."

While Juneclaire once more deliberated over her future on the way to Bramley, the Earl of St. Cloud was riding in the opposite direction, out of the little village. Vicar Broome was aghast to think that Miss Beaumont had not reached Springdale, but he was helpless to provide the earl with any other information. Poor fellow, he thought, the younger man was so smitten, he hadn't even stayed to have a sip of Madeira. Mr. Broome sipped it himself, in celebration of the handsome donation the lovesick earl had made to start up the poor box after the day's distribution. Reverend Broome wiped his spectacles and contemplated his own venality. Should he have reminded the mooncalf of his generous gift just the day before?

He wiped them again, then took them off altogether when the young lady in the rabbit-lined cloak walked into his study. "Miss, ah, Beaumont?" he mumbled, wishing his wife were there. He might know what to do with finances; affairs of the heart were Mrs. Broome's venue. While he was deliberating whether to send a boy after the earl—but who in town could ride at that neck-or-nothing pace?—or after Mrs. Broome, Juneclaire was thrusting a striped kitten into his arms.

"Because you and your wife have been so kind to me," she said, looking so sweet and innocent, he couldn't tell her how cats made him sneeze. And itch. And weep at the eyes.

"How happy I am to see you, Miss Beaumont. There was a gentleman here asking for you. We were all concerned for your welfare."

"A gentleman? Not a portly, middle-aged man who wears a bagwig? That would be my uncle Avery, and I never suspected he would make the least push to find me."

"No, this gentleman was not, ah, portly. He gave his name as Mr. Jordan."

"Oh, Merry!" Then she blushed. Her face was almost as red as the vicar's was becoming from stroking the cat.

"Oh, dear, Mr., ah, Jordan did not insult you in any way, did he? That is, your blushes and . . ." He blew his nose. Oh, how he wished Mrs. Broome did not have to visit the almshouse this afternoon!

"Mr. Jordan? Never! You mustn't think such a thing. He is a true gentleman."

Well, that relieved Mr. Broome's mind, if not his nose. "Have you decided not to go to London, then, Miss Beaumont?" he asked, changing the subject. "Mrs. Broome will be pleased." More pleased than she was going to be about the cat. "May I tell her your, ah, alternate plans, then, so she does not worry?"

"Thank her for her concern, sir, but I am not sure what I will do."

The vicar could feel a rash starting on his neck and

the check for the poor box itching in his pocket. "My child, have you ever heard of St. Cloud Priory?"

Juneclaire looked startled. "Why, Mr. Langbridge just mentioned it, that I might find a position with the dowager countess there. After what he said about her, though . . ."

"Perfect!" Broome wouldn't even have to consult his conscience about pitchforking this lovely young innocent into the arms of a hardened libertine. The old harridan would make sure nothing untoward took place, and if the young earl was as sincere as he seemed, Vicar Broome would be calling the banns next week, if his throat didn't close right up with cat hair.

Now the minister might believe in the efficacy of prayer, but he also believed in giving his prayers a helping hand, or a shove in the right direction. "I'll write a reference myself. I know the dowager has the reputation of being a holy terror, but I've seen worse reputations proved false, this very afternoon. She's just old and lonely. She needs you. The Lord must have sent you to Langbridge for just that purpose."

He was almost pleading. He was actually crying. Juneclaire was so touched, she said she would reconsider.

Then the reverend clinched her decision. He begged for divine forgiveness and lied through his teeth: "She likes cats."

*　　*　　*

So while the Earl of St. Cloud was racing past uninformative Springdale and heading for London, where he would knock on back doors himself if need be and haunt the coaching inns, Juneclaire was headed toward his own haunted house to knock on his own grandmother's door.

Chapter Fifteen

*N*o one answered the knock. Juneclaire thought they should leave.

"No, old Pennington must have the gout again. We'll just give him a few minutes to get here. He's Lady St. Cloud's butler, and he's older than dirt. So's her abigail, Nutley, who's too deaf to hear the door anyway. Mrs. Pennington is the cook-housekeeper and she, ah, tipples."

Juneclaire was positive they should leave. She set her carpetbag down on the steps of the gray stone house. "Goodness, no wonder you didn't tell me this before we got here. Why ever doesn't Lady St. Cloud retire them if they are so far beyond their work?"

"I asked the dowager once and almost had my head bitten off. They're like family, it seems, and have nowhere else they'd rather go. Help comes from the main house—you can't see it from here, but the Priory is just beyond those trees. They do the cleaning and such, so Lady St. Cloud's retainers' positions are more nearly pensions."

"Is there no one in the household younger than Methuselah? It cannot be very comfortable or even safe for the old lady."

Mr. Langbridge knocked again, harder. "There's a young maid, Sally Munch, and a footman. They are walking out, according to the dowager, and I am afraid they are walking out more often than they are working indoors. They're most likely off on holiday this afternoon anyway. But you mustn't think no one cares about the old lady's welfare. The earl has tried to get her to move to the Priory countless times, I understand, but the dowager and the present countess, the earl's mother, have never gotten on. Well, there is no point waiting out here any longer," he said, which Juneclaire was relieved to hear until he concluded, "We may as well go on in. I know the dowager is expecting me."

The solicitor guided Juneclaire to a bench along the wall of the long entry hall. The furnishings were old-fashioned but elegant, obviously expensive and scrupulously clean, from what she could see in the near dark. The dowager might be blind, but surely her staff needed more light than this? And there were no flowers or plants, not a holiday decoration of any kind. If *she* were here, Juneclaire speculated, there would be gar-

lands of fresh-smelling greens, bowls of dried lavender or crushed rose petals, and clove-studded apples.
Surely the dowager could smell what she could not
see. She'd light all the sconces, too, Juneclaire mused,
so the place felt warmer. Yes, she could be useful here.

When Mr. Langbridge came out of a room down the
hall, he seemed even more worried than before. "She's
agreed to see you," he said. "Alone. I beg you to try to
please her, Miss Beaumont, for I'm afraid the dowager
grows more addled in her wits every time I see her.
She sent for me today because the Angel of Death visited her last night, she claims, so she knows her time is
near. I fear for her, indeed I do."

"I heard that, you jobbernoll you," came an angry
voice from down the hall, accented by the pounding of
a cane. "Don't you know a person's hearing gets better
when they lose their sight? And I ain't dicked in the
nob, you paper-skulled paper pusher. Now are you going to send the female in, or are you going to sit in my
hallway gossiping about me all day?"

The old lady was still muttering when Juneclaire
went into the room and curtsied, even knowing the
small, white-haired woman didn't see her. The dowager sat perfectly erect, not the least bit frail or withered.
Juneclaire touched her on the hand and said, "How do
you do, my lady? I am Miss Beaumont. Thank you for
meeting me."

"Humph" was all the response she got back. "Thinks
I need a keeper, does he?"

"No, ma'am, just a companion."

"What for? To jaw me dead? Not much else for a companion to do around here. I can't play cards or go for a ride. Can't even do my needlework."

"But I could read to you, and I could drive you about if there's a cart. And I could teach you to knit. Once you get the hang of it, you don't need to watch the needles."

"Humph. Knitting ain't genteel. Ladies do fancy work, miss."

"Yes, but there are many people who need scarves and mittens more than they need another altar cloth in the church. I should think a lady might consider that, too."

"There's some sense in what you say, but you ain't going to be preaching to me about the poor, are you?"

Juneclaire laughed, a pleasing sound to the old lady's ears. "Not if I don't wish to join their ranks, it seems. But I am sure you think just as you ought, my lady."

"You're not one of those Methody Reformers, are you? I don't want any holier-than-thou reverencer sneering behind my back. Frank language ain't going to shock you, is it, Miss Beaumont?"

"My cousins cured me of that ages ago, my lady."

"Ages? How old are you, anyway? Langbridge said you were just a girl. I don't want any shriveled up prunes-and-prisms spinsters around me either. Let me touch your face, girl."

Juneclaire knelt so the old woman could touch her soft cheek, her straight nose, and heavy brows, the thick braids of her hair and the smile on her mouth.

"I am nineteen, my lady, and I haven't put on my caps yet." She laughed again. "In fact, I had a very attractive offer from a gentleman just recently."

Juneclaire jumped aside as Lady St. Cloud thumped her cane down. "What kind of offer, miss? I won't have any hanky-panky around here. It's bad enough with the lower orders sneaking off to the bushes and the pantry and the basement at all hours."

The laughter was gone from Juneclaire's voice. "You insult me, my lady, and also the gentleman. It was a very fine, very proper offer of marriage."

"Pish tosh, miss. If it was such a fine offer, why didn't you take it? You can't tell me you'd rather look after an old crone than have a house and husband of your own. Coming it too brown, my girl."

Juneclaire sighed. "I had to refuse, Lady St. Cloud. He offered out of honor, you see, not out of love. I couldn't hold such a fine gentleman to an empty marriage. It wouldn't be right." She sighed again.

"But you wanted to, didn't you, girl?" the old woman shrewdly interpreted.

"Oh yes, Merry was everything I ever thought a man should be."

Merry? The cane dropped from Lady St. Cloud's hand. "Miss Beaumont, what did you say your first name was?"

"Juneclaire," she answered hesitantly. What new quiz was this?

"And how many gals named Juneclaire do you think are running around Berkshire right now?"

"Why, none others, I should think. I was named after my mother, Claire, and my father, Jules. Why do you ask?"

The old lady didn't answer. She just laughed and laughed. "Turned him down, did you? Oh, how I am going to enjoy this!" She laughed some more, till Juneclaire began to worry about her sanity after all, especially when the dowager recovered and suddenly asked, "You ain't afraid of ghosts, are you?"

So confused was Juneclaire that she blurted out, "They cannot be more frightening than you."

The dowager laughed some more, then reached out to pat Juneclaire's hand. "You'll do, girl, you'll do."

"Does that mean I am hired, my lady?"

"Hired? I suppose it does, for now. Go send in that young solicitor of mine. I want to discuss your, ah, wages with him."

"Thank you, my lady. I'll try to please, I swear it. There's just one other thing, though. Do you really like cats?"

"Cats? Pesky creatures. Can't abide the beasts, always underfoot or carrying around dead things."

"Oh. I'm sorry, truly I am, for I should have liked to stay. But I have this kitten, you see, that no one wanted, and I cannot just abandon it with no home. So I'll have to—"

"I'll learn to love it."

When Mr. Langbridge came back out for her on her bench in the hall, he looked at Juneclaire as if she'd grown another head. Nevertheless, he silently beckoned her back to her ladyship's parlor.

"I have invited Langbridge to take potluck, Miss Beaumont. Are you too tired from your travels, or do you join us?"

"I, um . . . Oh, dear, I know this is not the proper way to start in my new position, my lady, but did you know that Mr. Langbridge's daughter was ill?"

"Of course I did. Asked first thing."

"Yes, but she needs to go to a warmer climate, and Mrs. Langbridge is traveling to Italy with her tomorrow."

"That's well and good. I wish them Godspeed, but what is that to—Oh, I see. We won't keep you then, Langbridge. I expect you to stay next week when you bring those papers back for my signature. I daresay you'll be glad for the company then. And as for you, miss, I suppose you think just as you ought. Just remember, I find it deuced uncomfortable being wrong." The dowager spoke with a smile, though, so Juneclaire went cheerfully off to get ready for her first dinner in her new home.

The three old retainers were in various somnolent stages in the kitchen. Juneclaire introduced herself and explained her new position to Pennington, the only one whose eyes opened at Juneclaire's entry. The butler instantly recognized her for a lady and slowly lowered his bandaged foot to the floor so he could rise and make her a proper bow. Juneclaire had to help him back to his seat. He shouted the news loudly enough to wake his wife from her post-tea, predinner stupor and for Nutley, the abigail, to hear. If Juneclaire worried her ladyship's longtime servants were going to be jealous of an upstart, she was soon dissuaded from that notion. The three were relieved someone else was going to help look after their mistress and thrilled someone else was going to be the butt of her temper. Mrs. Pennington vowed to fix a special dinner, and Nutley asked if miss needed help with her unpacking. What Juneclaire needed was a hot bath, but none of the servants looked fit enough to walk up the stairs, much less carry a tub and tins of water.

"Never you fear, miss," Mrs. Pennington said, wobbling to the door, "by the time we get a room aired and your things put away, young Sally Munch'll be back with her beau. They never stay away through supper."

Her room adjoining the dowager's was twice as big as the one Juneclaire had slept in most of her life. Did she just leave Stanton Hall a few days ago? It seemed a lifetime. There was a fire in the grate and lavender sachets in the drawers for her few belongings and a thick carpet for her feet. The kitten was being fussed over in the kitchen, and she was being fussed over here. Nutley insisted on brushing out her hair and taking her second-best gown to be pressed. The abigail had not even commented on the meager contents of her carpetbag.

As Nutley remarked to Lady St. Cloud as she helped her mistress change for dinner, "Young miss is Quality, anyone can see that, and if she had deep pockets, she wouldn't be going for a companion, now, would she?" Nutley did not hear the dowager's comments any more than the dowager could see Juneclaire's appearance. Mistress and maid were as one, though, in agreeing that Miss Beaumont was, on first meeting, a jewel.

The jewel was going to look far more brilliant without all the dust. Juneclaire looked at her bath when it came as a starving man looks at a slab of beef. Aunt Marta would call such sybaritic pleasure sinful, so Juneclaire would not think about Aunt Marta now. The morning was time enough to send her aunt a note that she was well. Juneclaire leaned back in the suds. She was very well indeed.

After dinner Juneclaire read the previous week's mail to the dowager and laughed at her stories about the people mentioned in her friends' *on-dits*. For a woman who did not do the Season, Lady St. Cloud used to keep abreast of the latest gossip with a vast network of correspondence. She was hoping her grandson did not return to steal the girl away before Miss Beaumont got halfway through the letters. Well, he could take the girl, but he wasn't getting the cat.

At first she was worried. "It's not going to trip me up, is it? Wouldn't do to fall at my age, you know."

"Cats are very good about things like that, my lady. And you do have your cane to sweep in front of you. You'll have to be more gentle with it, of course, not knowing the kitten's location. Here, hold it."

Silk and a sandpaper tongue and the rumble of tiny thunder that went on and on. It was love at first touch.

"What does he look like?"

Juneclaire wasn't quite sure what to say. This was the fourth kitten, the one no one wanted. "Well, his eyes were blue, but I think they are going to be yellow. He has a little gold on his chest and a black spot over one eye, and white feet, except for the back right one. That's kind of brownish. And there's a faint gray stripe down his back. He's a bit of this and a patch of that. But he has the sweetest personality!"

"Patches. I like that. Will that do for a name, do you think?"

Juneclaire laughed. "That cat is lucky to have a home. A name is icing on the cake."

"Lucky, then. No, what do the Irish call those patches

of lucky clover? Shamrocks! You did say he had green eyes?"

"Well . . ."

The dowager countess listened while Juneclaire played a few ragged carols. "I'm sorry, my lady. I never had many lessons; my aunt thought them a waste for a female with no prospects. I have no excuses for my poor voice, so I shan't subject you to that. Would you rather I read to you?"

"Perhaps tomorrow. This has already been a most pleasant evening, Miss Beaumont. I don't want to use all my treats in one day, like a child who cries when Christmas is past."

"But there are twelve days of Christmas, my lady," Juneclaire said with a smile in her voice. "What would you like to do now? Do you retire early?"

"What I would *like* to do is play cards." Lady St. Cloud reached for her cane to punctuate her vexation. She remembered the kitten asleep in her lap just in time.

Juneclaire thought a minute, and then her face cleared. "I'll be right back," she told the dowager, then ran off to find Nutley and shout until she had what she wanted. Out of breath but smiling, she came back with her prize, a sewing needle.

"What is it, girl? What are you giggling about?"

"Something else my scapegrace cousins taught me. Here, feel this." She held out a card. "The corner."

"Why, why, you're marking the cards! That's cheating!"

"Not if we both know the marks, it's not. I don't think we'll get so proficient that the dealer will have such an advantage, do you?"

"Miss Beaumont, I think I am going to learn to love you like a daughter. Or a granddaughter."

Chapter Sixteen

The dowager was having a nightmare. "Don't lie to me, Death. I know who you are and I'm not ready yet, I tell you. I have to make sure St. Cloud is settled before he's ruined for good and all. You'll see, the girl will be the making of the rogue."

Juneclaire heard the old lady's strident voice in the room next door. She had to recall which side held the bed stand before she fumbled for candle and flint in the unfamiliar room.

"You can't take me yet," the dowager was shouting. "He's already made mice feet of the thing. No, I don't want to hear any more of your wicked falsehoods about my sons. Go."

Trust Lady St. Cloud to tell the Devil to go to Hell, Juneclaire thought as she tied a wrapper Nutley had laid out for her over her own flannel nightdress. She hurried to the dowager's room and scratched on the door. When she got no answer, Juneclaire turned the knob and pushed the door open, shielding her candle. The dowager was fast asleep in a large bed. She was snoring gently, and she wore a satisfied smile on her face, having bested the Angel of Death for one more night.

Resisting the urge to peer in the corners or look under the bed, Juneclaire checked to make sure the silver bell was within the dowager's reach in case she needed to call for her companion during the night. Then Juneclaire went back toward her own room. Before she got to the doorway, though, she felt a prickle of sensation at the bottom of her spine. Someone was watching her. She whipped around, almost putting her candle out, but the steady sleep noises were still coming from the dowager's slightly open mouth.

It's just all the talk of death, Juneclaire chided herself, that and Sally Munch's chatter about the Priory ghosts stirring again. The slain monks were walking the ancient halls, Sally had declared as she slid the warming pan between Juneclaire's sheets . . . or something worse.

The young maid's imagination was as overheated as the rest of the little flirt, Juneclaire firmly told herself, blowing out the candle and getting between the long-cold sheets.

Then she heard a tapping noise, like the dowager's

cane but not quite. She had that same feeling of being observed. "There are no such things as ghosts," she declared out loud. Then she shouted, "Begone," figuring that if it worked for the dowager, it was worth a try, just in case. She thought she heard a chuckle, but she could not be sure, not with the covers pulled over her head.

The dowager never rose before eleven, but Juneclaire was up with the birds, so she looked around for other occupations to keep her busy. She helped Penny make bread and hid whatever bottles of wine she could find. She fetched the silver tea service, epergne, and sconces for Pennington, where he was polishing at the kitchen table, his leg propped on a stool. And she dragged Sally Munch and the footman out of an unused bedroom where they were checking the bedsprings, to help her gather greens.

The footman cut the holly and pine branches Juneclaire indicated, while she fashioned a wreath out of some vines. Sally, naturally, knew just where they could find some mistletoe. As they worked, Juneclaire tried not to listen to the servants' gossip about the doings at the Priory, some possibly scandalous goings-on between the master, a recognized rake, and his latest flirt. Bets were on in the servants' hall, it seemed, that a betrothal was all a hum, St. Cloud was never going to give up his profligate ways. The stable had it that the master was dead-set on the female, whoever and wherever she was. Juneclaire did not feel she could reprimand the maid for her chatter, but she found the whole conversation distasteful.

"It's worse than that, miss. What did he do yesterday but hare off in the middle of the tenants' visits? Castaway, they say he was. Left in a great rush without saying when he'd be back or nothing. Then what happens but stablemen start walking in the halls at night, with pistols. By hisself's orders, they say. Why, mistress was near swooning, they say. Then comes this morning. Molly, who comes to clean at the Dower House, says a whole herd of workmen arrived at dawn, on Lord St. Cloud's instructions, they say, to check for loose boards and such, banging on the walls. If that weren't bad enough to set the house on its ears, an army of sweeps comes looking for owls and squirrels and bats in the chimneys. So there can't be no fires!"

"And there are guests? I can see where that would upset even the most serene household."

"Which that one's not. Why, that cousin—"

Juneclaire did not wish to hear any more details of life at the Priory. She quickly asked the footman to carry a message to the sweeps to come check the Dower House flues if they got a chance. "I thought there must be woodpeckers, myself."

"Oh, no, miss. That be the ghost."

Juneclaire read the newspapers to the dowager before luncheon and answered some letters from her dictation. She thought about writing to her relatives. Later.

After luncheon the dowager announced it was time for her nap. "And I want you to go outside and get some exercise. Can't be healthy for a young thing like you to be cooped up inside with a parcel of old biddies, working so hard."

"What work?" Juneclaire laughed. "This has been the easiest day of my life."

"Doesn't say much for the rest of your life, but I'll hold my tongue on that. Can you ride?" Lady St. Cloud asked abruptly.

"Yes, but I did not bring my habit." Juneclaire knew the dowager was well aware of the fact. Nutley must have enumerated Juneclaire's scant wardrobe to her mistress the first day, thus the night robe. Juneclaire had two day dresses, the blue one she had on and the heavier gray one she'd worn on the road. She had the almost fashionable rose muslin castoff from Aunt Marta that she wore to dinner last night and, of course, her unworn white velvet gown. At least the dowager did not have to look at her companion in the same gowns day after day. She wasn't going to get as weary of them as Juneclaire was going to. Juneclaire supposed she could ask her uncle to send on her clothes when she wrote to him, but the gowns she had left behind were all faded and threadbare, and her habit was so thin in the saddle, one more gallop might have her petticoat showing. Perhaps when she got paid, Juneclaire would purchase a dress length or two. But wages had not been discussed, nor a possible day off for her to do any shopping. Since her employer was being almost pleasant, Juneclaire hated to bring up such awkward topics. Instead, she added, "I do like to walk."

"Humph. Walking's for peasants, girl, unless you're on the strut in Hyde Park or such. Nutley can alter one of my old habits for you. Certes, I don't need them anymore."

"If you wanted to ride, we could—"

"No, I'm not going to trot in a circle at the end of a lead line, by Jupiter. It used to be neck-or-nothing with me, and I ain't going to change now."

"Oh, then you weren't always . . . ?"

"Blind. No, I used to see fine, just saw too much, the specialists said. Too many birthdays, mostly. Now I'm too stiff to get on a horse and too old to chance breaking a bone anyway. So those habits are just taking space in the clothespress."

"But I couldn't—"

"Have to. There's no one else who can exercise my mare for me. Flame never held anything but a sidesaddle, don't you know. Prettiest little filly in the whole county, she was. Now go on, get. I need my rest if I'm to learn this knitting of yours tonight. Oh, and don't ride toward the Priory. No reason for you to face those spiteful cats up there without me. My daughter-in-law's relations, they are, and a worse pack of dirty dishes you'll never find."

"You haven't met the Root and the Newt."

"But they're just boys, you said. Fanny's niece is a

spoiled hoyden, and that other one is no better than she should be. The nevvy is a basket scrambler. You watch out for him, girl."

Juneclaire laughed. "I thank you, ma'am, but I'm not likely to tempt a man of that ilk. I don't have a fortune and I'm no dasher, as my cousins say."

The dowager had Nutley's opinion that miss would be a real diamond, with some careful dressing and a new hairstyle, should brunets come back in style. She also had the fact that one of England's premier bachelors had offered for the chit. "You be careful, that's all. When my grandson gets back is soon enough for you to meet the rest of the jackals. Now go."

"Yes, my lady." She curtsied, even though the dowager couldn't see.

"Why, that old—" She bit her lip, even if Nutley couldn't hear. A brown velvet habit was already altered, likely from measurements of her other day dress. The dowager had meant to have her way, no matter Juneclaire's feelings. "Thank you, Nutley," she shouted, giving the abigail a quick hug as she flew down the stairs in her eagerness for her ride. They were used to sending to the Priory for the rare times the dowager went out, Pennington explained while she filled her pockets with apples and sugar cubes (and hid another bottle of cooking sherry that was not destined for dinner). A carriage arrived every Sunday to carry the dowager to chapel at the Priory, he said, and a boy came every day to attend the small stable that served the Dower House.

He wasn't there now, so Juneclaire took down a gleaming ladies' saddle herself and went to lead the mare out of her stall. She did not have the heart to put the saddle on Flame's back. If ever the mare had a flame at all, it had sputtered and gone out before Juneclaire was born. Flame had barely enough teeth to crunch the apple, after Juneclaire found a knife to slice it, and barely enough energy to put one foot in front of the other.

"Still, you cannot be happy in this dark barn all day, and the dowager said we were both to get some exercise, so come along."

So Juneclaire, with the skirts of the most elegant riding habit she had ever worn trailing in the mud and the dust, ambled alongside the geriatric equine on the path where she'd been gathering holly that morning.

When Lady St. Cloud sent Juneclaire out for an airing, she hadn't been thinking of the chaos at the Priory. Lady Fanny was busy having spasms, Lord Wilmott was growing more bilious with each hammer blow, as if the search for defects were a personal affront to his care of the earl's property, and Florrie was in the attics, in the workmen's way, finding pig-size baby clothes. Things were in such a state there that even a ride to the Dower House appealed to the younger members of the house party, since it promised the diversion of investigating the new companion. On being informed by

Pennington—after a wait that had Lady Sydelle rapping her crop against her leather boots—that the dowager countess was resting and miss was riding through the holly path, they decided to ride after her. Niles wanted to wager the unfortunate creature wouldn't last a week; neither his sister nor Lady Pomeroy took the bet.

"I bet she is a perfect antidote," Elsbeth declared, "for even the poorest female can find a male to support her if she has any looks and is not fussy. I'd rather be married to a coal heaver than be Lady St. Cloud's galley slave."

"You mightn't have either choice, with that wasp tongue," the widow Pomeroy snapped at the younger girl, having married a dirty old man whose dirty fortune came from coal mines, although that fact was not well known among the ton.

Leaping to his intended's—his intentions, not hers—aid before Elsbeth could unleash even more venom, Niles taunted, "I don't notice you making any grand match, sister, now that your plans for St. Cloud are scotched."

"Unlike others I could mention, I am waiting for a love match. Not all females sell themselves for security, you know."

"And not all females are so totty-headed. I bet even the cipherous companion would jump at an offer to escape the drudgery."

"An honorable offer, of course," the widow agreed.

"But are you willing to back your wager on another kind of offer? Companions are notoriously virtuous. I'll bet my diamond pendant against—do you have anything worth wagering, Niles?—that this Miss Beaumont will accept something less."

"Do you mean you're betting that Niles can seduce the dowager's companion? Why . . . why, that's evil."

"And so entertaining. We have to do something to enliven the days till the New Year's ball, don't we? Niles, do you take me up?"

Niles was reflecting that the woman he wished to make his wife could show a little more interest in his fidelity to her. Not that he intended to remain faithful once the wedding vows were exchanged and the marriage settlements signed, but he hoped for some sign of jealousy, possessiveness even, before the fact. If there was to be a fact. "Sight unseen?" he asked. "I'm afraid I need longer odds, my sweet Sydelle. What say that if I succeed, I also succeed with you, my pet? My honorable offer, naturally."

"Naturally. And if you lose?"

"You can't do this, Niles, not the dowager's own servant. St. Cloud will kill you." Elsbeth was horrified, but not as horrified as Juneclaire, on the other side of the boxwood hedges where Flame was nibbling at the last grasses. And Elsbeth, it seemed, was more concerned with danger to her brother than any damage that might be done to the poor downtrodden companion! Juneclaire could not hear Lady Sydelle's answer as the group rode away.

The dowager was right. These people were scum. They were beautiful, Juneclaire's peeks through the branches told her that, but they were cold and cruel. They were as exquisite as swans, and just as vicious close up. Lady Sydelle wore a scarlet habit with a tiny veiled hat perched coquettishly on her guinea gold locks, and her horse had specks of blood on its flanks from her spur. Juneclaire had never seen a man dressed as elegantly as Mr. Wilmott, or heard one speak so casually of ruining an innocent female. She almost wept to think of Merry and his precious offer. These three did not have enough honor among them to be worthy to shine Merry's boots.

If they were representative of Lord St. Cloud's friends and relatives, Juneclaire wanted even less to do with the Priory than before. She'd had no great esteem for the libertine earl since Mr. Langbridge related the man's scandalous reputation, and that opinion was lowered a notch when she saw his grandmother's condition. He kept her in, if not outright penury, then straightened circumstances, unprotected and locked away where he never had to see her. His very behavior gave the poor woman nightmares; his associates would put even that rough-tongued lady to the blush. The earl did not seem to care what havoc he wreaked on his mother's delicate health either, or on his staff, from what she'd seen. Juneclaire, for one, wished he'd never get back from his latest mad jaunt, undertaken when he was in his cups. She pitied the poor girl he was going to marry and hoped he never found her.

Chapter Seventeen

St. Cloud returned two days later. Even before his horse was led away, the dowager knew he was home via the servants' grapevine. She calculated how long before Fanny or his man Todd filled St. Cloud's ears with gossip, sending him posthaste to her door-step demanding an explanation. She sent Juneclaire out early for her ride, saying that her old bones felt snow coming on. Miss Beaumont had better exercise the mare early, she claimed, lest Flame get too rambunctious from standing around all day.

Her grandson arrived not ten minutes later and managed to hold his patience in check for at least five minutes more.

"Grandmother," he said in an affected drawl after

the formal greetings, "there seems to be a small creature stalking the tassel of my new Hessians."

Lady St. Cloud was sure he'd have his quizzing
glass out, the fribble. "Adorable, ain't he?"

The earl did indeed have his glass out, but he was
swinging it on its ribbon to the delight of one of the
least prepossessing representatives of the feline species he'd ever seen. "Adorable is not quite the word I
would have chosen, my lady. But, pray tell, how does
it come about that you have a cat, no, any animal, in
the house? You surely never approved of such a thing
during my lifetime."

Oh, how the dowager wished she could see his face!
"I've changed my mind, St. Cloud, since my new companion insisted."

Aha! The new companion! St. Cloud was on his feet
and pacing. His forceful appearance was marred, had
the dowager only seen it, by the scrap-cat chasing after
him, intent on those dangling tassels. "Insisted, is it?
The Dowager Countess St. Cloud taking orders from
some encroaching female? They were right: you are
not fit to be living alone!"

"I am not living alone, you nodcock. That's what the
girl is for. And if any of those sponge-mongers up at
the Priory dared to suggest I am missing a few spokes
in my wheel, I'll have their guts for garters, see if I
won't."

The earl picked up the kitten and dropped it, with
his quizzing glass on its ribbon, into the dowager's lap

before his boots were irreparably scored with needle claws. He cleared his throat. "We were speaking of the companion, ma'am."

"No, St. Cloud, you were. I was speaking of the hangers-on and dirty dishes you permit to reside under your roof. Your grandfather, the earl, would be spinning in his grave."

"He'd be coming back to haunt me if I left you here with some strange female whose name nobody remembers! They can't tell me where she came from or why. For all I know, she's here to stab you in your bed and steal the silver. You don't understand about unscrupulous people, Grandmother, how they prey on the"—he was going to say old and infirm, thought better of it—"unsuspecting. She could cozen you into changing your will or—"

"Already have."

"What?! I'll see the bitch in jail first!" He struck his fist on the mantel.

"You'll sit down, boy, and mind your tongue in my parlor. You're giving me a headache."

The earl sat, took a deep breath, and tried again. "My apologies, Grandmother. But I have tried for years to hire you a companion, a respectable female to bear you company and look out for your welfare, since you refuse to move to the Priory. I found women from the best of families, with unimpeachable references. Young women, old women, women I personally knew, by Jupiter! And you refused to meet any of them. Dash it,

I would have hired one of the royal ladies-in-waiting if I thought you'd have her. But you, madam, without a word to anyone, take on a perfect stranger. Is it any wonder I am overset?"

The dowager hadn't enjoyed a conversation so much in years. She should have been an inquisitor. "You always were pigheaded, boy. Do you think no one else knows what's best for themselves? You're a fine one to speak, clunch. I have found myself the perfect companion, and we suit to a cow's thumb. Which is a lot more than I can say for you and your misbegotten engagement."

The dowager stroked the cat during the following silence. When St. Cloud finally spoke, she could hear the sorrow in his voice. "There is no engagement, Grandmother. That's the other thing I came to the Dower House to tell you. I haven't said anything to the others yet, but I couldn't find her. I left messages, deuce take it, I left enough bribes to finance Prinny's new pavilion. I found her old housekeeper in London, who didn't know what I was talking about. I promised Mother I'd get back to help with the blasted ball, but my staying in Town wouldn't have made a difference. There's nothing, Grandmother. She's gone."

Not even the dowager could enjoy torturing a broken man, even if he was her only grandson and a cowhanded chawbacon to boot. "About my companion . . ."

"You were right, Grandmother. It's none of my business. If you are pleased, then I am pleased."

"She was not entirely without references, you know. In fact, Langbridge, my man of business, brought her out to me . . . from Bramley."

"From . . . ?"

"With Reverend Broome's commendation. He mentioned something about church pews Mr. Langbridge couldn't quite—"

St. Cloud was gone. Then he was back. "Where the bloody hell is she?"

"Why, I believe she is taking Flame cross-country. There is nothing like a good gallop to put roses in a girl's cheeks."

This time he kissed her hand in farewell but said, "You know, my lady, you are lucky that only the good die young."

If the dowager thought to send him helter-skelter over the Priory's acreage, she sorely misjudged her grandson, and Flame. He left his own horse in the small stable and followed the only path that led away from it. If the old nag could make it farther than the second clearing, he'd eat his hat, which he'd left on the dowager's hall table in his rush out the door.

He did not see them on the path, but then he heard a familiar off-key carol. The angel choir in heaven couldn't have sounded sweeter to his ears. He followed the song through a break in the hedges, and there she was, leading the blasted horse like a dog on a leash. She was wearing the same tatty gray cloak—Juneclaire didn't bother with the long-skirted habit for Flame's daily constitutionals—and her nose was red from the cold. She was beautiful.

"Hallo, Junco," he called.

"Merry!"

Neither knew how the ground was covered, but she was in his arms, or almost, looking up into his face. He was looking as handsome as Juneclaire remembered, certainly neater, in fawn breeches and a bottle green jacket, but his eyes looked tired, and the planes of his face seemed harsher. He'd forgotten how to smile, again. He held her shoulders and said, "Wretched female, I don't know whether to shake you or kiss you."

"Do I get a choice?" was all she could think to say. She felt her face go red at her own ungoverned tongue, but he pulled her closer, then yelped.

"What the deuces?"

"Oh, I am sorry. It's a needle I've taken to carrying around with me." Niles Wilmott had not wasted much time making good on his boasts to Lady Pomeroy. He'd tracked her down yesterday while she was out with Flame. First he plied her with heavy-handed compliments, then barely disguised hints of a financial arrangement. Finally he tried physical enticements, as if she could ever be attracted to a snake in gentleman's clothing. Overdressed clothing at that. Forewarned was forearmed, however, and Niles would not be approaching her again soon. She hoped he died of blood poisoning. Merry raised one eyebrow, meanwhile, waiting for further explanation, so she said, "It's in case I ran into that dastard from the Priory again."

She instantly knew she'd made an error, for the hands on her shoulders tightened till she'd have bruises there. "What dastard? Who insulted you, June-claire? I'll—"

"Oh hush, silly. I'm fine. Everyone has been so nice to me. Well, almost everyone. I have so much to tell you, but you tell me first, instead of glowering at me so. What are you doing here and why are you in such a taking?"

"I am upset, goose, for I have been looking for you for days now, nights, too, in Bramley and Springdale and London and everywhere in between, and you've been right here. If I don't strangle you, it's just because I am too tired. You have led me a fine chase, girl."

"But why, Merry? We are friends, nothing more. I told you you were not responsible for me."

"Nothing more? After a night in a barn? That made you my responsibility, Miss Beaumont." That sounded too severe, even to the earl's ears, and hope made him add, "I cared."

Her hand touched the dent in his chin for an instant, and then she looked away, suddenly shy. "But . . . but how did you find me here?"

"I didn't. I came home to lick my wounds, and there you were."

"Home? You live here, at the Priory?" He nodded.

"You're not one of the earl's disreputable friends, are you?"

"Worse," he told her.

Juneclaire felt a hollowness in her stomach. "A relative?"

"Worse still."

She'd known he was an aristocrat. That assurance and, yes, arrogance of his just had to be matched to a title, but the Earl of St. Cloud? If Flame had an ounce of speed left in her, Juneclaire would jump on the mare's back and ride who-knows-where. Merry—the earl—could walk faster than Flame at her quickest, though. Juneclaire did the only thing possible. She kicked him in the shin with her heavy wooden-soled walking shoe. "You liar!"

The earl was wondering why he'd bothered to save his Hessians from the cat. "I am sorry about being the earl, Junco—sometimes sorrier than you can imagine—but I didn't lie. I am Merritt Jordan."

Juneclaire was limping away, at Flame's speed. "I am sorry, too, my lord, for the earl is not a person I wish to know."

"I did not lie to you about my reputation, Juneclaire, and I shall not lie now and say that it is undeserved. I am no longer that reckless, rebellious boy, however." He took Flame's lead out of Juneclaire's hand and walked beside her. "Besides, you can help me mend it."

Juneclaire ignored that last. "You're not caring about

your mother, from all I hear. Aunt Marta says you can judge a man's worth by how he treats his mama."

"That sounds like what a mother of sons would say. My mother has never been comfortable with me, June-claire, and I gave up trying years ago. It would take the patience of a saint to put up with her vapors, and I never lied about that. And didn't Aunt Marta tell you not to listen to gossip?"

"Well, you aren't kind to your grandmother either, and that is not hearsay. I can see for myself that you keep her on a tight budget. Those old servants, this one piti-ful excuse for a horse. If all this"—she waved one mit-tened hand around—"is yours, that is unforgivable."

He took that mittened hand in his gloved one and continued walking back to the stable. Juneclaire didn't remove her hand. "Now who told you that faradiddle about my holding the dowager's purse strings? Grand-mother is one of the wealthiest women in the county in her own right. She could hire an army and operate a racing stable if she wanted. Have you tried to get her to do anything she *didn't* want? She lives the way she does out of her choice, not mine."

Juneclaire was thinking of some of the other things she'd heard to the earl's disfavor when she remem-bered another item altogether. She pulled her hand away from his so fast, he was left holding her mitten, the odd, not-quite-finished one. "They say—and it is not gossip, for even Lady St. Cloud mentioned it—that you are engaged."

"Yes."

"Yes? That is all you can say, yes? You can hold my hand"—and make her heart beat faster, although she did not say that—"when everyone is waiting for you to bring your betrothed home as soon as you fi—oh."

"Yes." He kept walking but glanced at her out of the corner of his eye. She was biting on her lower lip and kicking at rocks, and her brows were lowered. He wanted to take her in his arms more than anything, needles and kicks and all. "I told them we were engaged."

She came to a standstill. "Were you disguised then, too? You must have been to say such a thing when you knew it wasn't true."

"I am not a drunkard, Juneclaire. You don't have to worry about that, at least. I said we were betrothed because it's right that we marry after you were so compromised."

"But no one knew that I was compromised at all, and it was my fault for being where I had no business being!"

"They'll find out. And I also said it because I wanted it to be true." There, he'd confessed.

Instead of being won over, Juneclaire stamped her foot. "Well, you're not Little Yerby to make it so because you say it, and I am not Jack!"

"I should hope not, dear heart, whoever Little Yerby and Jack are. Will you come for a walk with me?" They were back at the stable, and he handed Flame's lead to the stable boy.

"But the dowager . . ."

"Knows all about it. Come." He stuffed her unresisting hand back in the mitten and held it firmly, going in the opposite direction. "Are you warm enough?"

She just nodded, lost in her own thoughts. After a bit she said, with not much of a quiver in her voice, that she could not marry an earl.

"Why, my love, are you holding out for a duke? I understand there are few on the marriage market this year, and those are well into their dotage. You'd do much better with a young earl."

"How can you tease? I am a nobody, with no dowry and no connections. And . . . and my parents ran off to France to marry. I know I told you that, but it's worse. They . . . they didn't say their vows until they got to Calais, a week later!"

"Shocking, Junco, shocking. Someday, when I am not trying to convince you to join your name with mine, I shall describe my own parents' marriage. Suffice it to say that Lady Fanny has not been to London in over twenty years for fear of being cut. I have tried to convince her that the past is long forgotten, but Uncle Harmon cautions her otherwise. It is not in his interest to see her remarry, or even move to Town, for then he would have no place here. He knows I will not have him set one foot over the doorsill of Jordan House in London. Juneclaire, if I do not hold you responsible for your parents' sins, can you forgive me mine?"

She nodded, but her mind was only half attending. The other half was gazing in awe at the edifice sprawled across her horizon.

"I promised you a house of your own, remember? I, ah, never said it was small. Do you hate it? It's even worse inside. We don't have to live here, you know. There's London and the stud in Ireland, and I have a hunting box in Leicester. We could buy a cottage somewhere, damn it. Juneclaire, say something."

Something? "I want to go home." The Priory was surely the biggest building Juneclaire had seen since leaving France, where she'd visited some of the cathedrals with her parents. It was possibly the ugliest building she'd ever seen. Gray stone, tan brick, an Elizabethan wing and a modern wing, crenellated towers on one side, Roman columns supporting a two-story porch built right on top of the old Priory itself. One wing ended in the original chapel, another in a vast ballroom built in Henry's times. She could not see the conservatory from here, Merry—Lord St. Cloud—told her, but it formed the central wing.

Juneclaire had to laugh. He was teasing, of course.

"No, Junco, I am not bamming you. I need you."

"The dowager needs me."

"We'll share. I need you to convince her to move up here, where she'll be looked after better. There's a private suite all ready for her. I need you to keep peace between the countesses and referee the cricket matches between the Priory phantoms and the Angel of Death."

"Woodpeckers."

"You heard it, too? See, your calm good sense is just what they need. What I need. Please, Junco, at least consider my proposal. Say you'll come to dinner tonight, you and Grandmother, of course. The relatives mostly grow worse on closer acquaintance, but I swear no one shall insult you."

"I have nothing to wear to such a grand house."

"I believe you are turning craven on me, Junco. Is this the fearless amazon who attacked a bandit with a water bucket? Who fended off an amorous footman with a wine bottle? Who wears a blasted darning needle in her lapel? I happen to know you have a beautiful gown, a white velvet gown. I should love to buy you rubies to go with it, or emeralds. I should like to touch the softness of it, against your skin. But I can be patient. Not very, as you know. Come tonight, Junco. Come get to know us and give us a chance. Give me a chance."

Chapter Eighteen

*S*t. Cloud sent over red rosebuds from the hothouses. Nutley wove them through the wreath of holly Juneclaire wore as a headpiece, with her hair pulled up and back, tiny curls framing her face and a long sweep of brown waves trailing over one shoulder. The abigail pinned another of the roses to the green ribbon that sashed under the high waist, helped Miss Beaumont fasten her mother's pearls around her neck, and declared the young lady a diamond of the first water. The groom, draping the borrowed black velvet mantle with red satin lining over Juneclaire's pale shoulders, stared wide-eyed and openmouthed. Sally Munch gasped.

"Well, tell me, girl, tell me," the dowager demanded, banging her cane down once she knew Shamrock was tucked in the kitchen with Penny. "Will she do?"

Sally swore she was bang up to the mark, and Pennington, holding the door, added that miss was top of the trees, if my lady excused the cant. Juneclaire wanted to sink with embarrassment. "Really, ma'am, there is no need to make such a fuss."

"There's all the need in the world, miss, and you know it. Facing that pack of barracudas, you'll want all your defenses up, and a gel's best defense is looking her best."

Juneclaire was surely doing that, she acknowledged. She'd never felt so elegant, so pampered, or so unsure of herself. "Will they like me?" she asked, as the footman and Sally helped the dowager into an elegant carriage.

"What's that to the point?" the dowager replied as soon as the coach started moving. "Hell, they all hate me, and I've never lost a night's sleep over it. Besides, if you're worrying about St. Cloud, don't. He likes you enough to chase all over England after you, and he never cared what anyone else thought, especially not that parcel of flats. Oh, Fanny's just a flibbertigibbet, I suppose, afraid of her own shadow and that brother of hers, but the others are—Well, you'll see for yourself."

A very proper butler announced them to those assembled in the gold parlor: "Lady Georgette Jordan, Dowager Countess St. Cloud. Miss Juneclaire Beaumont."

They walked in to a sea of stunned faces. Then St. Cloud came forward and took Juneclaire's trembling hand. He squeezed it and winked. "Oh yes," he addressed the company at large, "I forgot to mention that Grandmother's new companion was my Juneclaire. With all the skimble-skamble over carriages and directions and such, she cleverly came ahead on her own to wait for me here, under the dowager's aegis, of course. Didn't you, my pet?"

His pet was wanting to box his ears, even if he was overwhelmingly attractive in his formal clothes! The devil had very nicely sidestepped awkward questions but also added to the impression that they were affianced. Juneclaire couldn't cause a scene, not when he was leading her to the two women on the sofa. One of them was weeping into her handkerchief. His mother hates me already, Juneclaire thought in despair. But he was bowing to the other woman.

"I am so glad," Lady Fanny trilled after introductions were made, and Juneclaire thought she meant it.

The other woman was moaning by now, and Juneclaire could not understand how everyone else in the room was ignoring her, even turning their backs.

"Aunt Florrie," St. Cloud was calling, "what's wrong? Aren't you happy I found Juneclaire and she is safe?"

"She'll want her pig back," Florrie wailed.

Juneclaire blinked, then said, "Oh, have you been taking care of Pansy? Isn't she a fine pig? I did give her to Mer—the earl, however, so I shan't be claiming her back. Did you know that we have a new kitten staying at the Dower House? Perhaps the dowager will invite you to tea so you can meet Shamrock."

Florrie was gone, skipping toward the dowager, who sat alone in a high-backed chair. It would be the first conversation between those two unlikely friends. Lady Fanny smiled her thanks and St. Cloud patted her hand, still firmly held on his arm, as he led her away.

"Why haven't you told your mother that we are not engaged?" she hissed at him, trying to maintain her smile.

"What, and cause another *crise de nerfs*? I thought you wanted me to be more careful of her sensibilities."

They were in front of the other two females in the room, and during the introductions, Juneclaire had to pretend she did not know their identities. Miss Elsbeth Wilmott's gaze was clearly speculative, then superior when she compared her own blond curls, lace overskirt, three tiers of ruffles and rhinestones to Miss Beaumont's rustic simplicity. The country drab would never have a fitting place in society, Elsbeth's curling lip seemed to say. If this sour-faced young woman was the girl Merry might have married, Juneclaire reflected, he was better out of it.

The other woman looked right through Juneclaire, judging her and finding her unworthy of notice. Lady Sydelle Pomeroy directed all of her attention on the earl, having decided that a nonesuch like St. Cloud would tire of the little nobody in weeks. Juneclaire was thinking much the same, observing the older woman's gold locks and nile blue gown, what there was of it. More bosom was showing out of Lady Pomeroy's bodice than Juneclaire had in hers. The woman made her feel like a gauche schoolgirl, and she was happy when someone placed a glass of sherry in her hand.

Then they were facing Niles, the toad. His face was as white as his high shirt collars, and he was tossing back sherries as if they were Blue Ruin. Juneclaire smiled as she held out her hand for his salute, forcing him to extend his own bandaged paw, which he was desperately trying to conceal from the earl. Trying to seduce a paid companion was one thing; attempting to have his way with his cousin's wife-to-be was another. He swallowed audibly. St. Cloud was such a deuced good shot. And had such a deuced short temper. Juneclaire took great satisfaction in letting him squirm a bit; then she inclined her head and said, "How do you do?"

"Magnificent, my lady," St. Cloud whispered in her ear after Niles scuttled away. "And I apologize. That performance was surely worthy of a duchess. I also apologize for my cousin," the earl added, having missed none of the byplay. "He'll never bother you again."

Niles, meanwhile, had attached himself to Lady Pomeroy's side. He needed a wealthy wife more than ever.

"What about our bet, Niles?" Sydelle asked, not bothering to lower her voice.

"What, are you dicked in the nob? Even if I succeeded, I'd not live long enough to enjoy my winnings. Besides, the fellow just paid all my debts."

The last two people in the room were the live-in curate, who welcomed her kindly, and St. Cloud's uncle Harmon, who uttered his greeting in form. Juneclaire did not have to be a mind reader to sense his disapproval. He wanted his daughter to be countess, she had that from the dowager, and he had an overweening sense of pride. If Juneclaire did not know she was unfit to be Lady St. Cloud, Lord Wilmott's slack-jowled sneer would have told her.

"Don't let Uncle Harmon bother you," the earl told her as they went in to dinner together, forgoing precedence. "He has digestive problems. An overabundance of spleen."

Someone, the earl most likely, had been very careful of the seating arrangements. Juneclaire sat on the earl's left, across from the dowager, with Mr. Hilloughby on her other side. The table was vast enough that she did not have to converse with any of the Wilmotts during the four courses and several removes, although she felt all their eyes upon her, waiting to see if she reached for the wrong fork or spoke with her mouth full. Aunt Marta would have scolded her for less.

Dinner was fairly pleasant, at her end at least, with the dowager quizzing the earl about her London acquaintances. They were quick to include Juneclaire, providing histories and reciting anecdotes that had her laughing. Juneclaire was glad to see the old lady happy and pleased to note how gracefully the earl made sure her food was cut and directions tactfully whispered.

Mr. Hilloughby was pleased to relate the history of the Priory chapel when she turned to him, and begged to show Juneclaire the fine rose window, at her convenience, of course. Then the dowager started recounting bits of her own London Seasons, which had Juneclaire in whoops. She *had* had a bit more wine with dinner than she was used to, on top of the sherry.

She needed it, to get her through the after-dinner gathering in the drawing room, before the men joined the ladies.

The dowager was drowsing near the fire, and Aunt Florrie was counting chair legs, "just to be sure." Countess Fanny had taken up her Bible and seemed to be praying; her lips were moving, at any rate, so Juneclaire did not want to intrude. That left her at the mercy of the two blond beauties.

"Did we hear you were from Strasmere? I suppose you know the baron, then, and his lady. So charming, don't you think?"

"Wherever did you find such a clever seamstress, my dear? So daring to set new styles, isn't it?"

"You are nineteen? Then you must have had your come-out. I do not recall seeing you in London. So many debutantes, you know."

St. Cloud would have seemed like an angel of mercy if he weren't scowling so. He took Juneclaire's arm to lead her away, but not before Lady Pomeroy asked if their newest member couldn't entertain them with a song and some music.

"*All* ladies can play, of course, and I am sure the company is bored with my poor offerings."

They'd be more than bored if Juneclaire sat at the pianoforte, she thought with just a tinge of hysteria, not wanting to shame Merry. She was saved this time by the dowager, who, rousing from her nap, declared that not all who could play well were ladies. "I wish more young gels knew their limits, instead of foisting their meager accomplishments on poor dolts with nothing better to do. Besides, Miss Beaumont has other talents, like teaching a blind woman how to play cards. I'll take you all on at whist, with her help. And my own deck."

Sydelle excused herself with a headache, rather than waste her time talking to Elsbeth or Lady Fanny. The men were all commandeered for the dowager's game, except the curate, who was aiding Fanny at her devotions. He didn't count anyway.

Juneclaire sat behind the dowager, whispering the discards. St. Cloud was partnering his grandmother, straight across from them, and Juneclaire could see his brows lift when he felt the rough edges of the pinpricks. Niles smiled; marked cards were nothing new to him.

Lord Wilmott, however, was furious. He threw his hand down and jumped to his feet. "This is an outrage!

These cards have been tampered with." He glared at Juneclaire. "We don't consider cardsharping a drawing-room accomplishment in our circles, miss."

Juneclaire felt the roast pheasant she'd enjoyed at dinner try to take wing. She couldn't look at Merry. It was the dowager who spoke first, though. "Of course the cards are marked, you popinjay. What did you think, I was reading my hands through Miss Beaumont's eye? And where was the advantage, Harmon? If I remember correctly, you had the deal."

Lord Wilmott sat down, red-faced and muttering. Juneclaire released her breath. Then St. Cloud spoke, every inch the earl. "I believe you owe the ladies an apology, sir. Lady St. Cloud has ever been the best whist player of my acquaintance; she has no need to cheat to beat you. And Miss Beaumont is many things, including a guest in this house, may I remind you, but she is not a Captain Sharp. I did not like your comments."

Lord Wilmott mumbled his apologies and took up his hand, ungracefully. His antipathy toward St. Cloud was barely concealed and was magnified when the earl suggested Lord Wilmott apply to Lady Fanny for a physic, if his stomach was in such an uproar it disordered his senses. The dowager cackled and Niles smirked. Lord Wilmott glared most at the outside witness to his humiliation, Juneclaire. Worse, in his eyes, he and Niles were sadly trounced. He excused himself before the tea tray was brought in.

Soon after, Juneclaire noticed that the dowager was looking peaked, exhausted by her triumph. "We should be going, my lord," she told the earl.

He walked with her toward the other side of the room, where the gold drapes were drawn against the night. "I, ah, took the liberty of having the dowager's and your things moved over to the Priory during dinner." He wisely stepped back.

"You what? Why, you arrogant, overbearing—"

"Now don't cut up stiff, Junco. You know it's best for the dowager."

"I know it suits your plans, my lord, and I know you like having your own way."

"Why, there have to be *some* advantages to having a title," he teased.

She was not amused. "I resent being forced to go along with your whims, willy-nilly."

"This, my little bird, is not a whim. I am trying to show you that. Since you are already up in the boughs, I may as well admit to the other decision I took on myself. I had my man Foley tell your people that you were safe here, with me."

Juneclaire had written three letters to her family, then ripped them up, not knowing what to say. She should be thankful, she supposed, that Merry had undertaken an unpleasant task, but Aunt Marta was not likely to consider her safe, not if she knew the earl's reputation, and not if he kept stroking the inside of Juneclaire's elbow, where her gloves ended. And certainly not if she knew how Juneclaire wanted to succumb to the gleam in Merry's green, green eyes. "Oh, dear."

Chapter Nineteen

*H*e was arrogant and overbearing and quite, quite wonderful! He led her himself to the family wing to a white-and-rose room with Chinese wallpaper. Pansy was waiting there, wearing a baby's bonnet, but clean and shiny and noisily ecstatic to see Juneclaire. Shamrock was curled in a basket by the fireplace, and a freckle-faced young maid sat sewing, ready to help her to bed. The dowager was installed in the suite next door, he explained, with Nutley and Sally Munch each assigned a bedchamber off the dressing room. Nutley was pleased so many more servants would be listening for the dowager's calls, and Sally was thrilled to have all the Priory footmen to practice her wiles upon. The Penningtons, St. Cloud continued, wanted to stay on as caretakers at the Dower House, where they were comfortable, rather than be interlopers in the Priory staff hierarchy. He was sending young Ned and his mother, who was feeling much better with the proper medicine, to help look after the house and the old couple. That should keep everybody out of trouble, the earl said. Then he kissed her hand good night, in view of the new maid, and thanked her for coming, as if she'd had a choice!

He thought of everything, Juneclaire had to admit. Her own three gowns hung in the wardrobe, with the brown habit and two simple gowns she and Sally and Nutley had managed to make over from the dowager's castoffs, and two other new dresses. These, her new maid Parker happily informed her, had been run up by the Priory's own resident seamstress that afternoon, with more to come since miss's trunks had so unfortunately gone astray in the carriage mishap.

There were powders and oils and hot towels, hothouse flowers and a stack of books on the bed stand, a dish of biscuits if she or Pansy got hungry during the night. What more could a poor orphan runaway want? Plenty.

Merry was kind. He cared for her. He wanted her and needed her, he said, and she believed him. He never mentioned love. Juneclaire could barely think in his presence, her blood pounded so loudly in her head. She thought he was the most splendid man in the world, if a trifle imperious and temper-prone. She thought she could make him happy, since the mere thought of him made her smile. She also thought she was halfway in love with him from the night at the barn, and the other half was a heartbeat away. But she was, indeed, a poor orphan runaway, and she would never burden him with such a wife, only to have him regret his good intentions later. Unless he loved her . . .

Merry asked for time to change her mind. Perhaps in time she could change his from just wanting to marry her to not wanting to live without her. It was possible. She thought she'd ask Mrs. Pennington to save her a wishbone when she visited them tomorrow. She went to sleep, smiling.

Tap, tap. Tap, tap. There it was again, Juneclaire thought in a muzzy fog. All those workmen and they never found the woodpeckers. Merry would be angry. She snuggled deeper in the covers.

Tap, crunch. Tap, crunch. Woodpeckers riding on rats? Merry would be very angry. Juneclaire turned over.

Tap, crunch, sigh. On remorseful rats? That was too much. She fumbled for the flint. Someone handed it to her, and she automatically said "Thank you" before lighting her candle.

Either there was a ghost in her room, or Juneclaire'd had too much wine. She opted for the wine. No self-respecting ghost ever looked like this. He had salt-and-pepper hair, a full gray beard and mustache, a brocaded coat from the last century—camphor-scented to prove it—that couldn't button across a wide paunch, and a peg leg.

Oh, good, Juneclaire thought, still half asleep, that explains the tapping. The empty plate of biscuits by her bed explained the crunching. Well, they were gone, so the ghost could leave and she could go back to sleep. She bent to blow out the candle, and the ghost sighed again, a mournful, graveyard sigh indeed. It occurred to Juneclaire that she should scream. She opened her mouth, but the ghost stopped her by saying, "So you're Merry's bride."

Merry? Only one person ever called him Merry, he'd said. "Uncle George?"

"Aye." He pulled a chair closer to her bed and fed the last biscuit to the pig when Pansy came to investigate. Then he sighed again, scratching behind Pansy's big ears poking through the baby bonnet, as though it were the most natural thing for a pig—or a ghost— to be in a lady's bedchamber at three in the morning. Juneclaire swore she would never take a sip of wine again.

Then she got a whiff of her guest, past the camphor. He'd been partaking of the grape, too, it seemed. "Um, Uncle George, how did you get in here?" Her door was locked; she didn't trust that Niles. The specter waved vaguely at the wardrobe against the far side of the room. Juneclaire nodded. That made sense. Ghosts didn't need to use doors. "Can you tell me why you've come? What it is that you want?" She was thinking in terms of revenge, or a better burial, typical ghostly reasons for haunting their ancestral homes.

"Someone to talk to, I guess." He sighed again. Life, or half life, was hard. "Fanny gets down on her hands and knees and starts praying every time I try to talk to her, when she doesn't swoon. I don't know how many more visits from me Mother's heart can take, what with her sure I'm Death come to carry her off. And Merry nearly ran me through with his sword tonight, thinking I was some nightmare from his French prison days. I tried old Pennington, but he drank down his wife's last bottle of rum and passed out next to her. Now he's taken to wearing garlic around his neck."

"Is that what it is? I noticed something. . . ."

"Don't want to go near the old fellow, and I can't ever rouse Nutley. I swear the woman sleeps like one of the dead."

He should know, but "She's deaf," Juneclaire told him.

"Oh. None of the other servants have been around long enough, so you see, there's no one to talk to. They all think I'm dead."

"Aren't you?"

"I don't think so. Are ghosts hungry?"

"How should I know? You're the first one I've met." Shamrock was now twining himself around the apparition's leg, and Pansy was wearing her idiotic grin of a hog in heaven. Juneclaire shrugged and slipped out of bed. She gingerly reached out her hand and touched

his arm with the tips of her fingers. Solid. She poked
her own arm to make sure. Solid, and awake. Unless
she was dreaming about pinching herself to see if she
was dreaming. She sat back down on the bed. "Uncle
George? That is, may I call you Uncle George?" He nodded, with another sigh. "Why don't you just come back
tomorrow, in the daylight, and have Talbot announce
you?"

"I wish it were that easy, lass. I wish it were. I can tell
you've a wise head on your shoulders, and I'd explain
all about it, if only I weren't so devilishly sharp set.
I'd go down to the kitchens, but Merry's got a guard
posted there with a pistol. One along the corridor here,
too."

"Someone's been stealing food and things and frightening the servants, to say nothing of poor Lady Fanny.
You should be ashamed, sir."

"I am, child. Very ashamed. And very hungry."

So Juneclaire went to find the kitchens, with Uncle
George's directions tumbling about in her head. She
was in the east wing; the kitchens were two stories
down, halfway along the central transverse in what
was the old Priory's refectory. She went in her bare feet
so as not to wake anybody, especially the guard who
was asleep at the end of the corridor. A hunting rifle
was propped alongside his chair, barrel pointing up.
Juneclaire shielded her candle and tiptoed past. So did
Pansy.

The kitchen guard was awake, playing patience and sipping an ale. He thought nothing odd about a barefoot houseguest in her white flannel nightgown helping herself to another dinner. Hell, he thought, everyone knew the gentry was peculiar. Once you got over the pig in the baby bonnet, the rest didn't make a halfpenny's difference.

Juneclaire found a hamper to fill, as if she and Pansy were going on a picnic, then covered the whole with a napkin so the guard couldn't tell how much food she was taking, she hoped. She could barely carry the basket as it was, with the candle in her other hand.

"I'd help you, miss, but it'd mean my job, were I to leave my post." The guard was back at his game.

"But you will tell them in the morning that I took the leftovers, won't you? I don't want anyone to think there were burglars or . . . ghosts."

"I'll be sure to mention it, lest they think I was eating more myself than Napoleon's army during the whole Russian campaign."

Juneclaire blushed but held her head high and retraced her steps. She thought she did, anyway. Somehow she found herself in the servants' quarters, built out of the old monks' cells. She turned around quickly and let Pansy lead the way, trusting the pig's unerring nose to get them . . . back to the kitchen. The guard sent her on her way in the other direction, shaking his head.

Her feet were cold, the basket was heavy, and June-

claire was sure she must have dreamed the whole thing.
She tiptoed carefully past the sleeping hall watchman
but was not quite as careful about Pansy, who stopped
to investigate. Her pink leathery nose whiffled into the
watchman's dangling hand to check for crumbs. The
guard jumped up and shouted and his chair fell back,
crashing. The pig ran away, screaming, and the leaning
gun went off, blowing a porcelain bust of Galileo into
cosmic dust indeed.

The first door to fly open was Lady Fanny's. Right
in front of her was a figure swathed in white cloth, surrounded by swirls of otherworldly clouds. Juneclaire
moaned. The countess collapsed onto the floor at her
feet, out cold.

The dowager was shouting to know what was going on and demanding to be taken home to the Dower
House, where a body wasn't likely to be shot in her
bed. Sally Munch poked her head out of the door, fireplace poker in hand.

Then St. Cloud was there, carrying his mother back
to her room, calling for her woman, shouting the dowager back to bed, dismissing the guard and the twenty
or thirty other servants in various stages of undress
who appeared from nowhere. And looking at Juneclaire in sorrow.

She held up the basket and pulled out a roll. "I . . . I
wanted it for the pig."

Elsbeth giggled until a glare from St. Cloud had her
scurrying away. He jerked his head to be rid of Niles,

too. But Uncle Harmon stayed, spluttering about harum-scarum chits and animals who should be in the stable or—with a dark look at Pansy—on the table. The look he gave Juneclaire was no better. "Milk-maids," he huffed, pulling his nightcap back down around his ears and stomping off to the other wing.

St. Cloud clenched his jaw and said he had to check on his grandmother. He would see Miss Beaumont in the morning. He tightened the sash on his paisley robe and bowed.

Juneclaire didn't doubt he was wishing the sash was around her neck. She fled to her own room and threw herself on the bed. Uncle George was gone, naturally. No one would believe her anyway, and now she had lost Merry's esteem.

His family hated her. They thought her a gapeseed, an unmannered bumpkin born in a cabbage patch. And they were right. She *had* been a milkmaid, just that one time for Little Yerby, true, but she was no fine lady like Sydelle and Elsbeth. She couldn't play or sing or flirt or fill a gown so well. Her friends were farmers and servants and barnyard animals, not lords and ladies and London luminaries.

And Merry was disappointed. She could see it in his angry face. He did not need another hysterical female in his household, or one who caused more ruckus and row than all the others combined—and on her first night there! Juneclaire sobbed into her pillow; the cat and the pig were already damp with her tears. She did not belong here, she thought, and she would have to leave before she disgraced Merry further. There was no way he could learn to love a milkmaid, and there was no way she could make a proper countess. You couldn't make a silk purse out of a sow's ear.

Chapter Twenty

*T*he food was gone in the morning. Juneclaire had put it on the desk, out of Pansy's reach, and the maids had not been in yet to light the fire, so Uncle George must have come back. Juneclaire wished he'd woken her up for a chat, for if he thought being dead was hard, he should try being Miss Beaumont. She was not *really* Merry's fiancée, she no longer had duties as the dowager's companion, and everyone, snooty relatives and well-trained servants, was treating her with polite condescension. They hated her. There was a hideous sculpture of some martyr being devoured by a lion in the niche where Galileo used to be. Lady Fanny most likely directed the maids to find the ugliest piece in the house, in hopes Juneclaire would relieve them of it next.

Breakfast was a disaster. Juneclaire and Aunt Florrie were the only women there. That court card Niles made oinking noises at her, while eating rasher after rasher of bacon. Lord Harmon barely concealed his disgust behind the newspapers, and Mr. Hilloughby kept his eyes firmly on his kippers. Merry pretended nothing had happened.

With his black curls damp from combing and his cravat loosely tied, Merry looked so handsome, June-claire had a hard time swallowing her toast past the lump in her throat. His brows seemed permanently puckered and his lips never turned up, but he was courteous, caring—and cold. He was too busy to show her around this morning, he apologized, what with the New Year's Eve ball just tomorrow night, and no, thank you, he said, there was nothing she could do to help; she was a guest. The weather was too inclement, at any rate, for her to accompany him on his rounds. He had arranged for Mr. Hilloughby to show her the chapel this morning and for Aunt Florrie to take June-claire to the attics to pick a costume in the afternoon. This was from the man who wanted her to spend time getting to know him, to see if they would suit. He had obviously decided.

Juneclaire was set to ask the dowager for a carriage ride back to Stanton Hall as soon as Lady St. Cloud awoke. That way Merry could have no worries about her safety, no embarrassing responsibilities toward her. Before she left, though, she was curious about one thing: "My lord, what happened to Uncle George?"

Niles dropped his coffee cup, and Mr. Hilloughby took a coughing fit. The footmen's eyes were all on the carved ceiling. Juneclaire barely registered all this. She was pinned in St. Cloud's stare like a mounted butterfly. She'd never seen him so angry, not even last night, when he walked barefoot over Galileo's remains, not even when Charlie Parrett had him in a death grip. Still, she would not look away. Let him think she was an unschooled hobbledehoyden. Let him think there was a breeze in her cockloft. He would *not* think she was a coward, unless he heard her knees knocking together.

He finally broke the silence by pronouncing, "We do not speak of George Jordan in this house," in the same tones he might have used to intone the eleventh commandment.

Then Aunt Florrie chirped, "We don't mention making water either."

Juneclaire would not stoop to questioning the servants, who were so in dread of the master's temper that they'd take the turnspit dog's place sooner than go against his wishes. She could not chance upsetting the dowager or Lady Fanny with her queries, and she was not about to ask Mr. Hilloughby, not after St. Cloud's edict.

She did, however, manage to check the family Bible in the old chapel, after dutifully admiring the age and architecture of the place. The stained-glass windows did not glow, not on such a dreary day outside, and the stone floors kept the sanctuary bitterly cold. Worse, Mr. Hilloughby was a historical scholar. While he described the life and last days of the original St. Jerome of the Clouds in excruciating detail, Juneclaire read through generations of Jordans. Uncle George was crossed out.

The dowager refused to hear of Juneclaire's leaving.

"That's a shabby return for my taking you on, girl, leaving me alone with the hyenas. No, I won't hear of it." She stabbed her cane halfway through the Turkish runner in her sitting room. "You will be happy here, and that's final."

The earl had inherited more than a title and wealth, it seemed.

Juneclaire was surprised at how well Florrie knew her way around the vast attics. She understood the earl's aunt was frequently lost in the Priory's warren of corridors, chambers, and alcoves. Aunt Florrie knew just what she wanted for Juneclaire, too, and knew right where it was, give or take a trunk or three or four. The St. Clouds must never have thrown anything out.

"Here, this will be perfect for you, dearie," Aunt Florrie said, holding up a wide-skirted shepherdess dress, complete with apron, crooked staff, and stuffed, fleece-covered lamb. "It's the best of all the costumes."

Juneclaire's heart was not in preparing for a mas-

querade. It was downstairs, brooding. She didn't care
what she wore. She didn't care if she attended, even
if she'd never been to a real ball in her life, much less
a masked one. Aunt Marta would convert to Hindi
before she let such wickedness occur under her roof.
Nonetheless, the outfit seemed to mean a great deal
to the older woman, so Juneclaire said, "Perhaps you
should be the shepherdess, Aunt Florrie, and I could
be something else." She looked around. "Queen Eliza-
beth, maybe, or Anne Boleyn." She felt like Anne Boleyn, after all.

"Oh, no, you have to be the shepherdess. It will
be wonderful. You'll see." She was cutting apart the
stuffed lamb with embroidery scissors from her pocket.
"Besides, I am going to be Yellow. Last year I was Rain,
but Harmon became angry when the floors got wet."

The dowager decided to have dinner on a tray in her
room. Juneclaire suspected the old lady was feigning
weariness for her sake, so she did not have to face the
company again, but she leaped at the excuse.

"It's no such thing, missy. I saw them Christmas and
last night, and I'll have to do the pretty for the ball tomorrow. That's three times in one week, and with that
bunch of counter jumpers, three times a year is enough.
Of course, you're free to go down if you want."

"Oh, no, I promised to teach you to knit cables, and
you promised to teach me vingt-et-un. And Lord St.
Cloud sent up Miss Austen's new novel and Scott's

ballads. I need to try on my costume for tomorrow and—"

"Cut line, girl. I'm glad for the company."

The dowager approved the theme of Juneclaire's costume. "Innocent and sweet, in case there's any talk. But pretty and feminine, too, if I remember correctly. Just the ticket. My costume? I'm going as a crotchety old lady, what else? No one'll recognize me, and that's only fair, for I sure as Harry won't recognize them!"

Juneclaire kept back all the uneaten food from dinner and asked for more to be sent up, for the pig. She let Parker help her into her night rail and brush out her long hair, and then she dismissed the maid for the night. She got into bed with a Gothic tale from the Minerva Press and waited for Uncle George.

The heroine was locked in a deserted tower. The steps were crumbly, the candle was low, small things chittered nearby. Everywhere she turned, spiderwebs stuck in her hair. Drafts blew through the cracked windows, and the door . . . slowly . . . creaked . . . open.

And there was Uncle George, stepping out of Juneclaire's wardrobe. Tonight he wore doublet and hose.

While he was eating, she told him her troubles. "They all think I'm a clodpoll, except for Merry. He thinks I'm a nightmare. The dowager won't let me go, and the rest of them will make fun of me if I stay. Tomorrow night at the ball they'll have all their friends to laugh and sneer at poor St. Cloud's goat girl. Elsbeth and Lady Pomeroy will be gorgeous, and I'll forget the dance steps. I've only practiced with my cousins, you know."

George waved a chicken leg. "Your problem, puss, is lack of confidence. Don't worry. I'll take care of it."

"You? How can you take care of it when you don't even exist?"

He sighed, feeding Pansy the cooked carrots. "Never could abide cooked carrots. Do you think a ghost cares what it eats? As a matter of fact, why would a ghost eat at all? I thought we'd settled that last night."

"Yes, but they won't talk about you, and they've struck your name out of the records. If you're not dead, why don't you just come back?"

"I promised I'd explain, but it's hard. You see, if I'm not dead, then I'm a murderer."

"A murderer?" she shrieked, louder than she intended, and suddenly there was a pounding at her door.

"Juneclaire, are you all right? Open the door."

St. Cloud would kick it open if he had to, she knew. She looked helplessly toward Uncle George, who shrugged and picked up another chicken leg. She unlocked the door and opened it a crack. "I am fine, my lord."

He was glaring at her again. "I thought I heard voices." He thought he'd heard a man's voice. He tried to look past her into the room.

She did not think this was a good time to mention Uncle George again. "I was, ah, reading."

"Out loud?"

"I was practicing, you know, for when I read to the dowager."

"And you are all right? Not frightened by those silly stories of the Priory ghosts?"

"Oh, no. Not at all. Are you?"

He snorted. "Hardly. I'll just be going, then. Good night, Miss Beaumont."

"Good night, Lord St. Cloud."

Juneclaire was almost as unhappy as the night before, until she started to hear screams and screeches from the far corridor, where the Wilmotts were installed. She tied on her robe and found her slippers and ran with St. Cloud and some of the servants to the east wing. Niles and Harmon Wilmott were already in the hall, trying to comfort Elsbeth, who was sobbing, and Lady Sydelle, who was raving hysterically about goblins, ghosts, and going home. Elsbeth had her hair tied in papers, and Lady Pomeroy had some yellow concoction spread all over her face. Juneclaire smiled. Uncle George was taking care of things for her.

The Earl of St. Cloud sat in his library, his head in his hands. Half a bottle of cognac hadn't helped. He was still in a deuce of a coil. He was fond of his Aunt Florrie, but he did not want his children to be like her. Juneclaire was touched, dicked in the nob, attics to let. Or else she was playing some deep game he did not know about. How could she look like such an angel and be so jingle-brained, if not downright evil? Nothing she said rang true anymore. He did not know what to think, except that she was turning his life and his household upside down.

And yet he was so attracted to her that just the memory of the chit in her virginal white nightgown, with her brown hair tumbling around her shoulders, set his juices flowing. Then he remembered how he was ready to commit mayhem at the thought of someone in the room with her. He was jealous of the blasted ghost! Botheration, he was jealous of the damn pig that got to spend the night with her. Life with Juneclaire would be hell.

But how could he cry off the engagement? A gentleman did not. And he was the one who had insisted, who had announced their betrothal to his family. He was obliged to marry her now, aside from the night in the barn. Blast her and the dashed pig. They had him by the shoat hairs.

Chapter Twenty-one

*J*uneclaire was walking the pig before breakfast when she heard the commotion. She followed the noise around the ballroom wing to find St. Cloud and a group of servants with axes, ladders, and hammers. They were searching for ways an intruder could have entered the house, Sally Munch explained to her, from her place at the fringes of the workers. Lord St. Cloud was directing the removal of climbing vines and overhanging branches. He walked ahead of the group, checking the loose ground under the windows for signs of recent disturbance. He paused to study an area under a balcony where a great many footsteps showed in the dirt. The workers gathered round, wondering if the master was going to order them to chop down the balcony.

Sally Munch was hanging back, so Juneclaire had a fairly good idea to whom at least half the prints belonged. Pansy snuffled around, then went straight to the new footman, the one with the shoulders of a prize fighter. Sally blushed, but the earl merely requested that Miss Beaumont kindly remove the pig from the field of investigation.

Juneclaire stepped closer and looked down. Thinking out loud, she said, "Those can't be his footprints anyway. Uncle George has a peg leg." She clapped her hand over her mouth. "Oh."

With one frigid glance the earl sent the workers off. Juneclaire shivered. Her words would be spread throughout the mansion along with the coffee cups and chocolate. She had to go explain to the dowager before Lady St. Cloud heard from that prattlebox Sally. Before she took one step, a steel-gripped hand clasped her wrist like a manacle, and she was silently pulled away from the house. That is, St. Cloud was silent, frowning fiercely down at the ground. Juneclaire protested, struggled, and ran to keep up lest he drag her facedown in the dirt if she fell.

He did not stop until they reached a high stone wall and a gate. St. Cloud released her hand, with a look daring Juneclaire to try to escape. She was too busy catching her breath and wondering where they were. He found the key under a loose stone and unlatched the gate, then pulled her through. They were in a small cemetery, and Juneclaire had a moment's fright that he meant to murder her and leave her body there. How awful to think her last sight of him was to be that terrible scowl. He wasn't even looking at her, though, continuing his long, angry strides toward the far corner.

"There," he said, stopping finally in front of a small grave site. "Uncle George."

Pansy was happily rooting in the leaves and stuff that had fallen on Uncle George's marker. Juneclaire pushed her aside and read the dates.

"He has been dead these four and twenty years," St. Cloud said. "My fifth birthday."

"There must have been a mistake."

A muscle flexed in the earl's jaw. "The only mistake, madam, was in my thinking you a sane, sensible type of female. You are upsetting my household with these idiotic ravings, and you will cease at once."

Juneclaire stood up. "I see. Uncle George is dead. Therefore I am seeing ghosts, talking to spirits, feeding phantoms."

"There are no such things as ghosts. You are either hallucinating or else you are the victim of some unscrupulous charlatan, preying on your weakness."

"Unless, of course, I am in league with this fiendish scheme to . . . what? To send your mother into a decline, to rout your houseguests, and terrorize your servants. Thank you, my lord."

He watched the pig. "I never said that."

"No, but you thought it. Did it never occur to you, my

lord, that you could be wrong for once? That someone, dead or alive, could act contrary to your wishes?"

"I saw him, dash it! I saw his body when they brought him in!"

"Tell me," she said quietly, holding out her hand.

St. Cloud took it, thinking he would air the dirty linen and then she would be gone. That was best for all. He looked around till he spotted a bench under a stand of bare-branched lilacs. "Come. It is not a short story." He did not sit down next to her but propped one Hessian-clad leg on the stone seat. He stared into the distance, into the past.

"The Wilmotts lived on the neighboring estate, Motthaven. They were minor gentry but, then as now, perpetually overextended. Uncle George and Mother were childhood sweethearts. The second son of an earl should have been a good enough match for his daughter, but Lord Wilmott wanted more, and Robert, the oldest son and heir, seemed interested. George was reckless, drinking, gambling, all the usual vices, so Wilmott had an excuse. He refused his permission. The two tried to elope but were brought back by Wilmott, his son Harmon, and Robert. Uncle George was shipped out to the army, more dead than alive, I understand. And Mother . . . Mother married Robert Jordan, the heir to St. Cloud and soon to be the earl.

"They were happy enough, I suppose. I seldom saw them, for they spent most of their time in London or traveling. Uncle George never visited." St. Cloud started pacing, kicking up leaves.

"Then he was gravely injured, and the army sent him home to St. Cloud. He was here over eight months, recuperating, and I got to know him well. He was full of stories and games to delight a little boy, when he felt well enough. We were nearly inseparable, they say. He was bored and I was . . . lonely. Then came Christmas and my birthday. My parents came here, with a large house party. And . . . something happened between the brothers."

Juneclaire knew he was not telling the whole story, but she did not interrupt.

"There was a confrontation, in view of the entire company, where Uncle George threatened to kill his brother. The two of them stormed out of the house, and Uncle George was never seen alive again."

"What happened? Did he kill your father?"

"My . . . father? No, but not from lack of trying, I fear. When neither came back that night, search parties were sent out in the morning. They found my father at the old quarry, grievously wounded and at death's door. They found George's body the next day, at the bottom of the quarry. I saw them bring him home. No one intended a small boy to be there, of course, but I was. It was a sight I shall never forget." He cleared his throat and went on: "The earl had a ball lodged against his spine, pneumonia, and severe loss of blood.

They feared for his life. Still, he managed to declare the disaster an accident. Lord Wilmott was magistrate and so proclaimed it, rather than let the county know the brothers had been fighting over his daughter, my mother. As if that could stop the gossip," he added bitterly.

"The earl partially recovered. He never walked again and was angry and pain-racked for two more years until he finally succumbed to an inflammation of the lungs. He never permitted George's name to be mentioned. Mother never recovered her spirits and never dared face the ton, beyond the narrow Berkshire society."

"Then George isn't a murderer at all?"

"Wasn't. Legally, no, for his shot did not actually kill my father. Morally? He is dead and better so for what he did to my parents' lives. Leave him rest, Juneclaire. Let my family's skeleton stay in the closet. Stop upsetting my mother."

But Juneclaire was not listening. She was wondering how to get word to Uncle George.

First she had to explain to the dowager.

"It really is George with a peg leg and not someone hammering nails in my coffin? That's a relief. You're sure it's George and not some other spook come back to life? I wouldn't want to see my late husband anytime soon."

"He won't eat cooked carrots."

"That's George. He tried to tell me, but I was too foolish to listen, I suppose. The boy never had a particle of sense anyway, always falling into one scrape or another. You tell him to stop playing off his tricks and get back here. Now go on, girl, I need to be alone to think about this."

Juneclaire locked her door so the servants would not think her more addled than ever, and then she tried calling Uncle George. She whispered his name in all the corners of her room and under her bed. She tried her best to find a secret door in the back of her wardrobe, dislodging everything and pounding on the bare wood. If there was a false wall, like in the Minerva Press books, it must catch from the other side. Finally she took to calling, "Uncle George" up the chimney and down the floor grates, unaware, of course, that the sound echoed throughout the family wing.

Countess Fanny was prostrate, too unnerved to attend her own preball dinner. Her frightened abigail let Juneclaire talk to her for a minute.

"No," the countess cried, "he has to be dead, or he'd have forgiven me by now. I said I would wait, and I did not. Now he's come back to haunt me."

Juneclaire wanted to kill the wretch herself, if he wasn't already dead, of course. She was no more kindly disposed to George's nephew either, especially when St. Cloud directed the footmen not to serve Juneclaire anymore wine with dinner. Her only satisfaction was seeing Elsbeth's pasty face and the black shadows under Sydelle's eyes.

Juneclaire was a success at her first ball. So was Pansy. The shepherdess costume was becoming, with the apron tied at her narrow waist, the short, ruffled petticoats allowing the merest glimpse of well-turned ankle, and the low bodice not as innocent as her flower-decked hair. Pansy, a ham in sheep's clothing, trotted alongside, to the delight of the company.

Since the ball was a masquerade, none of the sixty or so guests was announced, but everyone knew who she was. They had all come to inspect the female who rumor claimed had snabbled St. Cloud. The men were quick to sign the pretty gal's dance card, and the ladies were pleased to find her a well-behaved chit. With the dowager's approval, Miss Beaumont could be no less.

Precedence also went by the wayside. St. Cloud asked her to stand up for the first dance, instead of partnering the highest-ranking lady. He was dressed as Sir Philippe d'Guerdon, the sword-for-hire knight who first won the Priory of St. Jerome of the Clouds for the Crown. The Frenchman was wily enough not to wreck the place during the siege and wise enough to ask for it as his reward. He anglicized his name to Jordan and founded his own dynasty. His ancestors stayed wise and wily, increasing their holdings, filling their coffers, staying on the right side of whatever war or rebellion occurred. They prospered until this night, when the last Jordan stood in the guise of the first, bowing to the lady who would continue the line, God and Juneclaire willing. And if St. Cloud could get his heart and his head to come to the sticking point.

She was so damned beautiful, innocent and appealing at the same time, how could he doubt her? She greeted his neighbors as if she were truly glad to meet the stuffy old matrons, the giggly young girls, the spotted youths, and the snuff-covered squires. He was proud to lead her into the dance, he told himself, proud they all thought she was his.

His bow was as courtly as only a knight wearing a chain mesh tunic and scarlet tights could make it, and the broadsword at his side threatened only once to trip him up in the dance. Juneclaire thought this moment might be worth the rest of her lifetime listening to Aunt Marta's scolds. She smiled, and the sideline watchers shook their heads that another green girl had fallen for the elusive earl. Then he smiled, and they all sighed. St. Cloud was cotched at last.

Aware of their recent awkwardness, St. Cloud tried to reestablish some of the closeness he had felt with Juneclaire at first. "I suppose you have a New Year's wish all picked out, Junco. Does it have to be a secret?"

"New Year's is for resolutions, sir knight, not wishes, didn't you know? Instead of depending on luck and happenstance, resolutions depend on oneself."

"May a humble knight not wish for a favor from a pretty maid?"

She showed her dimples. "A man may wish all he wants, but a man resolved to have a thing works to make his own wishes come true. And a lady's favor is a paltry thing for a whole year's resolution."

"I believe that depends on the lady. But what is your resolve, Miss Beaumont?"

Juneclaire knew better than to interpret his words as a desire to win her heart; he was just a practiced rake. She also knew better than to admit her real resolution, which was to reunite Uncle George with his family. Instead she said, "I think I shall try not to be so impetuous. I've been in too many hobbles as is."

He gave her another of those rare smiles, so she impetuously went on: "And you, sir, should resolve to laugh more. Uncle George says you were a cheerful little imp of a lad."

Juneclaire found herself by the dowager's side before the music had quite finished. She excused herself to check on Pansy in the refreshment room with Aunt Florrie, who had changed her persona, not her costume, to Sunshine.

When she returned to the ballroom, St. Cloud was dancing with Sydelle Pomeroy, Cleopatra in a black wig and a cloth-of-gold gown held up by little more than asp venom. She had a bracelet on her upper arm and half of Egypt's kohl supply on her eyelids. And a crocodile smile on her lips. Niles was glaring from the sidelines, an unhappily togaed Marc Antony, the cost of persuading Sydelle to stay for the ball. His bare shoulders and hairy shins were sorely missing their buckram wadding and sawdust pads, all Juneclaire's fault, naturally.

"Dash it, puss, if you keep setting his back up like that, it's no wonder he turns to that high flier."

Juneclaire turned. Father Time was standing beside her, long beard, flowing robes, scythe in one hand, hourglass in the other. "Uncle George, I've been looking all over for you! Where have you been?"

"Hush, missy. Not now."

Her next partner was approaching, Sir Walter Raleigh with spindle-shanked legs. "But when? I have news."

"The library. Twelve o'clock. They'll all be busy with the unmasking. Sh."

Juneclaire had to let him go off to the refreshment room.

"Deuced fine costume, that," Sir Walter commented. "Even has the ancient's shuffle down perfect."

She danced with a cowled monk, Robin Hood, Henry the Eighth, and a Red Indian in face paint, feathers, and satin knee breeches. She watched the French knight dance with Elsbeth's wood nymph, a Columbine, and Diana the Huntress, complete with arrows that fell out of her quiver during the Roger de Coverly.

She also watched Father Time say a few words to the dowager, but mostly he stood near the windows, watching Lady Fanny where she held court on a divan. St. Cloud strolled over in his direction once, chain mail being devilishly warm to dance in, and Juneclaire held her breath.

St. Cloud thought it was too bad that the rules of a masquerade didn't permit him to quiz the guests, for he'd dearly like to know the identity of the fat joker in the fake beard. St. Cloud had first noticed Father Time because of Juneclaire's intense interest in him, but then the fellow kept eyeing the St. Cloud ladies. St. Cloud included Juneclaire in that small group, for he was determined to announce the engagement at the unmasking if she was willing. Everyone was expecting it, from the sly looks and innuendos he was receiving, and Juneclaire's name would be bandied about if there was no public notice. In the meantime, Father Time was as close as a clam, and St. Cloud had to partner the admiral's youngest daughter. He didn't know what she was supposed to be, but she looked like a lamp shade. No one else had asked her to dance this evening and, as host in his own home, swearing to be a reformed character, he knew his duty.

He knew his duty at twelve o'clock, too, when Juneclaire was not in the ballroom for the unmasking. He couldn't very well make the announcement without her, and he could not even kiss her happy New Year, damn it, when the infuriating chit had shabbed off on him. Again. Plainly his duty was to find her and hold a pillow over that beautiful face. He started looking for her as quietly as he could, considering he clanked with every step.

Juneclaire was in the library, explaining to Uncle George that he wasn't a murderer at all, but he was buried in the family cemetery.

"Must have been my man Hawkins. He was supposed to ride for the doctor. I never could figure what happened to him." Uncle George was sitting at the earl's desk, eating lobster patties and drinking champagne.

"But aren't you happy? You can come back now. Vicar Broome over at Bramley remembers you; he said so when he was sending me here. He can help you reestablish your identity if Lady Fanny won't. You can come home!"

Uncle George took another bite. "Old Boomer Broome still wears the collar, eh? Well, he can help with my soul, but that's not enough, I'm thinking, to keep my body from getting to hell via a hempen ladder. You see, I wasn't quite honest with you, poppet. Not that I didn't think I'd killed Robert. When Hawkins didn't send me word, I was sure I had, and I fled the country. And after that, nothing seemed to matter, so . . ."

Juneclaire's heart sank. "How bad?"

"Bad, puss. Did you ever hear of Captain Cleft, the pirate?"

"No."

"Good."

"Surely there's something we can do. Merry would know who to—"

"No, I won't hand the boy any more shame." He was up and using the scythe as a cane to limp toward the door. "Come on now, you're missing the ball. All those young fellows will be looking for the second-prettiest girl here."

"Who is the first?" she asked, dreading lest he name Sydelle.

"Why, Fanny, of course. I wonder if there are any macaroons?"

They were nearly to the supper room when June-claire begged him to consider consulting a lawyer. "Lady St. Cloud's man Langbridge is very kind. I'm sure he'd help. Please say you'll try. Otherwise I'll—"

She never got to say what she'd do, for just then St. Cloud spotted them. He was furious that Juneclaire had deserted him, and for a pillow-stuffed humbug at that! He was even more furious when Father Time limped into the refreshment room and his flowing robe billowed up to reveal a peg leg. This was the bastard who was haunting St. Cloud's house!

With a mighty bellow St. Cloud drew the broadsword from its sheath at his side. The bloody thing was so heavy, he needed both hands to hold the point up. Guests scattered; women screamed. Father Time saw Nemesis coming and reached out with his scythe. He swept the punch bowl to the floor, then the tub of raspberry ices, shipped out from Gunther's specially. Then he fled back to the library, while the French knight picked his way through the sticky mess past one happy pig in sherbet. When St. Cloud reached the library, followed by half the company, the old man was gone. Disappeared, vanished.

"Good show, St. Cloud," the admiral called out. "Out with the old year, eh? Happy New Year!"

Chapter Twenty-two

"*I*t's not Uncle George, I tell you!" The teacups were rattling again. St. Cloud wondered if he'd ever know another peaceful breakfast, with coffee and kippers—and no conversation. Why couldn't Juneclaire be like other women and sleep till noon? Why did she have to look so delicious in peach muslin, with a Kashmir shawl over her shoulders?

"He likes macaroons and hates carrots, just like the dowager said he would," she insisted.

"Juneclaire, *I* like macaroons and hate carrots. That does not make me Uncle George any more than it makes your impostor."

"But he knows the secret passages and the priests' holes. Not even you know them."

"I told you, my father died before he passed on the

information. He was afraid Niles and I would get lost in the tunnels."

"He knew you'd bedevil the housemaids, more likely," Lord Wilmott interrupted. "You were an undisciplined cub even then. I say this is outrageous. George Jordan, indeed! The fellow is gone and good riddance."

Juneclaire stuck doggedly to her argument. "But he would know the trick to getting into the hidden compartments. His father would have told him, my lord."

"Any number of servants could have known, even this Hawkins person he mentioned. Maybe that's who he is, some old employee come to blackmail the family or something. It won't wash. The dirty linen's been hung in public so long and so often, it's not worth a brass farthing. I told you I would have my man in London look into the matter of Hawkins."

"You won't find him. He's in the graveyard."

"Damn it, Juneclaire, you only have some actor's word for that!"

"But I wasn't seeing ghosts, was I? There really was a man with a peg leg?" He had to agree. "Then why can I not be right now? I'm not crazy, Merry. Why do you have to be right always, just because you are St. Cloud?"

Uncle Harmon's gorge was rising. "Why are you even listening to this rag-mannered fishwife, St. Cloud? George Jordan disgraced this family, miss, and it has taken over twenty years to rebuild our standing. Twenty years before *you* got here to stir things up."

Now St. Cloud pushed his plate away. "You forget yourself, Uncle," he said quietly. "Miss Beaumont is entitled to her opinions, and I respect her for expressing them. She and I may or may not quarrel over the coffee cups for the next twenty years. That is our decision. Where you break your fast is yours . . . for now."

Juneclaire was not sure if he meant they may or may not be married, or they may or may not argue, but she was content. He had stood up to his family for her.

Harmon Wilmott was not content. He knew better than to disparage the drab female who was ruining all his plans, but the thought of another uncle coming back from the beyond, this one with a more valid claim to St. Cloud's largess, stuck in his craw. Drooping jowls quivering in outrage, he declared, "George Jordan is better off dead. The man was a coward and a ne'er-do-well."

Before Juneclaire could say that Uncle George seemed to have done well enough on the high seas, St. Cloud stood up and tossed his napkin on the table. He may as well have thrown the gauntlet. "Uncle George was a soldier, a decorated hero. No one shall say else. If you are finished crumbling your muffin, Miss Beaumont, perhaps you would accompany me this morning."

He took her to the attics again, leading her gently this time, pointing out various ancestors' portraits along the way, telling her some of the history of the place. What he wanted her to see was in the lumber room with the broken bed frames and rickety tables. The earl pulled a gilt chair with only one armrest over toward the window and wiped the seat with his handkerchief for her. Then he pulled a painting out from behind a warped chest of drawers and turned it so Juneclaire could see.

Two young men looked back at her. Boys, really, they were cut from the same cloth as Merry. Both had black hair, worn long and tied in back as was the style, and both had green eyes. The seated one had Merry's serious look, as if he already knew the weight of his duties. The other, younger lad was smiling. He had Merry's chin. Captain Cleft.

"This is not the man I chased last night," St. Cloud said. "I knew Uncle George. I knew him well."

"But that was over twenty years ago, you clunch, and you were just a child. People change, especially when they lead hard lives. You said yourself the body they brought back was mangled. It could have been Hawkins, Merry. It could."

He sat on a stool next to her chair and looked out the window. "I said I will send to London, have my man-at-law look into the matter. But—"

"But you are not happy at the possibility. You'd prefer to think that I am a gullible nodcock and some plump old graybeard has fallen down your chimney and into the wainscoting by accident."

He took her hand. "I am sorry for thinking you were foxed or purposely trying to cause trouble. And

I swear I'll try to keep an open mind." He laughed at himself, bringing her fingers to his lips. "How is that for a resolution? Is it too late? I've already admitted I was wrong about you. But, Junco, there is more to the story than you know. My mother is weak, you know that. And she went through hell for the man, not once but twice. I cannot ask her to face him again."

"It has to be her decision, doesn't it?" She returned the pressure of his fingers, trying to give him strength and comfort.

"Then where is he? If he is George, why doesn't he walk through the front door and shake my hand like an honorable man? Why didn't he come forth and say what happened that night at the quarry? You said you convinced him he wasn't a murderer."

This was not the time to tell Merry his uncle was a pirate. Then again, she thought more cheerfully, if he could accept that, he could accept a penniless nobody in the family, too. "I, ah . . . believe he's working on that now. You St. Cloud men seem to have a surfeit of pride, you know. He has his own sense of honor."

St. Cloud stood and drew her up beside him, still holding her hand. "Speaking of honor, Miss Beaumont," he started.

She pulled her hand back. "No, my lord, I know what you are going to say and I don't want to hear it. I do not want your words of honor and duty and making things right."

He brushed a curl away from her cheek, but his

hand stayed to touch the soft skin there. "No? I thought marriage proposals were supposed to start that way. I am supposed to ask for the honor of your hand, and you are supposed to thank me for the honor of the offer. That's what I've always heard, anyway. I only did it that once before, you know, in the barn. But here, I've turned over a new leaf for the new year. I'll admit I could be wrong again. What words should I say instead?"

Words of love, you cloth-head, she wanted to shout. But she only whispered, "If I have to tell you, I do not want to hear them."

He was staring into her deep brown eyes as if the answers to the universe were hidden there. His fingers stroked her knitted brows, her chin, her lips, sending tremors where she did not know tremors could go. "Ah, my sweet, perhaps we do not need words after all." He bent his head. She raised hers and closed her eyes. His breath was warm on her lips. His hands had moved to her back, pulling her closer till their bodies were touching, the lean strength of his against the soft curves of hers. His breath came faster as their lips came to—

"Pardon, my lord, but there are two young persons come to see you and Miss Beaumont."

"Good grief," Juneclaire said, "what are you two doing here?"

Rupert and Newton Stanton were staring around

his lordship's library as though they'd never seen so many books in one place. For all the attention they spent to their schooling, likely they had not. Root was wearing a spotted Belcher neck cloth in imitation of the Four-Horse Club, and Newt was dressed in the height of absurdity in yellow pantaloons and shirt collars so high and so starched, his ears were in danger.

After Juneclaire's introduction, St. Cloud surveyed them through his quizzing glass like particularly unappealing specimens of insects suddenly come among his books. "Indeed, to what do we owe the unexpected pleasure?" he drawled.

Root squirmed and Newt felt his collar shrink. They knew Satan St. Cloud's reputation. Then again, it was his reputation that sent them here.

"Actually, Mama sent us," Root confessed. He was the eldest. He knew his duty. Hadn't Mama spent two days drumming it into him? "She got your note, saying Clarry was here under your protection."

Newt giggled nervously. "There's protection and there's protection," he continued, trying to sound worldly. Compared to St. Cloud he was as urbane as a newly hatched chick. "So Mama sent us to check."

Juneclaire was embarrassed for her family. "You gudgeons, you are insulting the earl," she hissed.

Root stood firm. "Reputation, you know. His. Yours."

"Well, of all the—"

"Excuse me, Miss Beaumont. I am not quite clear on the purpose of our guests."

Juneclaire knew from that sardonic tone that St. Cloud was very angry. "It's my fault, my lord. I should have written to Aunt Marta myself, to reassure her of my well-being. I'll just take my cousins to the kitchens, shall I, and get them a bite to eat for their return trip and send them—"

"I say, Clarry, we just got here!"

"Mama's not going to be happy, 'less she knows for sure there's nothing—"

"Miss Beaumont," the earl interrupted, in a quiet, smooth voice, "prefers to be called Juneclaire."

The boys nodded. "Yes, sir" and "Yes, my lord." Their tutors would have been shocked to see such instant obedience. Even Juneclaire was impressed.

"Now, Master Newton, Master Rupert, you shall answer me this: Did your esteemed parent really send two unlicked cubs to ask my intentions toward her niece?"

Juneclaire giggled, thinking of his intentions not ten minutes past. He sent her a quelling look. Both boys found the design in the carpet fascinating. Put like that, Mama'd sent them to their doom. And the earl was not finished. "Did she treat her responsibilities so negligently that she did not inquire into Miss Beaumont's health, how she came to be here, or her future plans, but only the state of her virtue? Did she think so ill of Miss Beaumont to think that she might consider *carte blanche?* That does not speak well of her upbringing at your mother's hands. Finally, did you, men-about-town that you are, think that I would bring my *chérie amour* here to my ancestral home to meet my mother and grandmother?"

"That's enough, my lord. Let them be. They're only boys. They meant no insult."

"No? I wonder what they were supposed to do if they found you dishonored. Call me out?"

Newt was quick to pipe up, "Oh, no, my lord, we were only supposed to tell Cla—Juneclaire not to come home again, ever. But if things were all right and tight, we were to invite you back to Stanton Hall."

"Hell will freeze over before I—" Then he noticed Juneclaire's scarlet mortification. "I am sorry, my dear, that you had to be witness to this." To the boys, he said, "You may tell your parents that Miss Beaumont is respectably established."

Root did not think such a bang-up Corinthian would shoot a fellow for doing his duty. He knew his mother would have his hide for not. "Don't see no chaperon," he stated. "Don't see no ring."

"If you want to see your next birthday, you'll—"

"With your permission, my lord, I'll introduce my cousins to Lady Fanny and the others in the morning room. Perhaps Mr. Hilloughby, the *curate,* will be there, Root."

The boys were in love, Root with St. Cloud's pastry chef and Newt with Niles Wilmott's hummingbird-embroidered waistcoat. Add to that heady mix tales of ghosts, secret passages, and lurking strangers, to say nothing of being able to tell their friends they were on intimate terms with Satan St. Cloud himself, and the Stanton boys would have sold their mother for a chance to stay at the Priory. Then Elsbeth walked in.

Miss Wilmott had been feeling sorely used, neglected, put upon, and cast in the shade. Her cousin was not going to marry her, and her father was not going to take her to London. Ordinarily two rustics barely her own age would not hold the young beauty's interest, but the Stantons treated Miss Beaumont with the greatest indifference and called Sydelle Pomeroy "ma'am," the same as Aunt Fanny! Elsbeth's Cupid's bow lips smiled at the brothers, and anyone in the room could hear two hearts fall at her feet.

"Please, Clarry—Juneclaire, ask him if we can stay. We are worried about you, really, no matter what Mama said."

"And it's snowing. You don't want us to have to ride out there in that, back to dreary old Stanton Hall, not while there's such jolly times here. Please ask him, and we will give Mama any story you want about how you got here."

His brother kicked him. "Not blackmail, cuz. Stick by you anyway."

Juneclaire had taken her cousins apart from the others. Aunt Florrie wanted to count their teeth. Now she had to laugh at their earnest entreaties. "Why don't you ask him yourself?"

Newt stammered, "He's not an . . . ah . . . easy man, Juneclaire. One look from him and I feel like checking my buttons. And his reputation ain't one to let a fellow rest easy if St. Cloud imagines some insult. Aren't you afraid of him?"

She smiled. "No, he's just a bear with a sore foot sometimes, especially when it comes to things like honor and family." And me, she thought fondly.

Root looked at her with respect for the first time in her memory. "Brave for a girl, Juneclaire. Proud to be kin."

So she walked the earl over to the window to note the heavy snowfall. "I know they're not much," she admitted, "but they are mine. And perhaps you'll be a good influence on them."

"Heaven help them." St. Cloud looked over to where the others sat, the two halflings vying with each other to bring a giddy Elsbeth the choicest tidbits. He smiled. "On the other hand, perhaps Uncle Harmon will have an apoplexy."

It snowed for two days and nights. There were no visits from neighbors, no mail in or out, and no Uncle George. St. Cloud put the Stanton sprigs to work in the library, looking for a hidden latch to the trick door. The proximity to so much learning might have had an effect if Elsbeth hadn't insisted on helping, for lack of anything better to do. Her father suddenly insisted Elsbeth get some fresh air, so all of the young people went on sleigh rides and indulged in snowball fights, even St. Cloud. Then Harmon thought Elsbeth should practice her needlework more, so the mooncalves sat at her feet, sorting yarns and making up absurd poems to her lips, her ears, her flaxen curls. Uncle Harmon was tearing his hair out, and it looked as if Elsbeth was getting to London after all, anything to get her out of the reach of the nimwit brothers.

At night there were card games with the dowager, charades, children's games of jackstraws and lotteries that turned into hilarious shouting matches, caroling round the piano. St. Cloud was enjoying every minute of his uncle's distress and every moment of the light-hearted games. Even if he did not participate, or when he made up a table for the dowager's whist, he watched Juneclaire and listened for her laughter. He imagined other holidays, real children playing at jackstraws and hide-and-seek in the mazelike Priory—their children. He smiled.

The third night he suggested dancing. He wanted to hold her in his arms. Between Root and Newt, the dowager and his own mother, the earl was finding it deuced hard to be alone with Juneclaire. The dowager, Harmon, and Mr. Hilloughby were at the deal table with Talbot, the butler, who had been drafted to make a fourth. Lady Fanny sat with her needlework behind her mother-in-law to call out the shown cards for Lady St. Cloud. This was the closest the two women had sat to each other since the former earl's funeral.

Aunt Florrie was playing the pianoforte, erratically but energetically. Niles danced with Sydelle, St. Cloud finally got to hold Juneclaire, and the Stantons took turns with Miss Wilmott. The other brother turned Aunt Florrie's pages, although she never seemed to be playing the same song as in front of her. Elsbeth begged for a waltz, and Root, the odd man that set, picked up Pansy, who was dressed for the occasion in diamond ear bobs and pearl choker. Everyone was laughing and gay, even Lady Pomeroy, for once, when a shrill scream rent the air.

"What is the meaning of this?" A sharp-featured woman pushed into the room, dragging a portly gentleman in a bagwig behind her past the inexperienced footman who'd been left holding the door. Rupert said, "Mama," and Juneclaire's face lost its pretty flush. Aunt Florrie kept playing.

Aunt Marta took a better look around, dripping snow on the carpet. There was a blind woman playing cards, one of her sons was dancing with a tousled hoyden, the other with a pig wearing jewels. Her niece was in the arms of the worst rake in England—with no ring on her finger! "I demand to know," she screeched, "just what is going on!"

St. Cloud bowed. He pulled Juneclaire closer to him with one hand and used the other to encompass the room. "Obviously an orgy, ma'am," he drawled. "You know, swine, women, and song."

Chapter Twenty-three

"*F*or your information, Lady Stanton, I have never seduced a female in my care, be she houseguest or housemaid." The earl chose not to recall that was before what almost happened in the attics. He had also never struck a female, but that was before meeting Aunt Marta. This was the outside of enough, being taken to task by an evil-minded old skinflint who never prized her niece in the first place and likely only wanted to wrest a healthy marriage settlement out of him. First she'd sent her husband, Avery, for a "man-to-man" talk. Avery got as far as "Nice gal, my niece. Want the best for her," before St. Cloud's frosty stare had him switching to a discussion of crop rotation. Lady Stanton was not so easily intimidated.

"We'll stay till Twelfth Night since the countess invited us. Then I am taking Claire home."

"Miss Juneclaire stays as long as she wishes, with the dowager's blessings."

"Humph. We'll see about that. What future does the gal have here, I'd like to know?"

"What future did she have at Stanton Hall? Mother to someone else's brats, or your unpaid servant? She is a valued guest here, better dressed, in more congenial company, and with far fewer demands on her time, Lady Stanton. Is her happiness worth nothing?"

"Not as much as the banns being called, and I don't care who you are! Lord Stanton is still her legal guardian, and *we'll* see where Claire goes and with whom."

St. Cloud was not worried about the harpy's threats as much as the idea that she might stay past Twelfth Night, three very long days away. No, Avery Stanton was not going to challenge St. Cloud. Not even that mouse of a man was so foolish. What concerned the earl more was Juneclaire's feelings.

After luncheon he asked her to visit Lady St. Cloud with him, knowing full well his grandmother was napping. Nutley made the perfect chaperon, sewing in the dowager's sitting room; she was busy and she was deaf.

Juneclaire sat on a brocade divan near the fireplace with the kitten on her lap playing with—Drat, so there's where his tassel had disappeared to. She looked the picture of innocence in a high-waisted sprigged muslin, a soft glow on her cheeks from the fire's warmth. He knew she was also a woman of great spirit and caring. He thought she was even coming to care for him. He did not want to hurt her, ever.

"Miss Beaumont, Junco, I, ah . . ." She looked up at him with those doe eyes, her dark brows raised in expectation. "Blasted expectations!" he muttered, pacing the width of the room.

"Oh, dear. I suppose Aunt Marta's been filling your head with her flummery, my lord. Believe me, I do not expect—"

"Well, you should, and it's not flummery! I should have offered for you in form days ago. I should have asked your uncle's permission the minute they stepped through the door."

"But you did offer. You were everything honorable, and so I told Aunt Marta. There was no need—"

"There was every need, and more every day you spend under my roof even if you are too green to see it. Now it's too late."

"Too late?" Her heart must have stopped because suddenly she could not breathe. Now that he'd seen her family, she realized how impossible an alliance was. Now that she was convinced she had to marry him for whatever reasons he chose to give if she was to be a whole person ever again, he had changed his mind. He was withdrawing his offer.

"Yes, and it's all that dastard George's fault! How can I offer you my name when it may not be an honorable one? How can I discuss marriage settlements when I don't know if I'll have a roof over my head?"

"I don't understand, but none of that matters." She was perilously close to tears. He hated vaporish women.

"Of course it doesn't matter to you, Junco. You'd live in a cow byre with your goats and pigs and sheep—only you'd starve to death because you'd never eat any of them! It matters to me that I can provide for you, that you can take your place in society with your head high, not stay hidden away like my mother."

She swallowed past the lump in her throat. "Uncle George?"

"Uncle George. I didn't tell you the whole, that day in the cemetery. You'll find out soon enough, if the cad has come back. I'm just surprised your aunt hasn't filled your ears with the tale. It's common knowledge." He kept pacing, not looking at her. "George came home from the wars injured, remember? My parents stayed away the whole time, until the holidays. I don't recall if they spoke then. I was in the nursery most of the time, of course, and there were other houseguests. I was brought down for luncheon that day. It was Christmas, you know, and my birthday. You have to realize that I was small for my age, and Uncle George had never been around children before. He said 'Merry Christmas, Merry. Happy fourth birthday.' And everyone laughed, because it was my fifth birthday. And then he must have counted back—I remember him mumbling while I waited for my cake. Suddenly he shouted, 'If he's five, he's mine!' and he lunged at my father, knocking him down. In front of forty *belle monde* busybodies. I have carried a certain unsavory stigma throughout my life, as you can imagine."

"But your—the earl acknowledged you."

"Who knows what he would have done if there had been another son? But he was paralyzed that day, and George was dead. I was the last Jordan. Until now. You, at least, are convinced that I am not. If George is alive, *he* is the earl."

"No," Juneclaire insisted. "You were baptized as Robert's son and reared as Robert's son. And Uncle George would never make that kind of trouble. I know he wouldn't."

"How do you know what he will and will not do? He left my father there to die, Juneclaire."

"No! Hawkins was to have gone for help. Uncle George has as much honor as you do! That's why he hasn't come back, Merry, because his past isn't quite . . . suitable."

Merry stopped pacing. "Pray tell, Miss Beaumont," he drawled in that slow, deadly tone he used to frighten lesser mortals, "precisely how . . . unsuitable is Uncle George's past? Where has he been all these years?"

"At sea."

"It could be worse. Other Jordans have gone into the navy, although I suppose he signed on as a common seaman."

"Not the navy," Juneclaire croaked.

"Then a merchant marine. Better still. Perhaps he joined the East India company and made his fortune."

"I believe he made his fortune," she said, barely above a whisper. "Have you ever heard of . . . Captain Cleft?"

"Oh, God, we're all ruined. You'll go home with your aunt. Uncle Harmon will have to find Elsbeth a husband before . . . and Mother. Hell and damnation, Mother."

Now it was even more important that they find Uncle George.

Luckily the company made a short evening of it so they could look. The dowager refused to join "those toadeaters" downstairs, and Lady Fanny had taken to her bed under Aunt Marta's aspersions that the countess was not a proper chaperon for a young girl. Uncle Harmon was closeted with vinegar water and digestive biscuits, and Aunt Florrie was busy writing a letter to her dear friend Richard. The Lion-Hearted.

Sydelle had excused herself after dinner. She was leaving in the morning, despite Niles Wilmott's fervent, nay, desperate, pleas. Lady Pomeroy saw no reason to stay. With that battle-ax of an aunt in the house, St. Cloud could never wriggle out of an engagement, and Lady Pomeroy was not cooling her heels until Twelfth Night, just to see a parcel of peasant urchins dress up as Magi and go around begging gifts. She'd had enough of those bucolic entertainments, thank you, and was anxious to get back to London, even if it was thin of company. So *la belle* Pomeroy used her packing as an excuse to avoid the gathering of puerile Stantons and lost-cause St. Clouds.

Root and Newt had escaped their mother's eye to the billiard room, forsaking even Elsbeth, who quickly claimed a headache. Niles took himself off to drown his sorrows with his cousin's excellent brandy, for lack of a better idea, and Mr. Hilloughby declared he had to work on his sermon.

All of which left Juneclaire and St. Cloud all alone in the gold parlor, except for Aunt Marta and Uncle Avery. Aunt Marta did not believe in gambling, so cards were out. Juneclaire did not play well enough to entertain with music. They had no mutual friends and no common interests, and the earl and Aunt Marta each represented what the other most despised. It was not a comfortable gathering, especially in contrast to the past few nights. St. Cloud as host could not retire before his guests, and Aunt Marta would have dyed her hair red and gone on the stage before leaving her niece alone with the earl. Therefore Juneclaire yawned, and yawned again until Lady Stanton decided they would all do better with an early night. She walked Juneclaire right to her door and would have locked her in if she weren't sure that the libertine had copies of all the keys to the house anyway.

Juneclaire would just have to do her hunting without

Merry. Under the heavy eyes of Pansy—Aunt Florrie had tried darkening the pig's lashes with bootblack to match Sydelle's—and with the assistance of a curious kitten, Juneclaire removed every single item from her wardrobe. When the closet was absolutely bare, she pulled and twisted, pushed and poked at every shelf, hinge, and hook. There had to be a way to get into the secret passage from her room. Uncle George had done it, at least twice. There were seams in the wood panels on the sides and back, but she could not get any of them to move. Nothing.

She rested her hands on the closet rod that held the hangers while she thought—and the bar turned under her hands. Then she rolled it the other way, away from her, and one of the panels slid back. She found it! Juneclaire poked her head through, hoping to see Uncle George on the other side, but she saw nothing, only darkness past the little circle of her own light. She thought she'd better go get Merry.

As Juneclaire backed out of the opening, though, the cat came to investigate and kept on going. "Oh, no, Shamrock. Here, kitty. Come back, kitty, kitty." Kitty did not come back. Shamrock would be lost forever, and the dowager would be heartbroken. There was nothing for it; Juneclaire had to go after the foolish furball.

She was *not* being impetuous. She made sure she had a fresh candle in her holder and another in her pocket, along with a flint. She put a hatbox in the opening to make sure it did not shut and checked the mechanism on the other side, a kick-wheel device, so she could get back in, in case.

Someone had swept the floor in the secret passage, but not well, and she could see footprints and, yes, the mark of Uncle George's peg leg going in both directions. Shamrock's went in only one. Juneclaire followed, trying to keep count of the doors, the turns, the side passages. She couldn't. She turned to check and no longer saw the light from her own room. For one awful minute she thought she'd be lost forever; maybe curiosity was going to kill more than the cat this night. Maybe Merry would be heartbroken. No, he would be relieved. Then reason reasserted itself: Merry would come after her in the morning and give her one of those dire looks and sarcastic comments. She'd better find Uncle George to lead her back.

She found the cat instead, sitting next to one of the wheel devices, licking its feet. Juneclaire picked the kitten up, hugging it more for her comfort than its. Now she had two choices: she could wander around these corridors looking for her own room for the next eight hours or so, or she could turn this wheel and pray. "Please let the room be unoccupied."

Her prayer was answered. Unfortunately, the answer was no. She found herself and the kitten in her hands in a closet so full of silks and satins and shoes and hats that there was hardly room for her to stand. A light shone through the crack in the door facing into the room, and she could hear voices. She took a deep breath. Hungary water . . . Niles. She decided to assay the dark passage again, with rats and bats and spiders, rather than come face-to-face with that slug in his bedroom.

As she was backing out of the narrow opening in the back of the closet, however, Pansy was coming in. The lonely pig's sharp nose had no trouble finding her mistress in the maze and no trouble detecting the wine and biscuits Niles had in his room. She pushed past Juneclaire, who lost her footing. Juneclaire reached up to save herself and the cat and the fop's expensive wardrobe from a fall, and grabbed onto the hanging bar, which turned, nearly shutting the rear panel on Pansy's curled tail. Pansy went flying forward, pushing open the doors.

Juneclaire followed. What else could she do? If a woman, a pig, and a cat flying out of an armoire astounded Niles and his companion, the sight that met Juneclaire's eyes was only slightly less shocking.

Somewhere in the middle of his second bottle downstairs, Niles had finally had a better idea. Instead of letting the widow Pomeroy and her voluptuous charms—not the least of which was her ample checkbook—hie off to London in the morning, Niles had one last card up his sleeve. And a cinder in his eye.

Juneclaire's garbled account of the cat, the secret passage, and "I'll just be going now" was lost as the elegant widow, *en déshabillé*, explained how poor Niles needed her assistance. What Niles needed was more time. The wine stood ready on the low table, the bed stood ready, and his flea-brained sister had dashed well better stand ready to burst in on them at the right moment. This wasn't it, so Niles shoved the damned interfering wench out the door.

Juneclaire leaned against the wall, breathing hard, her eyes closed.

"My, my, what do we have here?"

Her breathing stopped altogether, and her eyes snapped open. Merry, with his abominable quizzing glass, was surveying her disarranged hair, her heaving chest, her flaming cheeks. "Do you know what a good influence you have been, Miss Beaumont? I am still maintaining my New Year's resolution to keep an open mind. I find my affianced bride coming out of my loose-screw cousin's bedroom, looking, ah, shall we say, hot and bothered, and I haven't even skinned him alive yet. Aren't you pleased?"

Juneclaire was happy there was a wall holding her up; for sure her trembling knees were not. "We . . . we're not engaged," she quavered.

"True. Then I'll skin him after I murder him."

"No, he didn't . . . I wasn't . . . Don't go in there!"

"Why, did you already do him in with your darning needle? And here I thought you were going to be less impetuous."

"Stop it, you gudgeon. He's not—"

"Juneclaire Beaumont, what are you doing out of your room?" Aunt Marta yelled loudly enough that Uncle Avery peered out of his room across the hall. "And you, St. Cloud, how dare you carry on in this abandoned fashion right under my very nose? I'll—"

They were never to find out what Aunt Marta was going to do because a shriek came from inside Niles's room. The earl pushed past Juneclaire and flung the door open.

When Niles tossed Juneclaire out of his room, he forgot about the pig. Pansy didn't mind, as long as the biscuits were in reach. When they were gone, she went snuffling around, looking for Juneclaire or another friend. Her wanderings took her closer to the fire, where Sydelle was leaning over Niles, dabbing at his eye with a scrap of handkerchief. Pansy whiffled closer, right up Lady Pomeroy's skirt. Hence the shriek. Sydelle fell forward, and Niles, simply doing what came naturally to an immoral, licentious lecher, pulled her down on top of him.

"Congratulations, cousin," St. Cloud said from the doorway. "May I be the first to offer my felicitations."

And Elsbeth, tripping down the hall, said, "For heaven's sake, Niles, if you changed your plan, you should have told me."

Aunt Marta declared, "Well, I never," to which Uncle Avery sadly replied, "Twice, my dear, twice."

Chapter Twenty-four

*T*he dowager was so pleased with the match that she decided to go downstairs to see Niles and Sydelle off to London. Lady Pomeroy wanted to see the last of St. Cloud Priory, and Niles wanted to see the notice in the papers before Sydelle changed her mind. Juneclaire was walking the dowager down the long hall.

"Tell Talbot to serve champagne," Lady St. Cloud ordered. "That ought to ruffle your aunt's fur, the old hellcat. Maybe she'll take those scamps of hers and leave early."

Aunt Marta disapproved of the couple, among other things. She would not come down. Juneclaire was afraid St. Cloud really was going to send her off with the Stantons, though, so she tried to divert the old woman. "Do you actually think Niles and Sydelle will suit?"

"Like hand in glove. He'll have his glove in her pocket, and she'll have her hand on his—Well, she'll keep him under her thumb. They're both decorative, expensive fribbles, with less morality than alley cats. He'll have his gaming and clubs, she'll have her respectability and a title when Harmon sticks his spoon in the wall, and they'll both go their own ways. Perfect marriage, my dear, perfect."

"I think it sounds perfectly horrible, cold and mercenary."

"Wouldn't do for just everybody, mind, but those two? Besides, it'll get them out of my grandson's house. Now, if I can just remind Harmon that the older Stanton twit will inherit a tidy pig farm one day, and won't he and Elsbeth be happy in Farley's Grange, I might get them out of here also. What are you giggling about, girl? You don't think Harmon's already figuring that Sydelle has that London town house and the right connections to fire Elsbeth off? Trust me, the man's liver mightn't be up to snuff, but his wits ain't gone begging."

She was right. Lord Wilmott had decided that Sydelle needed his chaperonage on the journey to London and Elsbeth's help with the wedding plans. Root's and Newt's hearts were breaking as they stood on the steps waving farewell to their first love, until the earl invited them to help exercise his bloodstock. Lady Fanny waved her handkerchief to the departing coaches, and Aunt Florrie waved a dead halibut.

Juneclaire helped the dowager back inside and made her comfortable in the morning room with the rest of the champagne. "Fine day's work, my girl," the dowager said, lifting her glass to Juneclaire. "Now if we can just see the dust of your relatives, the place will be near livable again."

Juneclaire rearranged some figurines on the mantel. "I . . . I'm afraid I'll be leaving with them, my lady."

"Gammon, you're engaged to my grandson. You belong here."

"No, my lady. I am not really engaged. He just offered because he had to."

"Nonsense, girl. Satan St. Cloud hasn't done anything he hasn't wanted to since he was in short pants. You're good for him, miss. I could hear him laugh when you were dancing and such."

"But Uncle George . . ."

"Faugh, you haven't got your eyes on a man old enough to be your father, have you, girl? He's Fanny's. Always was and always will be, though heaven knows what he or his brother ever saw in the widgeon. Robert wanted her, too, you know. Always jealous, even if he had the title and estate. For the life of me I don't know how I raised two such bobbing-blocks. If you tell me my lobcock of a grandson is making mice feet of his future now, too, I'll take my cane to the both of you, I swear I will. But don't worry, girl. George'll bring him round."

"Then Uncle George is here, and he can tell Merry about—?"

"He said he'd make it right. Soon. Word of a Jordan."

Juneclaire couldn't wait, not if Aunt Marta was going to carry her away after tomorrow night's celebration marking the end of the holy season. It may as well be the end of Juneclaire's life, she thought dismally. Aunt Marta was already guarding her like a rabid sheepdog, not allowing her two minutes alone with Merry, following her to her bedroom and coming back an hour later to make sure Juneclaire was in bed, alone, with her door locked and bolted.

Locks and bolts on the bedroom door meant nothing to Juneclaire, of course, but no one had thought to ask how she came to be in or out of Niles Wilmott's bedroom last night. She had no chance to explain to Merry about the trick of the secret passage until now. It was his house; he should know.

Juneclaire wrapped a warm shawl over her shoulders and turned the bar. It was much harder, with the hangers all back in place, but the back panel finally slid aside. She counted doors until she was behind the master suite, she hoped. She turned the wheel and the door opened, revealing . . . nothing. She was in an empty closet. She mentally recounted doors and rooms, until she realized she must be in the mistress's chamber. The unused bedroom reserved for the countess, Merry's wife. Good. At least now she—and Pansy, of course—

wouldn't have to burst out of my lord's closet like blackbirds from a pie. She nudged the wardrobe door open, waiting for protests from unused hinges, but rust must be another one of those things unacceptable in an earl's residence. Edging her way out of the closet, she tiptoed toward the right, where light showed under a connecting door. Juneclaire listened for a minute, in case Merry's valet should be with him. Should she knock? Maybe this wasn't a good idea after all.

As usual, Pansy took matters into her own . . . knuckles. She knew a friend was on the other side of the door, and she knew her friend had something to eat. She grunted, loudly.

"What the bloody—"

Pansy trotted through the now open doorway, but Juneclaire stood where she was. She never thought he'd be naked! Or half naked, for he did have britches on, but his chest was bare except for dark curls that spread to where his hard muscles tapered into a lean vee that disappeared to where he *did* have britches on. She didn't trust that gleam in his green eyes, and why the rogue picked now to smile she never knew, but when she lowered her own, they saw—Oh, dear, this wasn't a good idea at all.

"It's not what you think, Merry," she hurried to say. "I am not here to compromise you like Niles. Not that *I* meant to compromise Niles, of course, for you know I did not."

His smile broadened. "If you are not here to cry foul on me, my dear, I am completely and devotedly at your service."

"I am not here for *that* either, you gamecock." If her cheeks were any warmer, they'd surely burst into flame.

He pressed his hand to his heart, reminding her that he had no shirt on, as if she needed a reminder, and said, "You wound me, Junco. I thought my last Christmas wish was coming true."

"Why . . . why you are foxed, my lord!"

"Either that or I must be fast asleep and dreaming, for the oh so proper niece of the redoubtable Lady Stanton could not be standing in my bedroom in her night rail. No, I must be jug-bitten because in my dreams you aren't wearing any heavy flannel wrapper. In fact, you aren't wearing—"

"Merry! I came to tell you about the secret passageway. I found the trick to opening the doors in the wardrobes."

"Did you? I always knew you were a clever girl." He had her hand and was leading her toward an enormous canopied bed in the center of the room.

"Merry, you don't understand. We have to go find Uncle George." She tugged to get her hand back.

"Oh yes, Uncle George." The name seemed to sober him, for he released her, but he sank down on the bench at the foot of the bed. He did not seem eager to go search for his missing relative. "Good old Uncle George, the pride of the Jordans."

Juneclaire sat beside him. "Merry, maybe the situation isn't so bad. Lady St. Cloud thinks he can fix things. He promised her."

"And Aunt Florrie thinks King George is going through a stage, like teething." He brushed her long braid back off her shoulder and put his arm there. "I'm sorry, Junco, truly I am. I wish things were different. I wish I could have made your wishes come true. You almost made mine, you know. You helped get the Wilmotts off my hands, and you showed me how happy this old pile could be." He pulled her closer.

"And I felt welcome here, as if I truly did belong, so my wish almost came true, too."

They were quiet for a moment, thinking of what might have been. Then they both started to say, "I wish . . ." at the same time. "You first," Juneclaire told him, nestling at his side.

"I wish there was a way, that's all, without dragging you through a scandalbroth. You?"

"I wish you weren't quite so honorable, my lord, because none of it matters to me." She turned her face up for his kiss, and not even the earl was noble enough to turn down what she was so sweetly offering. He did groan once, but that may not have been his conscience complaining.

Some while later, Juneclaire was half out of her

nightgown and more than half out of her mind with wonder at the strange new feelings throbbing through her. Somehow she and Merry were no longer on the bench but were in the middle of his wide, soft mattress. If Merry was whispering her name and nonsense in her ear—and he was, for she could feel the tickle of his breath—then someone else was in the room with them.

"Well, Pansy girl, looks like history repeats itself, all right. If this isn't the way the whole argle-bargle started, my name ain't Giorgio Giordanelli."

Juneclaire looked up. There was a Romany Gypsy at the foot of the bed, complete with flowing shirt, scarlet sash, and colorful scarf tied at his neck. He also had a thick gray beard, a fat belly, and a peg leg. She giggled. "It isn't."

He tossed her a blanket. "But it has been, puss, it has been."

The earl had been struggling to regain his composure if not his buttons. He sat up and made sure Juneclaire was decently covered before turning to the apparition. "Uncle George, I presume?"

"In the flesh. Or should I say in the nick of time?" He met the earl's hard, green-eyed stare with one of his own. "Are you going to make an honest woman out of her, or am I going to have to run you through?"

"That depends, *Uncle.* Do I have any honor? Are you going to leave me with a name I'd be proud to offer a woman?"

Uncle George sat on the bench and lifted the pig up next to him. "Are you proud of Satan St. Cloud?" he asked, and Juneclaire was astonished to see Merry flush. She was also amazed to see where the color started. Catching her glance, Uncle George snorted and threw the earl his paisley robe from the bottom of the bed. Merry's muffled curses did nothing to ease Juneclaire's embarrassment.

"Don't tease, Uncle George," she begged. "Just tell him what happened."

The earl crossed his arms over his chest and sat back against his pillow, like a pasha holding court. "Hold, Junco. I am not even convinced this . . . Gypsy is my uncle. He could be a horse thief or a fortune-teller."

George shook his head. "You know, Merry, I think I liked you a lot better when you were a curly-haired tyke."

"And I think I liked you a lot better when you were dead. Do you have papers? Proof?"

"I have friends working on the paper stuff. But proof?" He scratched the pig's ears while he thought. "You were just a wee lad. I'm not sure how much you remember. Then again, you weren't as young as I thought. Let's see. I found my lead knights for you in the nursery and we repainted them, but there was no red paint, so we stole one of your grandmother's rouge pots. Your pony's name was Thimble, but any of the old grooms would know that. They wouldn't know about the day you tried taking him over a hurdle without a saddle, a groom, or permission, because I promised I wouldn't tell, after I found you, picked you up, and brushed you off. Fanny'd have kept you off a horse till you were twenty if she knew you'd been thrown."

"And you brushed off the back of my pants a trifle more vigorously than necessary, if my memory holds."

"You didn't try that stunt again, did you?"

"No, Uncle George, I didn't. Do you still have the crescent scar from the wound that sent you home that time?"

"Still testing? You know it was shaped like a seven. Lucky seven, we called it. Want to see?" He reached for his sash.

Juneclaire hid her face against St. Cloud's robe. He laughed and she could hear the rumble in his chest. Then St. Cloud sighed.

"God, how I missed you when you died. No one would say why, just that you were too evil to talk about. What the hell happened?"

George got up and poured himself a glass from the decanter on an end table. "Two hotheaded fools, that's what happened. You know about the party?" They both nodded. "I was beside myself and dragged Robbie outside until he agreed to meet me at the old quarry. We went, with no surgeon, no seconds, no witnesses, only my man Hawkins to hold the horses. I cooled down along the way. He always loved Fanny, too, you know, and I hadn't been there when she needed me. He was.

So I was going to delope, I swear it. But he shot first, got me in the leg. As I fell, my gun discharged and the shot hit Robbie. It looked bad. He begged me to take what money he had and run away so I wasn't charged with murder, because all of the guests heard me threaten to kill him, and only Hawkins, my own batman, could say nay. I was scared, I was bleeding, I didn't know what to do. So we decided that Hawkins would ride for help and I'd head for Portsmouth and wait for Hawkins to come for me with news." He poured another drink and downed it in a swallow. "He never came. I was in no frame to do anything, delirious, sick, my leg turning uglier and uglier until some butcher amputated the thing and saved my life, I suppose. I cursed him enough at the time. I knew Robbie was dead or he'd have sent for me, even if something had happened to Hawkins. I couldn't face Fanny or my mother, not with one leg and a murder charge against me, so I signed on as junior purser with a cargo ship bound for Bermuda. After that I never wanted to ask about the St. Clouds because I never wanted to hurt more. We went aground, but that's another story. Just know I never meant to kill your father, Merry."

"I believe you, but why did you come home now, after all these years?"

"Not to steal your inheritance, boy, or cause trouble. Robbie called you his son, and you're the earl. I never wanted the title or the Priory either. I'm getting on, Merry, and I just wanted to see Fanny one more time.

But she ain't happy, and it fair breaks my heart all over again. I mean to have her this time, if she'll forgive me and if I can straighten up a few loose ends."

"Like a price on your head?"

"I have some friends working on that." He poured another glass but let Pansy slurp this one.

St. Cloud raised his brows. "What are you going to do, if you clear the minor detail of being a criminal, set Mother up in London for the gabblegrinders to picnic on, or take her on the high seas?"

"I'll take her to Town if she wants to go; there's nothing to be ashamed of. And I'm retired, boy, so you don't have to fear seeing her face on a reward poster. I thought she'd be happiest on my island in the Caribbean. You know, flowers and warm weather, beaches."

"You have your own island?" Juneclaire asked.

"I was a *very* good pirate, puss. As I see it, if I get those confounded papers, then I can try convincing Fanny. I daresay I've changed in the twenty years." He ignored Merry's rude noise and Juneclaire's giggle. "I should know by tomorrow. That ought to answer your questions about the family honor, Merry." He nodded toward Juneclaire. "You mind answering mine?"

Juneclaire blushed again, but Merry threw his uncle's words back at him: "I should know by tomorrow."

George laughed hard enough to shake the bed. "None of my business, right? In that case I think I'd better escort Miss Beaumont back to her room, Merry, since *you* ain't so clear about your intentions." He ignored the earl's furious scowl and turned to Juneclaire. "I'd wager you were the clever one to find the trick panels. This mutton-head must have looked for years. But you were lucky. There's another mechanism in the passageways—a trapdoor that drops trespassers right down to the cellars, unless you know the key." He winked at her. "I'll tell the bacon-brain *that* secret on your wedding night."

Chapter Twenty-five

$\mathcal{J}$uneclaire went to bed without worrying she'd have nightmares about falling through trapdoors. She had no more fear of being dragged back to Stanton Hall in disgrace; she'd stay here in disgrace if she had to. But she was not really worried. Juneclaire was not going to let Merry's pride, or hers, come between them, and no pitfalls either, no matter what Uncle George said.

She woke up smiling and eager. Today was Three Kings Day, Epiphany, Twelfth Night, when Christmas wishes came true. She crossed her fingers, rolled over in bed three times, and said, "Rabbit, rabbit, rabbit," before her feet touched the ground, although that was supposed to be for May Day. She hugged Shamrock for luck and Pansy for good measure.

St. Cloud was showing Uncle Avery the home farm,

and the boys were in the stables, most likely losing their allowances to Foley and the other grooms in dice games. The dowager and Lady Fanny were still abed, and Aunt Florrie was helping in the kitchen. Juneclaire took Pansy to visit the Penningtons and Ned rather than sit with Aunt Marta in the morning room listening to lectures. She still had too much bridled excitement after her visit, so she took Flame out for a walk to burn up some energy and minutes.

For dessert after lunch Talbot carried in the traditional Twelfth Night cake, which was supposed to have a pea and a bean hidden in the middle, denoting the king and queen for the day's festivities. Aunt Marta declared it a pagan ritual from pre-Christian days and refused to have anything to do with such rigmarole. Aunt Florrie looked near to crying, so St. Cloud ordered the footman to cut the cake quickly and pass the servings around. Florrie had been toiling all morning, helping make the batter, she told them in a reedy voice. She worked very hard, she said, making sure no one would be left out when the cake was cut. Why, she'd put in a cherry pit saved from last summer and a bit of a colored egg from Easter. A button, a pencil stub, a pussy willow catkin, one of her dear nephew's baby teeth, one of those pretty red mushrooms . . . Eight forks hit eight plates at once.

Late that afternoon they traveled in two carriages to the village of Ayn-Jerome for the local celebration.

Aunt Marta went, she said, sniffing in Mr. Hillough-by's direction, only to see a proper church. In truth she did not like being alone in the hulking Priory with no one but servants.

There was a candlelight parade down the main street, headed by three boys dressed in loose robes and paper crowns, followed by the other local children, some dressed as shepherds. They led the adults into St. Jerome's Church for the service and a reenactment of the arrival of the three kings bearing gifts for the Holy Child. Afterward, there were trinkets and pennies, sweets and fruits given to all the children, and mummers, acrobats, and jugglers performing in the torch-lit street. Food stalls were set up, ale was passed round with servings of roast venison or beef, St. Cloud's contribution. The villagers toasted him, his house, and one another.

Root and Newt got a trifle above par, Lady Stanton sat rigid as a rail in her carriage, Juneclaire searched every face for Uncle George, and Aunt Florrie brought home some holy water, since Pansy had never been baptized.

The evening lasted forever, it seemed to Juneclaire, sitting on tenterhooks next to the dowager in the gold parlor. Lady St. Cloud obviously knew something was in the offing, too, for she patted Juneclaire's hand and urged her to keep reading, when Juneclaire's eyes kept straying to the door. The earl was as stone-faced and serious as ever, except for the dancing light in his eyes when he glanced Miss Beaumont's way.

Finally Talbot walked into the room with his stately tread, his head held high. "My lord, my ladies," he pronounced, "there are callers." He paused and gulped audibly. "Lords Caspar, Melchior, and Balthasar." Then he turned and fled.

Aunt Marta's jaw hung open and Aunt Florrie clapped. The three wise men had indeed come, not in rough costumes, but in velvet and ermine and satin, with gold crowns and jewel-laden pendants, each bearing a silver casket on a pillow.

The youngest, Caspar, coughed and stepped forward. "We come from Lon—ah, the East, where, ah, great tidings are heard."

The oldest, Melchior, adjusted his spectacles and pulled down his fake beard so he could speak his piece. "We come bearing gifts."

Balthasar, his clean-shaven face blackened with cork, opened the chest he held to reveal a king's ransom in jewels and gold. Juneclaire squeezed the dowager's hand, quietly describing the scene. Then Balthasar hopped forward on his peg leg and laid the casket in the younger countess's lap. "For you, Fanny, all for you. And don't you dare swoon, because it took me long enough to coach my players and you have to pay attention."

Lady Fanny's lip trembled and she was shredding her handkerchief, but she did not go off in a faint. St. Cloud came to stand behind her, his hand on her shoulder.

Uncle George peered at her, then nodded. "Always knew you were stronger than you let on. Anyway, didn't know what you'd do with frankincense or myrrh. Buy you all you want, if you say so, of course. Thought you'd be happier with this." He directed Caspar forward.

Mr. Langbridge, the solicitor, bowed at Fanny's feet and lifted the lid of his chest. "A royal pardon, my lady."

"And a pretty penny it cost me too, Fanny. Half my island, the sugar plantations, and two of my ships. Don't worry, though, puss. There's plenty left. Oh, and Prinny might throw in a knighthood if I pay a few more of his debts." He beckoned to Melchior.

Melchior stepped forward with twinkling eyes and opened his offering. Then he started to sneeze so hard from the cat in the room that Uncle George had to take over Vicar Broome's lines.

"It's a special license, Fanny, with a dispensation from the archbishop for me to wed my brother's widow. Will you do it? Will you marry me at last?" He wasn't fool enough to get down on one knee, not when the other was a piece of ivory, but he sat next to her, reaching for her hand.

Tears were falling from Lady Fanny's eyes—and a few others in the room—but she raised her handkerchief to wipe the blackening from George's face, leaving him an older, heavier, gray-haired, and sun-weathered version of the boy in the portrait, but with the same straight nose and cleft chin, and the same love for her shining in laughing eyes. "Can you forgive me for not waiting, George? I tried, but I did not know where you were, and the baby . . ."

"Can you forgive me for doubting you? For staying away so long?" He suddenly recalled the avid audience, family, guests, servants crowded in the entry, and pulled Fanny to her feet. When they were near the door, he turned back and took another paper from one of the silver chests. George tossed it to the earl, saying, "I brought you a gift, too, my lord. It's another special license. Merry Christmas, Merry."

St. Cloud took two glasses, one of the champagne bottles opened in celebration, and Juneclaire's hand. "Come, my love." He frowned down Lady Stanton's incipient protests and smiled to Aunt Florrie, decking Pansy with the pirate's treasure like a porcine Christmas tree.

When they reached the library, he quickly looked around. "We never did find the secret panel for this door. I can only hope Mother keeps the old scoundrel busy for a while." He poured the wine and held a filled glass to Juneclaire. He raised his and toasted: "To happiness and laughter, and joy ever after, and you by my side. I cannot be as dramatic as Uncle George, but will you be my wife, Juneclaire? Will you make me the happiest of men?"

"To satisfy your sense of honor?" Juneclaire knew the answer, but she wanted to hear him say it.

"Honor be damned."

That was not good enough. "Because Uncle George gave you no choice?"

"Because my heart gave me no choice, Juneclaire."

He put the glass down and reached into his coat for a small box. "A gift for you."

Juneclaire waited while he opened the box. A ring rested on a satin bed, a square diamond crowned with an emerald, a ruby, and a sapphire. "It's the St. Cloud engagement ring. Will you accept it, my love?" He was putting it on her finger before she could answer. That was good enough.

"But I have no gift for you," Juneclaire protested.

"You have already given me so much, my family, my home. That's more than any man deserves. Yet I ask for the greatest gift of all. Will you give me your love, too, Juneclaire?"

"You don't have to ask, Merry. It's already yours and always has been."

He lifted his glass again but brought it to her lips. "To us." After she sipped, he turned the glass so his lips touched where hers had been. "Now all my wishes have come true." Then he shook his head, put the glass down, and went to lock the library door. He came back and took her in his arms. "On second thought, I still have one wish. . . ."

From
BARBARA METZGER

The Bargain Bride

It was a match not made in heaven, but in pound notes—an arranged engagement between a girl of thirteen and a lord's younger son. Since then, thirteen years have passed, and as her betrothed has been sowing his wild oats, Penny has grown up, grown impatient, and grown resentful. In fact, she's vowed never to marry the man who blighted her life and destroyed her dreams.

Viscount Westfield is happy enough to return the bridal dowry. But one look at Penny and Westfield knows he can never, ever let her go...

<u>Also Available</u>
The Scandalous Life of a True Lady
The Wicked Ways of a True Hero
Truly Yours

S0034